Acknowledgements

For advice, assistance, inspiration and support, my thanks go to Rupert Arrowsmith, Tim Dawtry, Paul Hazelgrave, Damien Hindmarch, Yvette Hoyle, Mick Lake, Mick McCann, Ciro Orsini, Roman Revkniv and Sue Weakley.

Blowback

John Lake

**The sequel to *Hot Knife*
and second part of The Leeds 6 Trilogy**

Published by Armley Press 2011

Cover Design: John Wheelhouse

Author cover photo by Sue Weakley

Layout: Ian Dobson

ISBN 0-9554699-4-5

Contents

1. Airedale Point

YOU COULD CATCH some arresting sights in the dying light of a winter's dusk on a Friday evening in Leeds. Stuff you wouldn't see anywhere else – incongruous snapshots of life in a unique northern city.

Up by the university, students drinking beer on the deck of a barge – but one docked on a grassy knoll of dry land, a good mile from any open water.

Down behind the Civic Hall, lusty teenagers ice-skating in the open air to blaring disco music – right across the road from a hospital where a neon sign read QUIET PLEASE.

Next to the river, a building like a giant glass spaghetti jar housed an Indian war elephant wearing the world's largest suit of animal armour.

And, farther along the banks of the Aire, twenty storeys up among the clean-cut, Lego-like structures of the city's newest and brightest housing developments, an upside-down Sri Lankan chemist dangled by his ankles over seventy metres of empty air between him and the rock-hard concrete of the street-level forecourt below.

Sanjeev Coomaraswamy, understandably, was wishing he wasn't there. He envisaged the thought as an egg within an egg within an egg, his Buddhist imagination's equivalent to a nest of Russian dolls, each shell representing a wish, each wish larger, more outlying and remoter in time, than the last: wishing that he'd never heard of dimethyltryptamine; wishing that he'd never met Dmitri Maximov; wishing that he'd never come to Leeds in the first place.

In summary, he was wishing himself 5,500 miles away, back in his native Kandy, by the steamy banks of the 'tank' – the big artificial lake constructed in the time of the ancient kings – where he would stroll as a student, occasionally stopping to gaze across the green flatness of the water, placing his hands together in the *namaste* prayer position and bowing his head towards the Temple of the Tooth of the Buddha on the opposite shore, while a swollen chorus of chanting priestly voices drifted over the water.

At the same time – more prosaically, and perhaps more realistically, given that this was a Friday night in Leeds – he was also wishing himself at home in Beeston, cuddling up with Tracy on the sofa in front of *Who Wants to Be a Millionaire*, while listening out for the sound of the back door telling him that Stephen was home and that he would have to resume the sort of good behaviour that characterised his tireless quest to win his partner's son's affection.

The memories, the taunt of nostalgia, the sudden terror-induced yearning for those innocent days long gone and far away, and for those intimate as well as intimidating moments so near and so recent, made him wonder if this was what they meant about your life flashing in front of your eyes before you die.

Where was all his childhood faith in karma and reincarnation now he was truly faced with what was happening to him right this minute? Maybe he'd been away too long. And maybe there was no going back.

'Please. . .'

Dmitri Maximov, standing not three feet away, on the sane and safe side of the railing of the penthouse balcony, laughed. More precisely, he snorted, like a bull dislodging a troublesome fly from its snout.

'"Please," he says,' said Dmitri.

Sanjeev deduced from the inclusion of the third person pronoun that this remark was directed not at him but at Cheslav, the hefty, smart-suited, bullet-headed underling whose meaty grip on Sanjeev's ankles was the only thing in the world keeping him alive. Sanjeev had just enough of Cheslav in his upended field of vision to see the cut of his suit jacket rucking up into his armpits and his expressionless face getting fatter and fatter and redder and redder.

Dmitri – also flashily dressed, a little less hefty and not quite so bull-necked as Cheslav, but less constrained and therefore freer to be ruthless in expression – stood by his underling's side, leaning out over the barrier to catch Sanjeev's eye. He rested his elbows casually on the rail like a man waiting to be served at a bar and clasped the gold-ringed fingers of his tattooed hands together.

'Please what? Or are you telling *me* to say please?' Dmitri grinned at Cheslav, who made no sign of getting the joke. A cold breeze riffled his fringe as he addressed his next question to the approaching night sky. 'OK. Where the fuck are my fucking drugs – *please*?'

'Please, Dmitri.'

Sanjeev couldn't help himself. It was the only word he could think of under the circumstances. It filled his mind, seducing him like a powerful fetish, an artefact of hope to cling to in the dizzying emptiness of the cold night air.

'Please.'

Dmitri allowed a puzzled look to cross his face, regardless of whether Sanjeev was able to appreciate it from the position he was currently in or not.

'What is this? Am I up here talking to myself? Because I'm certainly not talking to Cheslav here. I'm talking to you, Sanjeev.'

He leaned over the rail a little farther for emphasis and Sanjeev, against all his non-violent upbringing, wished he might lean out a little farther still, even just a little too far.

'You hear me, you fuck? Am I talking to myself, huh?'

'No. . . no. . . '

'No, what? Is this another way of saying "Please, please" or is it an answer to my fucking question?'

'Please, you must not do this. You cannot do this.'

Sanjeev was genuinely trying to reason with the man but perhaps he could have chosen the way he posed his words a little better. All the pleases in his head were squeezing out any sense of what was appropriate. A lifetime of practising humbleness, politeness and persuasiveness – none of it told him what should be appropriate now.

'Can't I? Can't I?' said Dmitri wildly. 'Don't look down! Don't you fucking look down, Sanjeev!'

Sanjeev wasn't looking down, and had never even thought of it until Dmitri had set the thought loose in his head, rampaging among all the pleases in there.

'There's no one there to help you,' said Dmitri. 'You know what's down there, huh? You see them? Down there? My boys, eh? My cleaners?'

Did Dmitri want him to look down now? Sanjeev didn't know what to do for the best – obey Dmitri's command and ignore his question or answer his question at the cost of disobeying the command. The Ukrainian had set either a clever trap or a stupid conundrum.

'They're waiting for you. No one will know. As soon as you hit that ground they're going to cover you up and clean you away before anyone knows about it. No one will know. You hear that? Huh? You see them down there, huh? They gonna clean you right off the ground and take you away and no one will ever know.'

As hideously sickening as it was to do so, Sanjeev couldn't resist peeking down below to see if this was true or a sick joke or both. Sure enough, a cluster of pale, distant, tiny blobs – the faces of men in overalls peering up at him – was visible in the glamorous light illuminating the long, swooping face of the building between him and them. Whoever they were – and Sanjeev knew who they were, that Dmitri would not be lying about this – they were clearly witnessing the event above them with remote and mute attention, their only interest being whether they got to do their work or not.

A rope of lights – a distant main road – swung across his gaze as he rotated his head away from the scene straight down: traffic, people, too far away in space to hear his cries. He squeezed his eyes shut against the horror of the impending plunge.

'It's not my fault, Dmitri, please.'

'Yes, yes, we've heard all that already. It isn't your fault. Someone stole them from you when you were looking the other way. Except you never should've looked the other way. You see what I'm saying here? You never should've looked the other way. You look away and – poof! –they're gone, huh? So whose fault is that, Sanjeev? Tell me. Whose fucking fault is that? Is it mine?'

Sanjeev gestured frantic appeasement.

'Don't waggle your head! I hate it when you fucking Pakis waggle your head like that. Is it a yes? Is it a no? Who the fuck knows? I ask you again, is it my fault?'

'No, no, of course not.'

Dmitri tried to bring his underling back into the conversation.

'Is it my fault, Cheslav?'

Cheslav strained at the gills and his face went a shade darker, touching crimson.

'Don't answer that, you might drop him. Or do you want to be dropped, Sanjeev, is that it? Ready to – how do they say it in

10

English? – give up the ghost?'

Sanjeev could feel his ankles slipping a millimetre at a time through the Ukrainian's powerful but not infallible grip. The blood in his head was pounding but it was the pain in his ankles and the Ukrainian's diminishing purchase on them that was occupying all his sensory awareness.

'It was the boy! It was the boy, I tell you!' There – he'd said it now. There was no going back. 'It was him! He took them! I know it was him!'

For the first time, Dmitri sounded interested.

'What boy?'

'Stephen. It was him. He took them. I know it was him. He hates me. He's always hated me. I know he does. I know it was him.'

'And who the fuck is Stephen?'

'My partner's boy.'

'What partner?' said Dmitiri suspiciously, thinking business partner, and mentally preparing to take on an unknown rival.

'My girlfriend's boy. He hates me. I know it was him. He's the only one who would have access to them. They were stolen from the house. It must have been him. But he's just a boy. He doesn't know any better. Only . . . he hates me in his mother's life.'

'Oh, boo-hoo. And where can we find this Stephen?'

'Please . . . I'll tell you. Just pull me in.'

Dmitri made no move to give the order, and Cheslav held fast, trying to ignore the build-up of lactic acid burning through his biceps.

'You tell me first,' said Dmitri. 'That's the way it works. But you better make it quick. Even a one-time champion wrestler like Cheslav here can hold on only so long. So where can we find your bitch's boy?'

'I have his mobile number. Here in my pocket, in my phone.'

'Bullshit. It would've fallen out by now.'

'The pocket has a flap held down by Velcro.'

It was such an unlikely thing for a man bargaining for his life to say that it struck Dmitri as being true. He looked at Cheslav.

'You mean you didn't search his pockets?'

Cheslav instinctively turned his head towards the boss. But a man whose head goes straight into his shoulders without the bother of anything you could call a neck needs to turn the whole upper torso to look left or right. The strain on Cheslav's jacket finally gave, a button popped, flipping away into the night, and the sudden shift in tension made him lose his grip.

Dmitri heard Sanjeev's fading scream before he realised what had just happened.

'Did I say to drop him?' he said, trying to sound patient.

'No, boss. Sorry, boss.'

Cheslav was panting for breath and rubbing and pumping circulation back into his upper arms. The Sri Lankan was only little but there was only so long you could hold on. He knew not to bother trying to excuse himself to Dmitri however, even though Dmitri had said the same thing himself not thirty seconds ago. Better to just apologise and take whatever was coming in the knowledge that it could've been worse if you'd whined like a peasant girl. He looked down crestfallenly at the missing button.

'It's Dolce and Gabbana. It shouldn't do that.'

'Dolce and Gabbana,' Dmitri scoffed, eyeing the cut of the cloth contemptuously. 'It's a fucking knock-off, you idiot.'

He peered over the rail. The team had already spread a tarpaulin sheet over the body and were screening off that bit of the forecourt from public view with instant fencing and high-sided vehicles. They worked quickly and were paid well. Everybody was paid well.

'I don't suppose there's any point in checking if his phone is still working.' Dmitri looked at Cheslav, fingering the weave now and fretting over his suit's authenticity. 'But get down there and check it anyway.'

'Yes, boss,' said Cheslav, hitching up his waistband.

'And find this fucking Stephen! Tonight!'

2. Swarfega

KELLY WAS WORKING down at the end of the shed in
Beeston, just down the road from the Elland Road football
ground, finishing a job on the transmission of a 1965 Triumph
T100SS and listening to Tommo tell one of his tall tales.

Tommo, his gaffer, the owner of the business, was sitting
cross-legged on the concrete floor with the engine of a 1971
Kawasaki Avenger dismantled and spread out in front of him like
a picnic.

'So I'm working at Barnbow, right? This is years ago, you
know? When I lived over in Cross Gates. Puttin' Chieftain tank
shells together on an assembly line. Anyway, one bloke, geezer
called Rob, only bets me I can't smuggle one a these things out
'n' so immediately I think, right, you're on. Wouldn't chance it
nowadays, like, they'd 'ave you locked up for terrorism before
you could spit, but back then security weren't all it were cracked
up to be an' I were young 'n' daft enough to think I could tek on
any kinda challenge, even if it were just to show willin'.
Anyway, took me a while to figure out how to do it but I
managed in t'end, an' he had to cough up. Wun't believe me till I
took him home an' showed it to him to prove I'd done it. Even
then I don't think he believed it. He paid though. Fifty quid, it
wa', which were a lot a money in them days. He never bet me
owt else after that.'

'Fuckinell,' said Kelly, playing along with the tale. 'A live
tank shell? What did you do with it?'

'Still gorrit. Sittin' in me shed at home, believe it or not.
'Snot exactly the sort a thing that's easy to get rid of without
drawin' embarrassin' questions, know what I mean?'

Tommo was not much older than Kelly and they got on well
together at work. The garage only needed the two of them and
turned over enough jobs to keep them both sufficiently happy.
There were a lot of bikers round here and most of them rode old
bikes either because they lacked the sponduliks to upgrade to a
newer model or because they were holding onto something they
considered a classic. Some were Angels, others were other kinds
of purists. Tommo specialised, found his niche market plus a
mechanic who knew his way around bikes, and it was enough to

13

keep them in business.

Tommo didn't feel like a boss to Kelly, not since the early days when he first took him on almost two years back, but he wasn't anything more than a workmate either. They'd shared many a lunchtime pint, of course, but each kept his personal life separate from the other for their different reasons.

Tommo liked to talk about his past though. He enjoyed and appreciated his position as a respectable garage owner now, but at work he liked to regale Kelly with his crazy, dangerous or illegal youthful exploits, maybe hoping to gain some kudos he thought it would buy him.

Kelly didn't mind. The tales, no matter how tall, were often amusing, and better to listen to than the shit they played on the radio. Occasionally he'd reciprocate with episodes of his own, mixed with a little imagination and changes of identity, and they'd riff an exchange of jokes and one-liners out of it for hours. It helped to pass the time. But mostly Kelly kept quiet about his past. The true parts, those that still meant something.

There were still ghosts that could come back to haunt him. Secrets that even Bea didn't know. Who was he trying to kid? Secrets that *only* Bea didn't know.

Those who were involved knew. Luckily, they were either gone away or out of his life now. But he saw no reason why Tommo should know either. So he stayed quiet about it, did his job, went home and kept a wall and a bunch of distance between himself and anyone from his past.

Apart from anything else, it was easier to stay off the smack that way.

At 4:30, Kelly's mobile rang. Shit. He'd forgotten to switch it to SILENT, something he tried to make a habit of doing while he was working. How many years had he had a mobile phone? And still, he didn't think he would ever get used to it. When he wanted it off it was on and when he wanted it on it was off. He wiped his oily hands on a rag and awkwardly dug it out of his overalls pocket.

'All right, love.' It was Bea ringing from home. 'What's up?'

'What's up?' she repeated. 'I don't know, but summat is.' She sounded serious. None of her usual dry sarcasm, just worry and weariness. 'You'd better get home, Kelly.'

14

'Why? What's happened?'

'It's all right, nobody's hurt or nowt. But you'd better come and see for yourself. I can't tell you over t'phone. Ask Tommo to let you off early. Please, Kel.'

'All right, calm down, love.'

He added that more for Tommo's benefit, sending him a look across the workshop that pre-empted objections: it's trouble, it's home, it's the missus – a man's touch urgently required. Hopefully say no more.

'I'll be there in a bit. It better be worth it.'

'Oh yeah, it'll be worth it all right.'

Kelly pushed END CALL and turned to Tommo, who already knew what was coming.

'Go on, then. Family emergency, is it?'

'Er, something like that.'

Tommo made a comic deal out of checking his watch.

'Only four-thirty? Ah well, I suppose it is a Friday night.' He pronounced it *Freedy neet*. 'But remember to stay on call Sat'day and Sunday in case any rush jobs come in.'

'Time an'alf if I have to give up me weekend,' Kelly reminded Tommo, as he did every Friday night when Tommo reminded him to stay on call. It was a ritual they repeated just to remind themselves that that was the situation, that remained the state of play, and nothing usually came of it.

Kelly removed his overalls to reveal his Motörhead T-shirt that he still wore from the 1995 'Bastards' tour. Tommo wondered if he'd ever taken that T-shirt off. He was an OK, decent bloke though, even if did have a dodgy past. He never talked much about it but Tommo wasn't born yesterday, he could recognise the signs. He'd noticed the old track marks in his arms when Kelly first started working for him – and he'd watched them fade over the many months since.

Kelly Swarfega'd and washed his hands at the sink before getting into his leathers, jamming his helmet on his head and climbing onto his own restored classic Triumph. Tommo knew enough about Kelly to know that he'd inherited that bike from some dead friend of his called Clint. That was one thing he did talk about, that bloke Clint and how he'd left him the bike. He'd done it up himself apparently and now it ran like a dream. Not that Tommo was jealous or anything – but it would look damn

15

good in his own collection if anything ever happened to Kelly.

'See you on Monday,' said Kelly.

'If not before,' said Tommo right on cue with the ritual response.

3. Tic Tacs

'YOU'D BETTER GET in here and take a look at this,' said Bea to Kelly, pushing the back door closed behind him and not noticing that it failed to sneck, the way it didn't sometimes when there was a draught blowing the wrong way through the house.

From the kitchen the house was quiet, just the two of them it seemed, no Casey or Damien. Paul and Nita, Bea's eldest two, had long since flown the coop. Paul had a flat and a job in Manchester, working for some computer company there, and Nita lived with her fella and their baby over in Hebden Bridge. They were grandparents now – little girl called Shona. Well, Bea was a grandmother anyway, which was weird, him dating a granny – if you could still call it dating after all the years they'd been together.

'What am I lookin' at?' said Kelly, and Bea pointed at a package on the kitchen table. It was a brown-paper sack, the kind that might contain a kilo of real coffee, standing upright, its top folded over to keep it shut and fresh. Kelly went and unfolded it and looked inside.

Pills. Little white pills. Maybe a couple of thousand of them, packed in loose like pick 'n' mix. He put the sack down gently and moved his hands away, afraid it might spill some of its contents.

'What the fuck's this?'

'I've no idea. I were 'opin' you might know.'

Kelly was fighting hard to stop himself from seeing red.

'Where the fuck did they come from?'

'Listen, Kelly, don't get angry.'

'Don't get angry? I'm tryin' to stay fuckin' clean 'n' suddenly there's a fuckin' big bag a drugs on the kitchen table? What's not to get angry about?'

'Well I din't fuckin' put 'em there,' said Bea. 'Well, I did actually – put them there on the kitchen table. But I din't bring 'em in the 'ouse.'

'Well who did then?'

'Well that's why I'm saying not to get angry. I think it were our Damien.'

'You think?'

17

'Well I don't think it coulda been Casey, do you?'

'Are you takin' the piss, Bea, or what? Course it wan't flamin' Casey! She'd never pull a stunt like this. Where is he?'

'He's out. But before you go gettin' all—'

'Where were they?'

'Hidden under his bed.'

Kelly couldn't help but grin but it wasn't entirely pleasant.

'Oh, he's gonna love you, Mum. The number a times he's told you to keep out of his room 'n' yer still at it.'

'Don't put the fuckin' blame on me, Kelly, cos I won't fuckin' have it.'

Bea wasn't emotional now, like what he worried she was gonna be like when he first walked in. She was steel, and that was somehow always better.

'D'you hear? I've been clean for two years as well, remember? I'm as fuckin' mad about this as you are. But he's my fuckin' son, all right? He's my kid an' I'll deal with him.'

Kelly felt like killing the little brat when he got hold of him but he made the struggle to control his anger. Try to look past that and see the bigger problem.

'And what about this?' He waved a hand contemptuously at the sack of pills like he was wafting flies away from a turd. 'Are you gonna take care of this an' all?'

'Yeah, if you tell me what to do. Yeah, I will.'

Her answer diffused his rage a little more. He needed to purge his emotions and think clearly about this.

He took a chair at the table and opened the sack again. He reached inside and picked out a pill and held it close to his eyes. Fuck, he was sure he needed glasses. He couldn't detect any marking on it at first. Then he spotted it, or what he thought was one. It could've been an imperfection in the surface, until he compared it with others and saw that they all bore the same stamp. The design was tiny and hard to make out. All it appeared to be was a cluster of minute scratches, a random squiggle. Or was there some organisation to it? Lines and curves criss-crossing. Possibly a number of letters imprinted one on top of another until they were individually unrecognisable. Other than that, it was simply a smooth white oval pill about the size of a Tic Tac. For all he knew it could *be* a Tic Tac. But this never came from any kind of sweet shop he'd heard about it, where they sold 'em wholesale by the kilo in a sack. Whatever they were, they didn't smell of mint and he instinctively knew that he didn't want them in the house.

'OK, so where could he have got 'em from? Are they from one of his mates? Is he runnin' errands for somebody? I mean they're not all his, whatever they are, are they? Unless he's dealing. An' if he is he must be in it big time judging by this lot. An' if he were in it big time we'd know by now already.'

'But we don't know what they are.'

'But we know there's a fuckin' lot of 'em though. And they must belong to somebody. And they must be worth something to somebody. And if he's nicked these—'

'He won'ta nicked 'em, he's not that flamin' stupid.'

'Fuckinell, Bea, this is why we fucking moved house in the first place,' Kelly snapped, 'to get away from all this shit.'

He got hold of himself. Calm down, gotta think clearly, remember?

'Well we know one thing. Somebody's either waiting for 'em or looking for 'em, that's for sure. And now we've found 'em. So it's our move. We can put 'em back where we found 'em and pretend it never happened or we can confront him when he gets back, see what he has to say for himself.'

'I'm not puttin' 'em back,' said Bea end-of-subjectly. 'I'm not shovin' a bag a drugs into my kid's bedroom, even if it *were* there in the first place.'

'Good,' said Kelly, 'cos it were never an option anyway.'

Outside the slightly ajar back door in the yard, Damien pulled his ear away from the gap and carefully turned around and retraced his steps away from the house without making a sound.

Shit! He could not believe that his mother would go in his fucking bedroom after so many fucking times he'd told her to stay the fuck out. It was so fucking outrageous. And now she'd gone and found the pills and told that cunt Kelly. This was all he fucking needed.

How the fuck was he gonna get them back? And in the meantime what the fuck was he gonna tell Stevo? Shit, man, this was all he fucking needed!

4. Switched On

NO POLICE – THAT was one thing they both agreed on instantly. They'd moved away from the old house to keep a low profile, stay away from certain people, and once the police get involved word gets around. Too many ghosts in both their pasts.

But when Kelly suggested he might have to get in touch with some of his contacts from the old days, Bea didn't like that either.

'What old contacts?'

'I dunno. Somebody who might know what this is or who it belongs to.'

'Christ, Kelly, you can't go running back to that old crowd.'

'Whaddya mean, running? D'you think I want to. Cos I fuckin' don't, I can tell ya.'

As the evening got later and there was still no Damien, the choice seemed to become more decided for them. If something had happened to Damien, if someone had done something to him, then the police would have to be involved.

At 8:30, long after they'd hidden the pills in a cupboard and Casey had come home and they'd eaten their tea together and Casey had gone out again and they'd put the sack of pills back in the centre of the table and tossed another hundred whys and wherefores back and forth, Bea's mobile rang.

It was Damien. Bea mimed for Kelly to stop pacing.

'Where are you?'

'Mam, I know you've found 'em.'

'Found what?'

'The pills, stupid. Listen, Mam, they're not mine, honest. I'm lookin' after 'em for someone, for a mate, that's all. So look after 'em, all right? Don't let Kelly do anything stupid with 'em. Please, Mam.'

'What the fuck have you got yourself involved with, Damien? Eh? You'd better get back 'ere now.'

'I can't. Not right now. You know Kelly'd give me a hard time and there's stuff I need to do right now.'

Bea shushed Kelly from talking, and he gestured a demand for the phone. She shook her head at him. They'd only fight and hang up.

'Ask him what it is!' Kelly hissed at her.

'Well what is this stuff? Is it Es or summat?'

'I dunno, honest,' said Damien. 'It's summat me mate's mam's boyfriend's working on. He's some sort a chemist. I don't know any more than that, Mam, truly. He just asked us to keep 'em for 'im.'

'Damien – why the fuck did you say yes? You don't know what you coulda got yerself involved in. Who does it belong to? Does it belong to your mate's boyfriend's . . . this chemist bloke? Was he keepin' it for somebody else? Why don't you come home now and we'll help you sort it out?'

'I'm sortin' it, Mam. I've got to go. But don't let Kelly do owt with 'em. Promise.'

'All right. Promise. But be careful. And phone me.'

She ended the call.

'Is he coming back?' said Kelly.

'He won't. There's no point in arguing with him. He's got his mind set on something.'

'So what is it?'

'He dun't know. He were looking after it for a mate.'

'Which mate?'

'As if he'd tell me that. Anyway he dun't know what it is. Summat some chemist were working on, he said.'

'Chemist?'

'That's what he said. He said not to do owt stupid with 'em. If he's looking after 'em then I suppose his mate's expecting 'em back. I promised him you'd look after 'em.'

Kelly looked cheesed off at not knowing what the pills were more than relieved at knowing that Damien was OK.

'I don't want these going back anywhere.'

'What you on about?'

'We don't know what the fuck they are. Oh, we know that they've just come out of some fuckin' laboratory though and there's thousands of the fuckin' things just in this one bag.'

'You saying there might be other bags?'

'I'm saying there's thousands here in just this one bag on our kitchen table that in two weeks might be out there fucking up kids' heads.'

'Who are you all of a sudden, fuckin' DS? It's only three years ago you were a smackhead, like me. Why should we care what happens to it? Like you said, there might be more bags out there anyway.'

'You said that.'

'And is it more important than protectin' our Damien? If we're not callin' the police then we should let him sort it out. It's between him and this flamin' mysterious mate of his.'

'Which is the option we both ruled out before. Put it back and forget about it. OK, I'm not ruling it out anymore but I still wanna know what this is before we just send it on its merry fucking way.'

'Why? Why interfere?'

'Because what if Damien's one a those kids who's gonna take one a these? Or what if Casey is? Wun't you rather know what they've taken in case summat went wrong?'

He closed the bag and picked it up from the table.

'What you doin'?'

'I'm gonna find somebody who can tell me what it is.'

'Who?'

'You don't wanna know.'

'Jesus, Kelly.'

She knew she couldn't stop him. She'd known all along that one day he'd find a strong enough excuse to look up his old bad buddies. Trouble is, this was as good an excuse as any in Kelly's mind, if she'd learned the half of how his mind worked over the years.

'Well at least don't take the whole bag, stupid. Leave it here. Just take a sample.'

Kelly dug a few pills out of the sack and stuffed them in his pocket.

Bea took the bag back from him.

'Put them somewhere safe. And hidden,' said Kelly to Bea.

'Keep your fuckin' mobile switched on,' said Bea to Kelly.

5. Entering and Breaking

DENNY WAS CROSSING the living room when his ring tone made him jump.

'Shit,' he whispered to himself, stumbling against something in the dark. He sensed a wobble and an object falling to the carpet, and in scrabbling to get his phone out of his pocket, he put his foot forward and heard and felt something crunch beneath his boot.

Meanwhile a polyphonic rendition of Isaac Hayes's theme from *Shaft* bounced off the walls. He pressed ANSWER to shut the damn thing up and got it to his ear before he'd even looked at the lighted panel to see who it was.

''Ello?'

'Denny.'

'Who's this?'

'It's Kelly.'

Kelly. Jesus. When had it last been? And what a time for him to call now.

'Y'all right, Kel?' As if he'd just spoken to him this morning, holding it back. 'What's up?'

'I know it's been a while but I've got a bit of a problem. Wondered if you might be able to help us out, do us a little favour.'

Normally Denny would've steamed in with a tongue-lashing after three years of silence then suddenly this from the cheeky bastard, but now wasn't the time. He'd swallow his pride for the better part of valour.

'Listen, I'll get back to you in about twenty minutes, all right? I'm in the middle a summat right now, I can't really talk.'

'Yeah, sound, mate. But get back to us, yeah?'

'Yeah, for sure.'

Denny ended the call and switched the ring tone to SILENT. He still didn't know if anyone else was in the house or not, upstairs, sleeping, though if there were he was sure they'd have stirred before now. His phone going off had put the shits up him but it had also boosted his confidence that the house was empty.

He switched on his pocket torch and started on the drawers and cupboards, working sloppily but quietly. After a quick scan of the surfaces – furniture tops, coffee table, mantelpiece – his beam fell across a desk, and he found what he was looking for in one of the drawers. Two mobile phones, a flash-looking men's bracelet watch and a digital camera.

That'll do.

He slipped the objects into his coat pockets, turned around without bothering to shut the drawer and tiptoed back to the kitchen and out the way he'd come, through the left-open window, out into the back yard and the streets and night beyond.

6. The Kremlin

WHEN DENNY GOT back to Kelly on the moby he wouldn't agree to meet in a pub or anywhere with people around, so Denny had to give him directions round to his new gaff. He'd moved out of Leeds 6 since the old days and all that business with Big Baz. He was in the Burmantofts now, in a flat in one of the old Shakespeare tower blocks – functional, modernist, utilitarian relics from the Sixties. Renting obviously. Well, getting the social to pay for it.

Up on the tenth floor, he had a commanding view of Quarry House, the national headquarters of the DSS, the ones stumping up the cash that paid for his place. With its hulking brick-house shoulders topped by a metal spike poking through a ring at the sky, the building squatting outside his window on the eastern edge of the city centre looked like some sinister ministry waiting for a new Soviet future. So, though it looked nothing like its namesake, the people of Leeds, knowing just so much to be not enough, labelled it the Kremlin.

It was getting late when Kelly rang the buzzer to come up.

Denny'd been back a while waiting for him, staring at the telly and imagining what they were going to say to each other. When he opened the door the figure behind it was immediately familiar but different.

Kelly was still Kelly, but he'd changed since Denny had last seen him. He'd grown a beard, or some bum fluff at least, grown his hair longer and gotten more into the biker leathers 'n' shit. But Denny thought *he* still came off the punkier of the two with his neck tattoo, short spiky haircut, UK Subs T-shirt and tight drainpipe trousers, which he'd just split at the crotch climbing through that open window that'd proven too tempting earlier on.

How punk was that? Spirit of '77, still alive and kicking against the pricks.

'Fuckin' come in then, you old cunt. 'An't seen you for fuckin' donkeys'.'

He gave his old mate a hearty slap on the shoulder. He was trying to be nice. Play it cool. Pretend nothing'd happened. For three fucking years.

'Y'all right, Denny, man? Good to see yer.'

They went through their old handshake routine – some things you just don't forget – and drew one another into a hug. Each could feel the defensive vibes coming off the other already though. It wasn't gonna be easy.

'What yer watchin'?'

Kelly nodded at the telly, the only real light in the room, dominating whatever meager street light was seeping in through the uncurtained windows this high up.

Denny flipped a hand at it.

'Fuck knoz. Just some shit. You know.'

'Right.'

Kelly looked into the screen while he thought up a line that would make him feel comfortable looking away from it.

'So how long you been round 'ere?' That would do.

'What, Burmantofts? Fuck, must be six months, summat like that.'

'Nice one.'

'Why?' said Denny. 'Cos I can see t'fuckin' DSS office out me winder every day?'

'Well it's not a bad fuckin' view, is it, you moanin' old cunt?' said Kelly.

They looked one another in the eye and laughed.

'You 'an't changed at all then, 'ave yer?' Kelly looked around him, thinking to pile on the insults while they were still being read as friendly. 'Lookin' after the place nice an' all.'

Around him, pizza cartons and brimming ashtrays on the floor, lager tins on top of the telly and what looked like a half-deflated, or half-inflated, rubber sex doll knotted in an impossible yoga position on a mattress on a floor in the corner of the room next to a stash of porn mags.

'Yer dirty old fucker,' Kelly said with a too-obvious grin.

Denny stepped forward and emptied his coat pockets on to the settee next to where Kelly'd parked his arse. Two mobile phones, a flash-looking bloke's watch and a camera tumbled out. One of them digital ones.

'Yer absolutely right, Kel. Same old Denny. How about you?'

Kelly looked down at the haul resting on the once-plush sofa stuffing at his side.

'You fuckin' been out robbin'?'

26

Denny didn't know how to answer that one.

'Well, no. Well, maybe yes. Sort of.'

'Fuckinell, man, you either 'ave or you 'aven't.'

'I was just walkin' past, honest, mindin' me own business. But the fuckin' winder were open, weren't it? An' I just knew it was a student house – it 'ad to be, around there. So, fuckinell, half-past-nine on a Friday night. All the lights off. They're not gonna be at home, are they? Probably been on t'fuckin' shandy before staggerin' out to t'pub, forgot to shut kitchen winder. End a term an' that. Know what I mean? It were a no-brainer. I'll be able to get two hundred quid for that lot. I mean look at that fuckin' watch. It's class, is that. '

'Two hundred fuckin' quid?' said Kelly. 'You'll get fuckin' eighty if you're lucky.'

He was taking a wild guess just to wind him up. It was Denny, for fuck's sake. Denny, after all this time.

'Still better than a kick in t'ribs, innit?'

The way he said it shut Kelly up. He didn't want to say anything more about it. This was no time to come on all high and mighty. He'd come round here expecting - no, hoping – that Denny was still up to his old dodgy ways and still had some of his old dodgy contacts, so he could hardly complain about it when the evidence was set before him. Maybe it'd be better if he just got straight to the point.

He put a hand in his pocket and tossed half a dozen of the white pills onto the settee next to Denny's haul.

'Er. . . what are they?' said Denny looking immediately interested.

'I were 'opin' you could tell me. Our lass found 'em in Damien's bedroom.'

Denny looked down at the pills on the settee cushion then looked up at Kelly and let out a splutter of laughter that left specks of spit in Kelly's beard.

'Fuckinell, Kelly, man, I thought you'd come round here to get ripped with your old mate for a minute there. Thought you was offerin' me a trip or a love-in or something, you know, for old times' sake.'

'I'm off drugs, man,' said Kelly. He could see Denny already grinning at the idea, thinking it was a joke. 'I mean it. Speed, smack – I 'an't touched any a that stuff in nearly three years.'

Denny sat down in an armchair at the end of the low table and reached for the handle of a drawer built into its edge.

'Bet you wouldn't say no to a smoke a this stuff though.'

He pulled out a small bundle of greenery swaddled in cling film. When he unwrapped it, the odour instantly filled the room like an air-bag full of wet nappies.

Kelly realised now that he'd smelt traces of it earlier as soon as Denny had opened the door into the flat, but he'd put it down to the neighbours pissing in the stairwell, or maybe that Denny was keeping an un-house-trained cat, God help them both.

'Jesus,' he said when the cannabis's olfactory event horizon struck him. His head snapped back as far as if he'd just sniffed the fabled pants that according to Frank Zappa broke Tommy Mars's neck. 'What the fuck is that?'

'Bit a skunk. You never smoked skunk? Gets you totally blasted.'

Skunk had been around for years but had only really taken off in a big way since Kelly had been off smoking blow. He was aware of it but didn't know what it was like, and he wasn't sure he wanted to be totally blasted right now. While Denny got busy building a spliff and waxing lyrical about the potency of the cannabis buds, Kelly wished he'd just take a look at the pills. He didn't have time for all this.

'So you 'an't tried one of 'em then?' Denny said eventually after much rolling and tweaking and prodding and licking of the tubular construction between his fingers.

'Are you going deaf in yer old age? I don't do drugs anymore. An' I certainly wouldn't do summat that I didn't know what it wa'.'

Denny sparked up the spliff with a Clipper then scooped all the doings back into the drawer and closed it. The smoke that he blew out and the smoke coming off the tip of the burning spliff produced a drier, harsher, stronger version of the wet-nappy smell that had billowed off the buds. When Denny passed it over to him, Kelly turned it down and took out his cigarettes instead.

'Never thought I'd see you say no to a smoke.'

'I wanna try 'n' keep me head together,' said Kelly, lighting a low-tar Lambert & Butler.

'Let's have a gander at these pills then.'

About time, Kelly thought. The sooner he got this sorted out, the sooner he could get back to Bea. He wasn't happy about leaving her alone. Not tonight. He picked one of them up and passed it over.

'What do you reckon they are?' said Denny.

'I 'an't gorra clue. Looks like there's some kind a mark on 'em though. Can yer see it?'

Denny rolled the pill between his finger and thumb, peering at its surface like Alexander Fleming looking at penicillin for the first time, void of realisation.

'Oh yeah. What the fuck is that?'

He opened the drawer again, this time pulling out a magnifying glass.

Kelly wondered what else was in that drawer. Although he didn't want to, he wondered whether Denny had ever gotten rid of that gun. Three years. You'd think he'd have learnt some sense in all that time. But then you never knew with Denny. His capacity for bad ideas had gone a long way in the old days, and the stolen gear on the settee didn't make it look like it went any shorter distance now.

'Fuck.' Denny said it under his breath first. Then he laughed a little, repeating the word louder. 'Fuck. Ha-ha. Fuck. Huh-huh. Fuck. Ha. Fuck.'

'Are yer gonna fuck all night or tell me what you're fucking at?'

'It's letters. Three letters overlappin' each other. D, M, T. Fuckin' DMT. 'Ere, 'ave a look for yersen.'

Kelly picked up one of the other pills from next to him on the settee and took the magnifying glass from Denny. It was hard to see by just the flicker of the telly.

'Have you got any fuckin' lights in 'ere? I can't see sod-all.'

Denny sprang up and put on the big light and a whole new dimension of domestic chaos and neglect jumped out of the corners of the room. Kelly ignored it and put the pill under the lens.

'How d'you know it's not TMD? Or DTM? Or MTD? Or—'

'Or MDT, yeah, you don't have to go through 'em all, I'm not fuckin' stupid,' Denny said tetchily.

'I'm not sayin' you are, am I?' Kelly snapped.

Fuck, this was hard work. Denny and he were both trying to

act like they last saw each other just yesterday, like today was just another day and three years had slipped into the crack between dusk and dawn. He needed Denny's help but being here with him wasn't helping. Neither was the stench of that stuff that Denny was smoking. It was all a bit too much like the old days, and it would be all too easy to fall back in. He took a long hard pull on his cigarette, shrivelling the last stump of it to a twist of paper and fibre before stubbing it out in an ashtray on the table.

'Look, I'm sorry, man—'

'And what's with all this *man* shit. Me name's Denny. Or 'ave you forgotten?'

'Fuck, Denny . . . I'm sorry. I'm just – I wanna know what it is. I wanna know what that little sod Damien's got himself involved with. Bea's desperate, you know? And – we're both tryin' to stay clean. Finding a bag a drugs under yer kid's bed dun't make it any easier.'

'I just don't want you comin' waltzin' in 'ere after all this time an' fuckin' takin' the piss, you know? I fuckin' did you an' Bea a favour that night. Seems like it's you who owes me a favour, not the other way round.'

'Well . . . what do you want?'

'Nothing. I don't want anything. Not from you. You're still a fuckin' mate, aren't yer? Well aren't yer?'

'Denny, course I fuckin' am. What can I say?'

'Nowt, yer soppy cunt. But just don't go takin' the piss, all right?'

'I'm not takin' the piss.'

'An' don't go moralisin'. I don't wanna hear about yer bein' clean, all right?'

'All right. Scout's honour. I won't fuckin' mention it again. Not a dickie-bird.'

After a sulky pause Denny said, 'All right,' like a kid who'd dared them to cancel Christmas and they'd only gone and done it. 'It'd help if you just had a sociable smoke with us.'

'All right, give us a blowback, then.'

Denny reversed the spliff and put the burning end inside his mouth, then Kelly leaned his face in close to Denny's and sucked in the trail of smoke that Denny blew out of the roach end. It only took a minute for the effect to go to Kelly's head, and though he thought of it as three years of hard effort going up in smoke, it also felt fucking great after all that time.

Denny finished the rest of it and ground out the end in the ashtray.

'So how d'you know it's DMT?' said Kelly.

'Cos it's the only one that's a drug, innit? Thought it mighta bin MDMA for a minute, burrit's not. It's fuckin' DMT.'

'DMT? Never heard of it.'

'Fuckinell, Kel, I know you 'an't been doin' drugs but 'ave yer been livin' in a cave or summat? Your drugs knowledge needs some serious updatin'.'

'So educate me. What is it?'

'Well that's the weird one. It says it's DMT but I've only ever heard of smokin' it or injectin' it. If you eat it it's not supposed to do owt.'

'So what does it do if you smoke it or inject it?'

'I dunno, I've never done it. Trippy stuff though. It's hallucinogenic. An' if you pipe it it's supposed to burn your throat 'n' lungs like a bastard. Like smokin' plastic, apparently.'

'D'you know somebody who's done it?'

'Only kids off the estate 'n' that. Don't know anybody our age who's into it. You don't hear of it often though. They're mostly doin' glue 'n' ketamine round 'ere.'

'Hang on, so you said it dun't do owt to you if you eat it. So how come they can make it into pills?'

'That's what's weird, innit? I've never heard of it before.'

'I'd never even heard of it in the first place. Damien told our lass that they came from some chemist bloke. Maybe he's found a way a turning this DMT stuff into pills that actually work when you swallow 'em.'

'You said Damien had a bag a these things?' said Denny.

'Yeah.'

'How many is a bag?'

'Mebbe a couple a thousand.'

'Fuck.'

'I know. It's a fuckin' lot.'

'No. Fuck. I've just thought of something else. About DMT.'

'What about it?'

'Not the drug. The letters, D – M – T.'

Kelly looked at Denny under the harsh light dangling from

the ceiling and wondered if it was the skunk that had sent him a slim shade paler, or something else.

Something that he wasn't going to like.

7. The Tyranny of Friday Night

DMITRI MAXIMOV WAS checking his BlackBerry for up-to-the-minute reports as he walked from the garage where he'd just parked and locked away the Merc to the front door of his detached house in Roundhay.

Nothing.

Nothing about that damn dead Sri Lankan chemist or his bitch girlfriend or wife or whatever she'd been to him.

Nothing about her runt offspring.

Nothing about his missing consignment of dimethyl-fucking-triptamine.

Nothing at all.

'Shit,' he said before pocketing the BlackBerry and fitting his key in the Yale lock. He'd find a moment to check again later. If there was nothing then, maybe he'd make a few calls and rattle a few chains.

He'd bought the house for a good price in the late Nineties off an old Russian Jewish tailor who was retiring to the homeland. Some English called it a mansion; to him it wasn't quite big enough to qualify. It had an acre of garden, a quaint English exterior, plenty of Victorian space inside and more rooms than they ever needed. The Maximovs rarely had guests who stayed over, and the kind of partying Dmitri enjoyed was best done elsewhere – away from the home and the family.

As he stepped into the hall he glanced at his wristwatch. 9:30. Not a bad time to get home for a Friday night. One should always try to spend Friday night with one's family, he had always believed. It scored you credit and deflected attention away from your absences on other nights of the week. It seemed a fair price to pay for a quiet life and a little peace of mind. At work, in front of the boys, he called it 'the tyranny of Friday night', but mostly as a joke.

'Jimmy, is that you?'

His wife's head popped out from the recess of a doorway. She looked as beautiful as the day he married her. Better. She looked as beautiful as the day he met her. She was that kind of woman. Always beautiful. Even at home. Mostly.

She stepped out towards him. She'd changed already from

her daytime clothes into slacks and a T-shirt. Of course she had. It was 9:30. The public part of the day was over, it was night – no need to dress up unless you were going out. He never really understood that about English women. A Ukrainian woman would always want to look her best both outside and at home. But then again would he want a Ukrainian woman? Not for a wife anyway. God forbid. Too high maintenance.

'Have you eaten?' she said, helping him slip out of his jacket. It was their little ritual, one of many. It was how he knew he was home at last.

As he turned to release his arm for her he slipped the other around her waist and drew her close to him.

'Come here,' he said and kissed her directly on the lips. His eyes were closed; he felt her lips slide open into a smile then her tongue entered his mouth. Briefly. Just a flicker.

'I've eaten,' he said as she drew away.

'Good. Because we ate hours ago. And you don't smell too much of vodka. So you can say good night to the kids before they go to sleep.'

'They're still up?'

'They're waiting for you in their rooms. When I say waiting, I mean playing on their computers.'

'Playing the stock markets, I hope,' he said.

Donna gave him one of her looks.

'But just playing, of course,' he said, holding up his hands to show he wasn't serious. She would insist on them being allowed to have their childhood.

He took his jacket from her, making sure to retrieve the BlackBerry from the pocket before draping it over a wooden coat-hanger and hooking it on the coat rack. Then he followed her through into the main reception room where a hump of embers was seething in the fireplace.

She was already at the drinks cabinet pouring him a vodka and herself a gin and tonic. It wouldn't be his first tonight but it would be hers, unless she'd grown very skilful at deceiving him: something you had to watch out for in the English.

'Busy day?' said Donna, handing Dmitri the shot glass.

'Busy day,' he said, briskly tipping the hot, smooth fluid down his throat.

'We received a dinner invitation earlier this evening,' said

Donna, 'from the Woods.'

'And who the hell are the Woods?' said Dmitri, heading for a refill.

'The Woods, our neighbours? Tim and Eileen from round the corner?'

Donna liked to use that kind of question-style upspeak from the Australian soaps when she thought he wasn't listening to her.

'Oh, right, we met them at—'

'Exactly. Those Woods.'

'But you didn't call me. Did you? Have we already blown it?'

'Relax, Jimmy. I didn't want to go. And I'm damn sure you didn't either. If I want to spend the evening with a bunch of stuck-up old fogeys I'll go see my parents. Anyway, I think they only rang because another couple'd let them down.'

While a part of Dmitri's mind was relieved that he'd avoided the prospect of an uncommonly tedious dinner party, another part was contemplating what arrogant old fucks these people were – *We'll keep the Ukrainian and his nouveau riche whore on the reserve bench until someone more important pulls out* – and the different ways he could make them pay with just a click of his fingers, the old-fashioned equivalent of a text message. But now wasn't the time. He needed to let go of all that. He needed to relax and focus on his family if he was to keep some order in his life. He made himself a promise though that he would never go into the Woods' again.

'So what are we watching tonight?' he said, watching Donna spread herself on the couch.

'Don't forget you're putting the kids to bed first.'

'I know, I know. I just want to know what we're going to be cuddling up to.'

'We-e-l-l-l . . . I rented a couple of DVDs. One for you and one for me.'

'I'll be asleep for the second one. What are they?'

'*Hannibal* – '

'What's that?'

'It's a sequel to *Silence of the Lambs*. You know? With Anthony Hopkins?'

'What's the other one?'

'*Chocolat.*'

'I've been waiting to see that!' said Dmitri. 'Juliet Binoche. And Lena Olin. And Johnny Depp. It's a love story, isn't it?'

'But what if I fall asleep?' said Donna. 'I want to see *Hannibal* just as much as you want to see your silly love story.'

'Please,' said Dmitri. 'Please.'

It was all he could think to say.

'Well, it's just as well I watched *Hannibal* earlier then, isn't it?' said Donna, smirking.

'Thank you,' said Dmitri. 'Thank you, thank you.'

On the way upstairs to put the kids to bed he checked his BlackBerry and at last there was a message from Cheslav. It looked like he'd found a lead to Sanjeev's bitch. This was good news but it was something he'd have to let that blockhead take care of himself till morning.

At least it cheered him up and allowed him to look forward with equanimity to kissing the kids good night and snuggling up in front of the fire afterwards with Juliette Binoche and Lena Olin. And his wife, of course.

8. Teddy Roosevelt

'WHAT ABOUT DMT?' said Kelly.

He was getting a little impatient with Denny now. He wanted to get back to Bea. He wanted to know she was OK. And Casey – though she was probably still out.

Being stoned and not used to it had set his nerves on edge. He took his fags out and the minute he'd stuck one between his lips, Denny was on the scrounge. He tugged another out of the packet and tossed it across, half-wishing it was a grenade. At a much greater distance from himself obviously.

'Oh fuck, man, I shoulda twigged earlier,' said Denny.

'Twigged what?'

'When you said summat about a chemist. I've remembered now. Baz's sister's lives with a bloke who's a chemist—'

'Hang on,' said Kelly. 'Did you just say Baz's sister?'

'Yeah, Tracy. You remember Tracy.'

'Hang on. Fuckin' Baz's sister? Don't tell me she's got summat to do with all this.'

'Er . . . that's what I am tryin' to tell yer if you'll let me. I need another fuckin' spliff.'

He stretched for the drawer handle.

'Aw, come on, Denny.'

Kelly reached out and stayed Denny's hand and he wasn't sure that Denny liked it. More bad vibes.

'Stop getting' fuckin' distracted 'n' explain to us what yer on about. Is this the same Baz's sister whose kid all that fuss were about?'

'Yeah. I'm only telling' yer what I've heard, if you'll shurrup 'n' let me.'

Kelly removed his hand from Denny's wrist.

'Go on then.'

'Tracy shacked up wi' this Paki bloke or Indian or summat who's got a degree in chemistry. I heard he were doin' some dodgy work for some dodgy geezers – prob'ly ones that she set 'im up with.'

''Old on. I thought she were straight. I remember Baz tellin' us she din't want her kid turnin' out like him.'

'So? Does Bea want her kids turnin' into speed dealers like

she is?'

'Was,' Kelly corrected.

'Whatever. Just cos she wants a better life for her kids dun't mean she won't do owt it takes to get by. She's got to live, like the rest of us.'

'So where d'you hear all this? Have yer seen her?'

'Nah. Gorrit off a lad I know. You won't know him though. Since your time.'

'Who?'

'Teddy Roosevelt.'

'Teddy Roosevelt?' said Kelly.

'Yeah. Small skinny little ginger fucker.'

'Teddy Roosevelt?'

Meaning, *You've gotta be kidding me.*

'Yeah. D'you know him?'

'*Teddy* fuckin' *Roosevelt?*'

Meaning, *Explanation, please.*

'Yeah. *Do* yer know him?'

'No,' said Kelly, giving up.

'Used to be a student at the uni but I reckon he musta dropped out a while ago cos he's dealing full time now, man. Like I say, small skinny little ginger fucker, looks like he wun't say boo to a goose, but I tell yer what, he's got a short fuse 'n' he can be fuckin' tasty with his fists. Tough as nails, like a lot a these little 'uns. Dun't stand for no shit. D'yer remember Ryan? He musta been five-foot nowt 'n' have to run around in t'shower to get wet. But you fuckin' land a good punch on the cunt 'n' yer could guarantee he'd be up off that floor 'n' back at you in a second. He were like a fuckin' Weeble. He wun't give in an' he always kept on till he got the better of 'em. Teddy Roosevelt's like that.'

Ryan's death from an overdose, like the deaths of many others, had been on the balance sheet of pros and cons when Kelly and Bea were pitting their brains against their demons in the fight to quit drugs. He recalled the time at Clint's funeral when Ryan took offence because he hadn't been asked to be a pall bearer and after the first few beers at the wake picking a fight with the tallest bloke in the pub, an inoffensive guy who didn't deserve it.

Kelly found his mind flooded with memories he'd rather

forget. They'd still be in there but sealed away. Like they had been, until tonight.

'So you learnt all this from Teddy Roosevelt?' said Kelly, unable to believe what he was saying.

'Yeah. Teddy Roosevelt.'

Kelly buried his face in his hands. Fuck, he felt stoned – skunk-stoned, something he'd never been before. He had to force himself to think back to what they'd been talking about before Teddy Roosevelt had risen up into the conversation from the fucking bone yard of dead American presidents.

'So what's all this got to do with the letters D – M – T?' he said at last, unmasking his face at Denny.

'Well Teddy Roosevelt—'

Kelly stopped him with a mad bark of laughter. It was like he couldn't help himself. He thought he'd go insane if he heard that name again.

Denny left it a beat without comment then carried on.

'He said one bloke Tracy's fella were workin' for were this Ukrainian. Into drugs. Sellin' 'em, not doin' 'em, least not as far as I know—'

'Denny, are you fuckin' whizzin'?'

'No. Wish I wa'.'

'Cos yer fuckin' babblin'. Will yer fuckin' gerron with it?'

'It's his nickname,' said Denny. 'He's called Dmitri, right, but I just remembered his nickname. "DMT Dmitri". These could well be his fuckin' drugs, man. If it's DMT, you can guarantee it'll have summat to do wi' DMT Dmitri.'

'What d'you know about him?' said Kelly, focused now.

'Nothin'. Except that he sells drugs 'n' he's Ukrainian so he's probably a fuckin' mad bastard.'

'Well what does your mate know about him?'

'I dunno. Probably as much as me or you. Teddy Roosevelt dun't move in that kind a circle. I doubt he'll know owt.'

Denny paused while Kelly watched the workings of his brain on his face.

'I bet I know somebody who does though.'

Kelly waited, and waited. *Is that it?* he thought. *Is this where he keeps me in suspense indefinitely?*

'Who?'

'Guy I know. It's too late now though. Don't wanna disturb

him at this time a night. Gunner 'ave to leave it till tomorrow, I reckon. Give us a ring early to wake me up an' I'll give him a call. He's a good bloke, I'm sure he'll help you out if he can.'

Kelly didn't know how to feel: deflated at the trail coming to an end for the night or relieved that he could go home at last.

'Are you sure about this?'

'About what?'

'That this geezer's gonna – what? What is he gonna do?'

'Kelly, will ya stop yer fuckin' cluckin', woman? Give us a ring in the mornin' an' I'll fuckin' sort it. All right?'

'Promise?' said Kelly.

'Promise.' Denny stuck his hand out and Kelly grasped it. 'My word is my fuckin' Brooke Bond PG Tips an' all that, all right? So unless yer plannin' on stickin' around for another spliff . . .'

'No, man,' said Kelly, rising up with determination. 'I'm gonna get off. I wanna make sure Bea's OK.'

Denny watched Kelly gather up the pills from beside him on the sofa and replace them in his pocket. Then Denny observed him going through the motions that bikers go through – zipping up the leathers, checking for keys, fiddling with the helmet – as a general prologue to leave-taking. He'd changed a lot in that three-year fissure between today and yesterday.

'Listen take care, Denny, yeah? Thanks a lot for this, man. I really appreciate yer 'elp on this one. You know what it's like when you've got kids. Even when you 'an't gorrem. An' I'll give you a bell early tomorrer, yeah?'

'No probs, Kel. Early as yer like. I'm a changed man meself these days.'

'Nice one. I'll catch yer later.'

After Kelly had left and closed the door behind him, Denny got to his feet and switched off the big light. He sat back down in the armchair at the end of the low table facing the telly screen, thinking about building another spliff, and leaned forward to get his stash out of the drawer.

And there it was in front of him.

He'd forgotten about it for a second, not before Kelly had left, but between standing up to put the light out and sitting back down again.

There it was on the table top.

40

The pill that Kelly had given him to study.
The pill that Kelly had forgotten to take away with him.
The little white pill of temptation.

9. The Lib

CHESLAV HAD LEARNT from a helpful old *babushka* neighbour of Tracy's that Tracy would more than likely be in the Lib tonight.

Cheslav for a moment had no idea what that could be.

'The Liberal Club, dear. Two hundred yards down the road. That's where she usually is on a Friday night. I usually go meself for the bingo but my chap's not available tonight. Don't suppose you'd like to take me, would you?' she said with a wink of a wrinkly eyelid.

'Sorry – better not,' said Cheslav, beating a quick retreat, leaving the old woman to the rest of her solitary evening at home and returning to the car.

They spotted the club set back from the main road, a one-storey red-brick building with tall windows, a flat tarpaulin roof and a faded sign over the door: LIBERAL WORKING MEN'S CLUB. They turned into, and pulled up in, the car park.

From here, through a window, Cheslav could see people inside in a big concert room with musicians on a stage: a drummer and an organist. The sight reminded him of his teenage years at the Ukrainian Club: a sad place for entertainment but a good place for cheap drinks and to make useful contacts.

'Wait in the car,' he said to Olek, his driver.

'Are you sure?' said Olek. It was just the two of them, he was thinking; they should've brought three, one to drive and two for the heavy stuff. There were a lot of large drunken men in there if this bitch decided to create a scene. Still, Cheslav was good at this kind of work. He knew what he was doing.

'Wait in the car,' Cheslav repeated, climbing out.

The car park was empty. Everyone who was going to be inside tonight was already in there. As he walked toward the doors of the building, his hands went to the front of his jacket to hide the holster visible against his shirt beneath. He'd forgotten about the missing button though. Damn. He stopped to look down at himself. The remaining buttons, when fastened, failed to hide the gun enough.

'Shit.'

He turned around and walked back to the car. He opened the

door and climbed into the back seat. Olek looked round at him.

'What's happening?'

'When that button came off my jacket it spoiled the line of the suit.'

He slipped off his jacket and wriggled out of the holster, tossing it on the back seat and removing the pistol.

'The holster was visible. It looks bad going into a place like this showing you have a gun. Bad form.'

He shrugged and fidgeted his way back into the jacket, mumbling 'Fucking knock-off', then dropped the gun in the side pocket. If he wore the jacket open it wouldn't show.

'Is there anything you want me to do?' said the driver.

'Wait in the car.'

Inside there was an old man in a flat cap and National Health glasses sitting behind a table nursing a bottle of Guinness in one hand and a smouldering cigarette between the yellow fingers of the other. In front of him on the table were a beer mat, an ashtray, a pen, a book of tickets, a tin cash box and a large glass jar of once-loose change labelled 'Non-members 50p'.

'Fifty pee for non-members,' said the old man, indicating the jar – clearly a devotee of the belt and braces approach. He put his Guinness down and transferred his cigarette to the other hand so he could write.

Cheslav took out his wallet and tossed the old man a twenty-pound note.

'Keep the change,' he said moving past the table.

''Ey, 'ang on, I've still got to sign you in.'

But Cheslav was already striding down the hall towards the concert room ignoring the cry of the old man behind him.

When he opened the concert-room door the harsh blare of the organ and drums hit his ears and the cigarette smoke rasped at the back of his throat. He stepped inside and looked around.

People on the dance floor shuffling to the tune of 'Blue Spanish Eyes' beneath a glitter-ball; elderly couples mostly, and some children. Others sitting at tables, some queuing at the bar. The room was small enough and lighted enough for him to recognise her if he saw her, and open enough to see everyone from the same spot. But she wasn't among them. He would come back in a few minutes and look again if necessary. Maybe she'd gone out to the toilet.

In the meantime he followed a short corridor that led him to the public bar. In clubs, they didn't call it a tap room. That much he remembered too from his teenage years. It was a long time since he'd last been in a place like this.

It'd been a long time since Cheslav had last seen Tracy Croft too but he recognised her immediately. She struck him now as she had on the few occasions they'd met before. She'd lost some weight but not too much. There was still something sensuous about her. It wasn't just her figure though but her personality. It was defiant, fiery. Of course, she was as rough as a bitch in a whorehouse kennel but he liked that too. Not that she would even remember him.

Anyway, he had to forget all that tonight. It was a job and it was for the boss. If he screwed up again he'd be in real trouble. Proper Siberian-style trouble.

There were maybe fifteen, twenty people in the room. As he walked across to the table where she was sitting talking to a man and a woman, she happened to glance in his direction incidentally in mid-conversation. She looked at her friends again for a second then looked back up, double-taking, her mouth slowing to a halt.

So she did recognise him after all. He mustn't forget that she didn't know about Sanjeev.

'What the hell are *you* doin' 'ere?' she said as he approached her table.

'Come with me, please,' he said.

'I beg your pardon.'

'I'd like you to come with me. Please stand up.'

'Who's this, Tracy?' said the man sitting at her table.

He was a man, not a boy. He hadn't made a move yet but he looked as though he thought he could.

The other woman at the table was staring at Tracy with her mouth open.

'That's a point, who are yer?' said Tracy. 'I don't even know yer name.'

'I'll tell you on the way.'

'I'm not goin' anywhere,' said Tracy. 'And certainly not wi' you.'

'I'm sorry,' said Cheslav. 'Please, finish your drink first.'

''E's a joker, in't he?' said the man. 'Look, pal, I don't know who you are but she wants to stay 'ere. You heard 'er, din't yer?'

'This has nothing to do with you,' said Cheslav, not looking at the man, looking at Tracy.

'Well—'

That was as far as the man got. As soon as he started to rise from his chair Cheslav put him back down on it with a flip of his hand. One hand, like a butcher's slap.

'Don't – be stupid,' he said, looking at the man now.

The room had fallen quiet.

'Hey, what's goin' on 'ere?'

A male voice behind him, coming around from behind the bar.

'It's all right, Colin,' said Tracy.

'No, it's not all right,' said the voice.

Cheslav turned to look. A man of about fifty, big, an ex-miner or boxer, by the look of him, but out of shape.

'I run this club 'n' I say what's all right. All right? So what's goin' on?' He was addressing the big bloke in the suit now, the stranger with a funny accent.

''E's tryin' to make Tracy go somewhere with him,' said the man Cheslav had restrained.

'I've had enough of this,' Cheslav muttered to himself, and grabbed Tracy by the arm, lifting her from her chair. 'We're going. Now.'

The sitting man was up again, all the way up this time on his feet, but Cheslav kept a hold on Tracy's arm as he head-butted him out of the way.

The bar room was a frenzy of shouting and commotion now. He wished it hadn't come to this.

As the manager of the club came at him Cheslav had to let go of Tracy to block a punch before sidestepping and ramming his knuckles into the man's kidneys. The man crumpled to the floor gagging for breath and Cheslav decided it was time to get the gun out.

'Please,' he said, waving it around for everyone to see.

After a couple of shrieks the noise in the room fell to a panicked murmur before Cheslav called for silence. He bent down and put his hand through the crook of the manager's arm, coaxing him up on his feet.

'Come on. Get up. Stand up. You'll feel better in a minute.

Stand up and breathe.'

He looked across at Tracy.

'It's all right, Colin,' she said as the manager wobbled up with the support of his attacker's arm. She turned and helped her friend, the other one who'd tried to intervene, up to his feet. 'Are you OK, Don?' she said, producing a tissue from her cuff for his bloody nose.

'Yer not fuckin' goin' anywhere wi' that mad bastard,' said Don through his hands. 'Some'dy call the fuckin' police!'

'No!' said Tracy. 'Don. It's all right, OK? Just leave it. I'll be all right.'

She gave him a hug to calm him down and whispered something soothing in his ear. Her woman friend across the table looked emotionally threatened as she watched this semblance of intimacy pass between them. Cheslav could see it in her posture and in her eyes – the dagger of jealousy in the look. Don's wife, perhaps.

'Can we go now?'

'Come on then, yer Russian fucker,' she said gathering up her coat and belongings and strutting past him. She knew he was Ukrainian, she remembered that much, but calling him Russian was the only way she could think of to piss him off to his face.

Cheslav put the gun back in his pocket and leaned in close to the manager's ear.

'Any police, I'll come back and blow your club up. You understand?'

Colin just gave him a look, half agony, half malice.

'D'you understand? Say yes or no.'

'Yes.'

The whole room was like a frieze in a museum, maybe from the future – a museum of working men's clubs. As he walked Tracy to the door, movement returned as people parted out of their way. It was like some kind of red carpet treatment and they were the celebrity couple. Except that there was a button missing from his suit. That spoiled the effect.

The gawping old man on the door holding out his pen took one look at Tracy and said, 'Are you signin' him in, love?' then gawped some more as they strutted wordlessly past him and out the door.

Once outside Cheslav put her in the back seat of the car and climbed in next to her. The driver turned round to her as if to say good evening but, at one look from Cheslav, correctly thought the better of it.

'Drive,' said Cheslav, watching all the time for trouble hunting him out of the club.

'Where are we going?' said the driver. 'To the boss?'

'No. He'll be watching his film now. We'll take her up to the penthouse. Now drive.'

The car U-turned its way out of the car park and joined the main road, accelerating to a moderate speed.

'Give me your mobile phone,' he said to Tracy.

'What? What the fuck d'you want that for?'

'Just give me it, please.'

She didn't move.

'Look,' said Cheslav, 'you know who we are. You know who I am, even though it's been a long time. You remember. You know what we're willing to do.'

'I 'an't gorrit.'

'What do you mean, you haven't got it?'

'What d'you think I mean? Your English is good enough.'

He said nothing. He was good, she thought. He wasn't going to let himself be drawn into her efforts at stalling for time.

'I left it at 'ome. When I went to the club. I forgot it. I din't even realise till halfway through t'night when I went for it to check me texts.'

She shut up. She was explaining too much, she realised.

'Show me your handbag. And your pockets. Come on, turn them out.'

'What the fuck is this all about?'

'We can talk about that later. Give me your handbag, please.'

She slapped it at him. He didn't even flinch, the cool bastard.

He opened it up, prising its jaws apart with both of his big fists like a crocodile wrestler. She'd seen one the other day on the telly put his head inside a croc's mouth and it had snapped shut on him. Silly sod. In Florida or somewhere exotic. He was a big macho idiot too, like this one.

To be fair though he was considerate enough not to tip her handbag's contents out all over the back of the car, he just rummaged through it, finding no phone and nothing dangerous. He started searching her coat pockets but he knew from the look she was giving him that he wasn't going to find anything there either.

'Who is at home now?' he said handing her back her things.

'No one.'

'You're lying. Who?'

'I dunno. Depends who you're looking for, dunnit? You lookin' for Sanjeev? Well you won't find him. Is that who yer lookin' for, eh? You must remember Sanjeev. In fact, didn't I introduce 'im to you once? A long time ago.'

Cheslav remembered.

'But how could you?' he said to her. 'You don't even know my name.'

'Yeah, that's right. I never caught it properly the first time. An' I don't wanna know it now.'

'Are we going back to her house, Cheslav?' said Olek from behind the wheel.

She caught it this time and Cheslav looked her in the eye to make sure she had, but she said nothing, playing it cool.

'No. We've disturbed the locals enough for now. We don't want to run into a posse.'

Cheslav was aware that he was explaining himself too much – excusing his decisions to the driver. Really it was for her. Better that Sanjeev wasn't on her mind for the time being. The dead Sri Lankan was on his mind enough for both of them.

'Continue to the penthouse.'

Penthouse, thought Tracy, trying to convince herself this wasn't going to be so bad after all.

One thing she didn't understand though. What did they want from her that they wouldn't want from Sanjeev? And if they knew or even suspected he was at home why didn't they go and look for him there? It'd be a lot easier than grabbing her the way they had done in front of a bar full of witnesses.

Cheslav or whatever the fuck he was called had fallen into silence. While Tracy glared at his profile watching the traffic on the road ahead she thought back to what had happened in the Lib.

She thought back to when she'd given Don a hug after the Ukrainian had busted his nose and how she'd secretly pushed her mobile phone into his hand, whispering to him to phone Sanjeev, the number was in the phone, and tell him to get out of the house now and not to worry, she'd be all right – please, Don, just do it for me.

10. Jimmy Savile

DENNY'S THROAT WAS parched from smoking the skunk weed and it felt like it was getting drier even though he hadn't smoked any more of it since he'd popped the tablet that Kelly had left behind. He wished he had some beer. He looked around the room for empty tins lying around.

Next to his mattress there were a couple of bedsides, but when he rattled them they proved even drier than his throat. He picked his way through the debris to the kitchen and managed to find a glass clean enough to drink from. He poured some tap water and swallowed it down but it clicked past his Adam's apple like dice rolling on a wooden game board. If anything he felt more parched.

He stumbled back into the bed-sitting room. Jesus, he had to sit down before he fell down.

When he flopped back down onto the armchair the floor of the room rippled like a water bed. There was no sound to it, just the rippling motion, like he'd jumped on to a mattress full of water. He lifted his feet up instinctively so they wouldn't get wet and he felt the armchair cast off like a raft untied at sea.

He looked over the edge and saw the rubber doll, which had drifted over from the corner of the room, floating past. She lifted her arm towards him, drowning not waving, and he reached down and pulled her aboard.

'There you go, you're safe now,' Denny murmured.

He hugged her close to his body and waited to see what would happen to the two of them next. Just as the floor had turned into something resembling the ocean, he saw the walls around him buckling and dissolving into the waves of light thrown off the TV screen, producing an effect similar to a heat haze.

'Now then, it's all right, son' the television was saying directly to him.

There was no picture as such anymore but the screen was a face; not showing him a face; it had become a face in itself, neither male nor female but a talking cartoon television, like the talking anthropomorphic telephones they put in mobile phone commercials. There was no longer any programme being broadcast. The TV set was a human-like presence now, squatting and talking to him in the corner of the room, so that Denny expected it to sprout a set of little legs and paddle towards him. And still there was a part of his mind that told him such a thing would be ridiculous.

'I totally agree,' said the rubber doll in his arms before kissing him on the cheek and snuggling her face into the side of his neck.

'It's all right, son,' said the TV. 'We're coming. Just hang on and stay put.'

The walls shimmered like photonic curtains of energy and directed Denny's attention to the light pouring down from the ceiling. He looked up, wondering if the ceiling would still be there or if the building above him had opened up to the heavens yet. That was the deal, wasn't it? That was what the TV was counting down to.

'Five . . . four . . . three . . . two . . . one . . . '

Here we go, Denny thought, *here we fucking go.*

The light was a flower, a cosmic stamen pointed straight at him and zooming towards his head at a thousand miles an hour.

Two thousand.

Five thousand.

Mach ten.

As the dart of pure light hurtled down faster and faster, it got no nearer. It was as if Denny's armchair raft were retreating before it just as fast as it advanced, keeping the same distance between them, except that the chair wasn't moving at all, not even bobbing on the waves of the floor anymore, but held dead still at the centre of the universe.

Denny was a vast planet-sized bull's eye, a gas giant, and the dart of light was penetrating deeper towards a core it would never reach.

'Now then, it's all right, son. We're coming for you.'

He knew that voice from somewhere.

The walls, floor and ceiling fizzled away completely now.

The chair fizzled away.

The doll was gone. The TV was gone. The light was gone.

There was only Denny left, scooped into the rounded spoon-like cup of a featureless grey cell like the inside of an egg, and he was dead.

He observed himself lying there completely still and useless and stone cold dead for some minutes, wondering what he was going to do about it and knowing that there was nothing he could do. But it was all right, as the voice kept telling him.

'It's all right, son. We're coming.'

He knew he recognised that voice.

Jimmy Savile, complete with lilac shell-suit, gold medallion and a fat cigar, materialised through the formless grey wall of the egg. For a moment he stood over Denny's corpse looking down at it, then he bent over, took hold of it by the scruff of the neck and stepped away, dragging the lifeless body one-handedly behind him, like a caveman with his kill.

Jimmy Savile and Denny's corpse passed through the wall as though it were a fog bank.

When they reached the other side, they had left the block of flats and were on top of the Kremlin, and Jimmy Saville lay down his burden, spreading it out ceremoniously beneath the antenna-like spiked circle that crowned the building, pointed at the night sky above.

Jimmy Savile transferred his cigar from between his teeth to between his fingers and spread his arms out wide, his face turned towards the stars, a cosmic shaman performing the ritual he was born to carry out.

'And there,' he called out to the face of the wind buffeting around them, 'reigning supreme at number two . . .'

Stars coalesced into a pattern of lights above them. The lights slowly began to wheel around them, the speed of their revolution accelerating till they were whizzing like a Catherine wheel.

A beam of energy shot down from the centre, connecting in a blinding flash with the tip of the spike, and when the corona of light subsided back into the night like the afterglow of an atom bomb, Denny was gone.

11. Park Life

DAMIEN WAS CROUCHING in the shadows of the bushes at the edge of the park and it was fucking freezing. Even though he'd got his jacket on and a baseball cap, the cold was starting to get to him now.

He didn't have any gloves but his hands were still OK – he'd been keeping them buried in his trouser pockets, nice and near the warmth from his groin. He took them out to check the clock on the screen of his mobile.

Shit, man, it was nearly eleven o'clock. When was Stevo gonna call him? He'd left loadsa messages. He gave his number another go, punching in the redial with a thumb that was already starting to feel bitten by Jack Frost. If he wasn't answering by now Damien didn't know what the fuck he was gonna do.

Just when he thought it was gonna go to voicemail again, Stevo picked up.

'Y'all right, bro',' said Stevo straight away. 'Man, you won't believe the night I'm having. I can't find my mum anywhere. I'm getting well worried, D-Man.'

'An' you won't believe the night I'm 'avin'.' Damien thought he'd better come straight out with it. 'They've found your gear.'

'What? Who have?'

'Me folks. Me mam. An' Kelly.'

'What, your stepdad?'

'He's not me stepdad. He's me mam's boyfriend, partner, whatever.'

'He's not gonna do anything stupid with 'em, is he?'

'No, it's all right, I've sorted it.'

'What d'you mean, you've sorted it. How've you sorted it?'

'Look, it doesn't matter, Stevo, I said it's sorted. For now, anyway. Thing is, I can't go back there. Not tonight, anyway. I wanna let things cool down overnight. But I 'an't got anywhere to stay. In any case, I think we need to meet up an' discuss this, don't you?'

'Listen, D-Man, I can't right now, all right? I'm really worried about my mother. I got a call from this geezer earlier tonight from *her* phone, right? One of our neighbours, right, but from *my mum's* phone, man, 'n' he's sayin' someone's bin in the club where she goes drinkin', right, 'n' they've like . . . I dunno, fuckin' kidnapped her or summing. An' I can't get hold a fuckin' Sanjeev, that Paki bastard.'

'I thought you said he was from Sri Lanka.'

'Yeah, whatever. But he ain't around, man. His phone's dead so that's just something else to worry about, innit?'

'Look, Stevo, we need to get together. Summat's 'app'nin', man. At least, let me help ya find yer mam.'

There was a pause while he gave Stevo space to think.

'Yeah, all right, D-Man, we'd better meet up. Bu you've got the gear, yeah?'

'No, it's still at 'ome.'

'But it's OK, right? Your old man's not gonna call Five-O or anything like that?'

'Nah, it's cool, man. 'E used to be a druggy. So did me mam. They're not gonna involve the police. They know I'm OK.'

'All right, let's hook up. But not at my place, not at the house, yeah? Think of another place.'

Damien thought and thought hard. He had an idea, but it was desperate and he wasn't sure how much he liked it. More than that, he wasn't sure how much Chloe was gonna like it.

Fuck it, though. He'd rather be anywhere than in this fucking freezing park all night.

12. Sanjeev's Ghost

IT WAS LATE, far into the early hours of Saturday morning. Cheslav could never really figure that one out, how it could be late and early at the same time, and his brain was too tired to think about it now. He was awake though still, his eyes resting on the big TV screen across the room while he let the sound of Russian voices from the movie drift into his consciousness.

Funny. He had spent more years of his life living in England, surrounded by the sounds of English, than he had spent living in his homeland, and still he could follow the dialogue without effort.

What was even funnier was that Russian wasn't even the natural language of his homeland, yet it remained his linguistic touchstone, something he still used with one person or another every day.

In fact, it was so long since he'd used Ukrainian that he doubted his ability to speak it any longer with any confidence and fluency. Here he was, a Ukrainian, and he felt as though Ukrainian were his third language.

Sitting there contemplating his own identity, Cheslav became conscious of the plush apartment around him, and the woman sleeping in the bedroom behind the closed door down the hall.

This wasn't where he lived, he had his own apartment elsewhere, but this place felt as much like home as his own place – or, more accurately, as little. Today, this night, he had washed up here as aimlessly, just as much at the behest of other people and other forces, as Sanjeev had done earlier, and tomorrow, who knew where he would next find himself. He certainly felt no compunction to gravitate to his own place, which contained little or nothing that defined who he was.

At least, he was pretty sure, there was going to be a tomorrow for him – that, unlike for Sanjeev, this was not going to be the last place he would ever see.

His eyes flickered away from the film on the TV screen to an armchair across the room, and the little Sri Lankan man was there, sitting in it.

It was the Sanjeev that he had brought up here, thankfully,

not the Sanjeev whose wet, pulpy clothes he'd searched afterwards for a mobile phone down at the bottom.

Cheslav didn't flinch. He just sat there looking at Sanjeev and Sanjeev sat there looking at him. Then he thought that someone had to talk first and it might as well be him.

'I'm sorry.'

'I thought we were friends,' said Sanjeev calmly, less of an accusation, more of a lament.

'We knew each other, that's all.'

'When I first met you, I thought I could trust you because you knew Tracy.'

'I didn't know her. I only knew some people that she knew.'

'You let me down' said Sanjeev.

'It was Dmitri who put you up there. You know I had to obey his orders. I didn't mean to—'

He thought he heard a movement from down the hall – Sanjeev's woman stirring in the bedroom – and he tensed, ready to move, in case she thought he might have abandoned his vigil and she could attempt to depart. He listened more carefully but there was nothing.

When he looked back at the armchair, it was empty.

The Sri Lankan was gone.

Cheslav returned his attention to the Russian film, but he couldn't concentrate on it anymore. After ten minutes, he felt his eyes growing tired and he clicked the remote impatiently, switching off the TV in disgust.

13. Blues Brothers

ON THE SATURDAY morning Kelly phoned Denny at nine and Denny told Kelly to meet him at ten in the Blues Brothers Café at Hyde Park Corner, and to bring a spare helmet if he was coming on his bike.

By the time Kelly arrived Denny was already tucking into a Full English Breakfast and swilling it down with a cup of sweet milky tea.

'Sit yerself down,' he said to Kelly, gesturing at the chair across the table. 'Have you eaten?'

'Nah, I'm all right. Thought we'd be meeting near yours rather than this old neck a the woods.'

'He works near 'ere, though – the guy we're off to see.'

'Workin' on a Saturday?'

'Yeah, he does weird hours. Sure you don't want owt to eat?'

'I'm not 'ungry. Our fuckin' Damien din't come 'ome all night.'

Denny stopped chewing his sausage for a moment.

''E'll be all right. He's streetwise is Damien. Has he not called?'

'Not yet. Bea's hangin' on' telephone like fuckin' Debbie 'Arry.'

Denny paused in his chewing for a moment longer to ponder, like Archimedes thinking about the bath-tub water in the penultimate bath before his eureka moment.

''E'll be all right,' he finally said, the phrase playing piggy in the middle between platitude and philosophy. He resumed his chewing of the sausage.

'I fuckin' 'ope so. I don't know how Bea'd cope if owt happened to 'im.'

'Take it easy, man. We'll go see this mate a mine 'n' see what he sez.'

'Would you like me to bring you anything?'

It was the waitress, suddenly arrived at the table unnoticed, addressing Kelly.

'Cup a coffee, please, love.'

'Latte, cappuccino, Americano, espresso . . .'

'Just hot 'n' brown 'n' wet wi' two sugars, please.'

'Just a normal filter coffee then?'

She was obviously bored and wanting to play with the Gaggia machine just for something to do.

'Anything to eat?'

'What? No, I'm all right, ta.'

She drifted off and Kelly hunkered over the table towards Denny, who was eyeing the girl's bum as she walked away.

'So what's the score? What we doin'?'

'Give us a chance to finish me breakfast.'

'I've seen yer talk with yer mouth full before.'

'We're gonna go see a mate a mine called Ilko. Well, when I say a mate – Did yer come on yer bike?'

'Course I came on me bike.'

'Did yer bring a spare helmet?'

'Yer just saw me walk in with it.'

'Oh yeah, sorry. Did I? I'm still half asleep. Yeah, Ilko. I reckon he'll be able to help us out.'

'Ilko? What, like Sergeant Bilko?'

'Bilko, Wilko,' said Denny, thinking of the old Leeds United manager back in the day. 'Yeah. But I think he was higher up than a sergeant.'

'Jesus. He's not another mercenary, is he? Where do you meet all these SAS types?'

'No, man, he's a social worker. He was in the army though. Russian army, I think. I suppose. Though he's actually Ukrainian. Well, they all are in Leeds, aren't they? Either that or Russian Jews.'

'Hang on, he's a social worker? What, you mean like he's your parole officer or summat?'

'What yer givin' it, fuckin' parole officer? I never said 'e were *my* social worker.'

'Well I don't know, do I?'

Kelly noticed Denny wasn't saying that he wasn't his social worker either.

'He works at that hostel for ex-offenders on Brudenell Road, all right. Used to go drinking in t'Brudenell Social Club. That's where I know him from.'

'All right, so how can he help us?'

'He'll know Dmitri, for one thing. Or he'll've heard of him.

So if those pills *are* Dmitri's, at least you can find out who you're up against. He knows a lot about what goes on in Leeds – 'specially wit' East Europeans.'

Kelly's coffee arrived just as Denny was mopping up the last of the baked bean juice with his bread and butter.

'Right,' he said clattering his knife and fork down on the empty plate, 'drink that quick and let's get off.'

Jesus, thought Kelly, *now who's doing all the rushing?*

14. Penthouse

TRACY AWOKE FUZZILY and looked around her, not knowing where she was. Everything smelt and looked too clean and bright. It wasn't home, that was for sure.

A memory of violence jolted through her brain and it all came flooding back. The Lib, the Ukrainian turning up. Poor Don and Colin.

She hoped Don had managed to contact Sanjeev. Hope was all she could do; without her mobile she had no immediate way of finding out. And no way of letting anyone know where she was. Which she now remembered.

She moved her limbs and felt smooth silk sheets rubbing against the skin of her unstockinged legs. For a moment she panicked, thinking someone – that mad fucking Ukrainian – must have undressed her before putting her into the bed, because she couldn't remember undressing herself.

She pushed a hand under the covers, could feel that she was still fully clothed, breathed a sigh of relief.

It was all coming back to her. The drive from the Lib to one of the new buildings in town down by the riverside; alighting from the car in an underground car park; a smooth, swift ride in a lift up to one of the penthouse suites and the kind of luxury she'd only ever seen on TV.

Cheslav had dismissed the driver for the night, instructing him to wait for a call in the morning. When they got up to the penthouse and the Ukrainian let himself in with his own set of keys, she realised that it was going to be just the two of them. Once they were inside with the door locked behind them, he could have done anything he wanted with her.

Instead he'd poured them both a drink – vodka of course, not what she'd have chosen but she wasn't offered a choice – switched on the television, an enormous widescreen set, slipped in some DVD of a film in Russian with no subtitles, and told her where the bedroom was for whenever she was ready to go to sleep.

She noticed it wasn't the only bedroom in the apartment and assumed and hoped that the other one was where the Ukrainian would be sleeping.

She also didn't fail to notice the touch of a woman's presence about the place – a pair of earrings on a side table, a bottle of expensive perfume in the corner of a bookshelf, a magazine rack with magazines she was sure this man wouldn't be caught dead reading – but they were certainly the only two here and she kept shtumm, stopping herself from enquiring further, keeping conversation to a minimum.

Understanding that she was there for the night whether she liked it or not, she had gulped down the vodka and just hoped it would help blot it all out and put her under.

Later, in the night, she would swear that she heard the Ukrainian talking to someone, but when she listened more closely there was no one else there. He must've been talking to himself. First sign of madness, she reflected automatically, then tried to push the thought out of her head.

She got out of bed now, stood up, straightened her skirt, which had twisted round in the night, and fastened some buttons that had come undone at the front of her blouse.

Without her mobile she'd no idea what time it was, having stopped wearing a watch years ago. Outside it was daylight. She walked over to the floor-to-ceiling windows. The curtains were open, not that it mattered – the buildings opposite were low-lying commercial properties from which no one could see her because she was high above them, and which were closed and empty for the weekend in any case.

Her shoes were on the floor next to the bed. As she returned to them and slipped them onto her feet she looked around the bedroom, taking it all in.

Whereas the living room that she'd seen last night had betrayed a woman's hand, this room looked reserved for a man's use. The bed was massive, one of those kingsize ones that she'd seen in catalogues and shop windows but never expected to sleep in. There was another widescreen TV set at the foot of it, blank-eyed, just a tiny red standby light showing, awaiting a command from the zapper on the nightstand to bring it to life. She'd ignored it last night, too worried to think about watching telly, her brain soon fatigued by distress. When she slid open the doors of the built-in wardrobe, she saw two expensive men's suits hanging from the rail, a couple of shirts, new-looking, and little else. The soft furnishings were all freshly laundered, unmarked black silk and velvet, and the walls were slabs of spotless snow-white space interrupted only by a large framed colour print of a photograph hanging above the bed-head – a twenty-year-old Nastassja Kinski lying on her side facing the camera and wearing nothing but a live python: the one thing in the room that Tracy recognised as being tacky as hell.

Just as she was about to test the bedroom door to see if she was locked in, a knock from the other side made her jump.

'Are you decent?'

It was Cheslav's voice.

'If you mean am I dressed, then yes,' she said back. 'If you mean owt else, you can go fuck yourself. How's that for an answer?'

The door opened and he was standing there. At first he looked no different from yesterday, same clothes, same demeanour, as though he could have been sitting in the same position watching the TV all night long. Then she noticed that he was clean-shaven and his suit jacket had a button where one was missing yesterday. She could remember him making some silly fuss about it at some point to the driver in the car on the way here.

'Get ready.'

He pointed to a door behind her across the bedroom that she remembered looking behind last night.

'There's a bathroom through there if you want to freshen up. Wash.'

She glared at him, resenting the implication that she wasn't already as fragrant as a lily.

'Clean your teeth.'

Her resentment melted a little when he held out a new toothbrush still in its packaging, as if he'd just conjured it specially for her out of thin air.

'We leave in ten minutes.'

She resisted the temptation to ask where they were going. She knew what his answer would be. *I'll tell you on the way. You'll see when we get there.* She wasn't going to give him the satisfaction.

She had a pretty good idea anyway. What was it that driver had said last night? Something about going to the boss. Somebody was pulling Cheslav's strings, that was for sure. She didn't know what the fuck was going on or what this was all about but she sure as hell knew that it was something this dumb bunny hadn't cooked up by himself, so there was no point asking him anyway.

In the meantime, she might as well take full advantage of the hospitality. After all, it could be the first and last time that she had her own penthouse bedroom with an en suite bathroom. She should enjoy it while she had the chance.

She snatched the toothbrush out of Cheslav's hand and shut the door in his face without a word of thanks.

15. Sergeant Ilko

'NO, NOT TRUE,' Ilko Pogrebinsky was saying to Denny. 'I never rose above rank of sergeant. I didn't want to anyway. I would've lost respect of my comrades-in-arms. You have to remember what a vicious war that was. Now history praises Gorbachev for pulling Soviets out of Afghanistan but when he first came to power in '85 actually he sent in *more* troops, willing to give it another year before pulling the plug. We were last wave to be sent in but we weren't the dregs. They trained us long and hard before they sent us into that shit-storm. None of us had much respect for officers though. We obeyed them, we had to, but we didn't respect them. Especially those of us who weren't Russian anyway.'

All very nice, Kelly was thinking, but time was moving on, there was stuff to be sorted while they were still relatively young, and he hadn't come here for a history lesson. In any case he didn't know the first thing about the Soviets in Afghanistan and figured it was a bit late to start learning now.

He looked up from the bench that the three of them were occupying and swept an impatient gaze across the park. Ilko hadn't wanted to talk to them in front of the lads at the hostel where he worked so they'd come here for some privacy. It reminded Kelly of something out of a spy story, except he wasn't sure who'd be the joes and who the runners. Meanwhile children played on swings and people walked their dogs at a distance impossible to eavesdrop from and Kelly waited for the old guy to finish his reminiscing. Well not old exactly, but definitely in the decade above theirs.

'How come you were there then if you're not Russian?' said Denny, who seemed to be taking pains to show an unnecessary interest in the subject.

'It was before Ukrainian independence. Maybe we thought ourselves as Ukrainians but to Red Army we were Soviet citizens. They could conscript us as easily as anyone else and we had no choice in the matter. We had to go and do our duty.'

'So how come you know this Dmitri?' Kelly said, prising an opening for himself in the conversation. 'Was he there as well?'

Ilko glanced at Denny as though checking with him – *Is this guy OK to talk to?* – then looked at Kelly with a mixture of suspicion and warning in eyes that had clearly seen a lot of life – and death.

'Denny said something to me about this man Dmitri. No, if he was in Afghanistan I never knew him there. He's the right age, so it's possible. I was in east, in Paktia Province. We had it hard there towards the end. Maybe he was in some other part of the country. It's possible. But I know of him from here. He is a bad man. If you are at all involved with him I would advise you to get uninvolved as quickly as possible.'

'How's he a bad man? I mean what's he done? What does he do?'

Ilko laughed. It was short and bleak, hardly the product of pleasantry.

'What doesn't he do?'

Kelly was expecting more but Ilko stopped short as if no further explanation were necessary.

'Such as?'

Ilko looked around, taking pains that no one was within earshot. Kelly was finding it all a touch melodramatic, meaning a touch irritating. He wondered if all Russians or Ukrainians or whatever they were went in for this kind of cloak-and-dagger pantomime. Or was it really himself being naïve?

'From what I know, Dmitri Maximov came to this country long time ago. Ten, fifteen years at least, maybe more. Long time before me. Already then he had relatives here in England, here in Leeds. When he get here they help him out. Help him set up in the family business. But business was already going back in Kiev. Dmitri came over to run it this end.'

'Run what?' said Kelly.

'Black market. How do they call it? Racketeering. If Ukrainian wanted to come to England, gangsters like Dmitri provide him with Polish passport so he can find job in this country. In early days it was good for them. Lots of people with more money than love of Ukraine's independence. Independence is a nice dream but it doesn't put bread on the table. Under Soviets, people were looked after, under independence they must look after themselves, and they have a word for what happened then: shitocracy. Later, of course, Poland joined EU so Ukrainians must go to Polish mafia if they want identity card.

But no matter for Dmitri. By then his business was expanding into other areas. Guns. Drugs. Prostitutes. You name it.'

'I'm not being funny,' said Kelly, 'but how do you know all this?'

'You tell me something,' said Ilko. 'You ever take drugs? Eh? I'm not being funny either but you look like someone who maybe take drugs sometime. You a friend of Denny here and I know damn well he take drugs.'

Kelly didn't deny it.

'So you know where to buy drugs, right? Now you tell me. How do you know where to buy drugs? How do you know where to go to buy them?'

Kelly had no answer.

'See? Same for me. You just know. Since many years ago you just know, right? So. You know your people, I know mine. That's how it is.'

'OK,' said Kelly at last, 'so why do they call him "DMT Dmitri"?'

Ilko laughed.

'You hear that too, huh?'

'I heard that's his nickname. I'm askin' you about it.'

'Stories, stories,' said Ilko lyrically, 'bedtime stories to frighten little children.'

'So tell me these stories,' said Kelly, feeling bolder now in front of this stranger.

'Why you wanna know this stuff?' said Ilko. 'Denny here tell me you want to know this stuff but he not tell me why.'

Kelly sensed he could get away with a degree of cheek.

'Indulge me for a while.'

'You wanna know about DMT Dmitri? Like I say, this Dmitri is a bad man. But it only serves his purpose if word gets round just how bad he is. So he go out of his way to make himself look even badder. Just to show how bad he really can be.'

'Like I said,' said Kelly, 'you'll have to indulge me cos I've never heard o' this Dmitri before yesterday so I 'an't got a clue how bad he is.'

'OK,' said Ilko warming up to his subject. 'You ever take this drug? DMT?'

'No. I'd never heard o' that till yesterday either.'

Blowback

Ilko looked at Denny.
'You?'
'Nah. Me? Nah.'
Kelly could tell from his shiftiness that Denny was lying. He didn't know if Ilko could tell and he didn't say anything – for now.
'I never take it either,' said Ilko, 'but kids who have tell me it's like dying. Like dying and living at the same time. I don't understand this. Why would anyone want to feel like they die? Why would they pay money to do this? Maybe I don't want to understand, right? But one thing they all say is, this is a scary experience, 'specially if you never done it before. So Dmitri thinks to himself, Hey, maybe I can use this to – shit, how you say in English? To make his reputation more – more – '
Ilko gestured an increase in size with his waving hands.
'To enhance his reputation?' said Kelly.
'That's it. That's the one. To enhance his reputation. Make him even badder to all the people who fear him already. Make them fear him more.'
'How?' said Kelly.
'Few years back Dmitri kept dogs. Not for fun or pets. Fighting dogs. You know, illegal dog fights. That small vicious breed they use.'
'Pit bulls.'
This was Denny chipping in now to help fill the gaps in Ilko's vocabulary.
'Yeah, those. Dmitri kept a stable of them—'
'Kennel,' Kelly and Denny both interrupted at once.
'Dmitri kept a whole bunch of these motherfucking little brutes,' said Ilko paraphrasing capably now, 'on a farm outside town somewhere. Made a lot of money on dog fights out in the country till the business started getting too much attention in the papers and the police cracked down hard. He got out while the going was still good. But while he had those dogs, dog fighting wasn't the only thing he use them for.
'Around that time there was a guy who tried to double-cross Dmitri on a drug deal. Everyone on the estates knew him, or said they did, and everyone told the same story about what happened to him when Dmitri found out. The story involved Dmitri starving those dogs for two days before he toss the guy in with

67

them.'

'I don't get it,' said Kelly. 'How does that explain why he's called DMT Dmitri?'

'Because before he threw the guy in with the dogs he injected him with DMT just to make it worse for him.'

Denny shuddered visibly and it only seemed to confirm to Kelly that he *had* done DMT himself after all. But last night he said he hadn't and Kelly had believed him. Then it twigged. He must've left one of those pills behind when he left Denny's place last night. And if Denny and drugs were left in the same room together, you could safely bet your last penny that Denny would do them in.

It was up to Kelly now to do some explaining on his side of the bargain. He pulled one of the pills out of his pocket and showed it to Ilko.

'I think this Dmitri character has found a way to produce this stuff in pill form, which is supposed to be impossible, right?'

Ilko held the pill up to his scrutiny between a thumb and forefinger, analysing the marking that Denny had deciphered for Kelly the night before.

'What's the connection?' he said at last. 'This could be anything. How d'you know it is DMT? How d'you know it has anything to do with the same man we are talking about?'

'I don't,' said Kelly. 'But there are two ways we can find out. One, swallow it and see what happens.'

'And the other way?'

'You ever heard of a—' Kelly stopped himself from saying 'Paki' at the last minute – 'an Asian chemist who works for Dmitri?'

'Sanjeev,' said Ilko. 'Yeah, I know him. Nice man, clever, but weak. Foolish to involve himself with Dmitri.'

'Well I'm pretty sure this is something he made. So I'm guessing he made it for this DMT Dmitri character.'

'So? You're buying drugs supplied by Dmitri. What's unusual about that?'

'I didn't buy it and I've got no intention of taking it. But about two thousand of the fucking things've ended up in my house.'

'How?'

It was Kelly's turn now to look at Denny and wonder how

far he could trust this Ukrainian that he'd only just met with information that could bring a shit-storm down on all their heads.

Denny got the message and nodded that it was OK.

'My partner's lad brought 'em home. But he claims he's just lookin' after 'em for some'dy else. Bottom line, I think they were stolen by this guy Sanjeev's partner's kid. Which suggests to me that somebody's gonna be lookin' for 'em. If we're lucky, it'll be Sanjeev. If we're unlucky, it'll be Dmitri.'

'That is not good, my friend,' said Ilko. 'If it's Dmitri he won't just want the pills back, he'll want some payback on who stole them from him. That could mean Sanjeev or his partner's boy or your partner's boy. It could mean all of them or anyone else who's been involved. He won't want to leave a trail of witnesses if it's something illegal. I assume these pills are not meant to be sold legally over the counter.'

Shit, thought Kelly, why the fuck did Damien have to go and get himself mixed up with these people? Kids were a right pain in the arse, especially when they weren't your own, but the last thing he wanted was to see the little bugger wind up as street kill. He had to do something, for Bea's sake if nothing else.

'So what do you suggest we do about it?'

'You want my advice?' said Ilko.

'You seem to know what you're talking about, so yeah.'

'First thing: hide the pills somewhere Dmitri will never think of looking.'

'If he finds out who's had their hands on 'em, then none a their places is gonna be safe, is it?'

'No,' said Ilko.

'So where do you suggest?'

'You'll probably think it's crazy but it's somewhere he'll never think to look.'

'Where?'

'Bring the pills to me and I'll do the rest. Better that way.'

Kelly looked doubtful.

'I don't like the idea of not knowing where they are, just in case.'

'In case what?'

'In case something 'appens. In case I need to get back hold of 'em quick.'

'You worried he gonna find you and when he do you gonna

spill him the beans.'

'Like I said, who knows what can happen? How do I know, for instance, what you're gonna do with 'em?'

'You don't. But you came looking for my help. Who else are you going to trust? Once they're hidden we can work out the next step.'

'Fine, let's hide 'em, but I still wanna know where they are.'

'OK. Just get them. In the meantime I'll try to contact Sanjeev. If he knows what's going on, maybe he can help us.'

'But if he's the one who's had them stolen from him—'

'Trust me. He is not a bad man. He won't want anyone to get hurt.'

'Fair enough. If you say so.'

Kelly agreed a time and place to meet Ilko later with the pills. In fact, the thing he was least happy about was Denny ear-wigging on the plan and tagging along, but he thought it best to follow this guy's advice for now and just hope that in the process they could persuade Denny to keep his hands off anymore of the merchandise.

16. One Stone

FIRST THING SATURDAY morning Dmitri was on his
BlackBerry arranging for Cheslav to transport Sanjeev's bitch
from the penthouse to one of his warehouses, situated on York
Road. He was expecting a shipment of parts there today that he
needed to take delivery of in person and in the meantime there
was a back room where he could have a nice chat with the
woman about this wayward son of hers – thus killing two birds
with one stone. The more time he could save in sorting out this
DMT fuck-up, the more time he could devote to managing his
other burgeoning assets, both illegal and otherwise.

Dmitri's seven-year-old daughter Charlotte, who he called
Carla for short, had her usual Saturday-morning piano lesson to
attend and it was his habit to drop her off at the piano teacher's
house himself but have a man parked outside on watch who'd
then drive her home two hours later. A check of the BlackBerry
told him that today it was Gordy, a reliable Leeds lad who'd been
with the firm for a few years now. He hated his christened name
Gordon but could just about put up with this short form that had a
vaguely Slavic ring to it. Dmitri knew he'd make sure his
princess was well guarded and delivered home safely, or face the
consequences otherwise.

Carla was Dmitri's firstborn. He loved her, to him she was
his Princess Carlotta, but naturally what he'd really wanted was a
boy, so he made sure to get Donna pregnant again as soon as
possible and a year later Joshua was born. It wasn't a name he'd
have chosen himself but after putting her through the strain of
two births little more than twelve months apart and thanking his
lucky stars that the second one was the boy he'd been praying
for, it was a concession to Donna that he was prepared to make.
Keeping the peace. That was what family life was all about.
Donna and Carla insisted on calling him Josh, a form Dmitri
disliked and refused to use. Joshua had his roster of Saturday
morning TV programmes that he liked to watch, something
called Dick and Dom or something, and that's what he'd be
doing this morning under the watchful eye of the maid who came
in at weekends to give their German au pair Lillian some well-
earned time to herself. Two men stationed in the grounds would

also be on hand to protect Josh and deal with any eventualities while Donna went off and did whatever it was she spent her Saturdays doing – shopping, spa treatments or some other way of spending his money.

It was mid-morning when Dmitri parked his car outside the lock-up warehouse. The driver who'd transported Cheslav and the woman here was parked up and sitting behind the wheel. Dmitri and he nodded at one another without speaking. He was a fellow Ukrainian but he was Cheslav's man and Dmitri wasn't even sure he knew the guy's name.

Also parked outside was an unmarked blue Ford Transit, which indicated that the two birds had landed at the same time. That could be inconvenient. Dmitri would've preferred the van driver to have called ahead with a specific rendezvous time but he was obviously insufficiently clued up to have thought of that. Normally Dmitri would've given him a hard time about that but this guy was on someone else's payroll and he had a strong vested interest in maintaining good relations with the other party that the delivery driver worked for.

When he got inside, the van driver, a young guy in his twenties who could've been either British or East European until he opened his mouth to reveal a Yorkshire accent as thick as suet dumplings, was sitting on a small packing case smoking a cigarette while Cheslav loitered near by with his hands folded together across the front of his knock-off suit. Dmitri noticed that he or someone else had sewn a replacement button on the jacket since yesterday.

He gave Cheslav a significant look – *Where's the woman?* – and Cheslav nodded towards the locked door of the small room in the back of the building.

'You should've let me know you'd arrived,' he said to the delivery guy, trying hard not to sound unfriendly.

'I think your pal 'ere were just about to do that,' said the guy, gesturing at Cheslav.

Cheslav unfolded his hands to show that he was clutching a mobile phone in one of them.

'He just got here, boss, just before you.'

'Dr Livingstone, I presume,' said the driver rather self-consciously to Dmitri.

'Mr Stanley, I presume,' said Dmitri back.

It was a formality, an agreed code to establish the correct trading participants without any real names being bandied about. They didn't bother to shake hands. Once it was done there was little more to be said. The driver was just a driver; his job was to deliver the case, that was all. Payment for the goods would take place elsewhere between other parties as soon as Dmitri had verified the contents.

He turned to Cheslav.

'Take "Mr Stanley" into the kitchen for a moment. Offer him a cup of tea.'

Dmitri waited until Cheslav and the driver had disappeared into the small fluorescent-lit scullery built into a corner of the warehouse space. There was a small window in the scullery door through which Dmitri could see when the driver wasn't looking at him. Then he prised open the lid of the case, noting it had been properly nailed down, and looked inside. Pushing aside a layer of padding revealed ten objects stored beneath. He lifted one of them out of the case and tore off its polythene shrink-wrapping. The pistol sat snugly in the palm of his hand, smaller than he expected, almost like a child's toy, like he should take one home for Joshua. Ha, Donna would love that.

The Baikal IZH-79 was a design based on the Makarov 9mm police handgun used in Russia and the Baltics and manufactured in Izhevsk to fire tear-gas pellets in self-defence – a gun for women to ward off would-be muggers and rapists. In Vilnius, the Baikals were illegally modified to fire real bullets. In Russia, they might change hands for what, three hundred dollars? It was a price Dmitri was more than willing to pay. On the streets of South Manchester they would sell for £2,500 apiece. Already there were gangs lining up in a bidding war for the first ones to come into the country.

He unloaded the cartridge, squinted down the barrel to check it was empty, tested the firing mechanism with a dry metallic snap. Dmitri knew the market for guns here in Leeds wasn't big enough to bother with, that it had a long way to go before it acquired the glamour it enjoyed in Longsight or Moss Side; his intention was to sell these on across the Pennines. First though he had to provide the ammunition and fit them with silencers. These young British gangsters all wanted silencers and that was where he came in as a middle man. If silencers were what they wanted, silencers were what he would get them – at a healthy mark-up to the final reserve price, naturally.

Satisfied, he took a linen handkerchief from his pocket and wiped his prints off the gun before replacing it in the case with the other nine and shutting the lid. Then he took out his BlackBerry and keyed in a phone number.

After the agreed two rings it was answered and a voice said to him, 'Dr Livingstone, I presume.'

'OK,' said Dmitri. 'Do it.'

The money was changing hands. He killed the connection and deleted the record of the call then put the BlackBerry away and walked over to the scullery where the driver was just about to sip the tea that Cheslav had poured for him in a styrofoam cup.

'You can go,' Dmitri told him.

The young man looked longingly at the drink poised in his hand.

'Take the tea with you,' said Dmitri.

After he'd left the building Dmitri turned to Cheslav.

'Did they meet?' he said, meaning the delivery guy and Sanjeev's bitch.

'I got her locked away before he came in,' said Cheslav.

'Does she know where she is?'

'No, boss. I blindfolded her in the car. I didn't take it off until we were inside.'

Other than frosted-glass skylights, the warehouse had no exterior windows except for two tiny barred ones for ventilation, one in the kitchen and one in the toilet. Even if she were somehow able to get to them, they were positioned too high up to see through without standing on something, and even then both of them looked out the back onto unidentifiable scrubland. It would be impossible for her to recognise the location.

'OK,' said Dmitri. 'Go and make sure the van has gone, then lock the outside door.'

Cheslav did as he was ordered. Then the two of them sauntered over to the door of the back room.

Cheslav unlocked it with a key and stepped inside ahead of the boss. As he did so, a wooden chair came crashing down on the back of his head.

He staggered for a second before regaining his balance. When he turned round, Dmitri had Tracy in a hold that pinioned her arms against her body but she was still struggling and screaming.

'Get the fuck off me! Get yer fucking 'ands off!'

'Whoa,' Dmitri was saying, 'you're a lively one.'

'Who the fuck are you?' Tracy said, trying to crane her head round to see. 'Another fucking Russkie. What is this, fuckin' Moscow all of a sudden?'

Dmitri laughed and said, 'Shut up, bitch,' and threw her across the little room from one side to the other.

Tracy hit the wall hard but seemed to bounce straight back off it with her fists raised for a renewed attack.

'No you don't,' said Cheslav, grabbing hold of her from behind and bringing her under control.

'You,' said Dmitri, stepping towards her with a finger pointing in her face, 'need to fucking calm down.'

He slapped her hard across the left side of her jaw and Cheslav stepped back in shock as if it was he who'd received the blow. He felt her body sag, and let go of her as she slid to the floor. She was still conscious, sobbing maybe, her face hidden, but quietly.

Dmitri picked up the wooden chair, which miraculously was still in one piece, then motioned Cheslav to sit her on it. Cheslav took hold of her arm, trying to be firm but not rough.

'Come on,' he said. 'Sit. Come on, Tracy.'

Dmitri shot Cheslav a glance of faint contempt that the ex-wrestler failed to notice because he was too busy fussing over Sanjeev's bitch. Tracy. He made it sound tender. Maybe he was getting soft. Dmitri hoped he still had the stomach for this kind of work.

Cheslav positioned her on the chair and she let him. A little of the fight seemed to have gone out of her; at least she wasn't screaming and spitting like a cornered wolverine anymore.

'If she moves,' said Dmitri, 'hold her. If she struggles, tie her up.'

'What the fuck do you want, Boris?' said Tracy, suddenly looking up at Dmitri with defiance glaring through the wetness of the tears.

'Not to waste time. So tell me. Where is your boy?'

This was a question Tracy wasn't expecting, but she had to pull it together now and not show them anything, least of all surprise.

'Which boy? I've got three and they're all trouble.'

Dmitri looked at Cheslav and snapped his fingers.

'What's the kid's name?'

'Stephen.'

'Yes, Stephen. Where is he?'

'How should I know? I don't even know where I am. How the fuck am I supposed to know where he is?'

'Don't fuck around with me. I'm a busy man and I need to find this Stephen of yours now.'

'What for?'

'Like you don't know?'

'I 'an't got a fuckin' clue, mate.'

Dmitri thought silently for a moment, choosing his words judiciously.

'It seems he has something of mine.'

'What? He's never even fuckin' met you.'

Tracy gripped the edges of the seat of the chair with her hands, trying to keep them still, trying to keep herself calm and expressionless. Not expressionless exactly but without fear. She didn't mind expressing contempt but it needed to be done coldly and with control.

'Let's stop beating around the bush,' said Dmitri. 'He took something from that boyfriend of yours, the Asian. Something that belonged to me.'

Cheslav felt his insides contract as they skirted the topic of Sanjeev. He noticed that Dmitri had slipped into alluding to him in the past tense. Tracy still didn't know what had happened to him and for some reason he dreaded the full details coming out now.

'Sanjeev doesn't discuss his business with me. He says it's better that way.'

'Ah, but you know he worked for me then?'

'I've just told you, I don't know jack shit. Why not ask Sanjeev?'

'I did. Who do you think told me to look for Stephen?'

Tracy's head snapped up and she regarded him with a curled lip.

'You're a lyin' cunt. Sanjeev wouldn't do owt to harm my lads.'

'Not even when he knew the boy hated him?'

'That's not true. That's not fuckin' true.'

Tracy felt vulnerable all of a sudden. Even she could hear the tone she was using to convince herself. OK, they didn't get on. But Sanjeev was a good man and he'd never deliberately or voluntarily put the boy in harm's way. That she knew to be true at least, regardless of how Steve felt about Sanjeev.

'Where is he?' she demanded. 'Where's Sanjeev?'

'Boss,' said Cheslav, edging forward nervously.

Tracy was gripping the chair tighter than ever now. No wonder this sack of shit didn't bother to look for Sanjeev last night after he'd dragged her out of the Lib if they'd already spoken to him. But there was something more, wasn't there? Something these cunts weren't telling her. She could feel the knowledge of what was to come already building inside her.

'Where the fuck is Sanjeev?'

Cheslav stopped himself from saying 'Boss' again and swallowed on a dry throat as he watched Dmitri lean over and push his face close to Tracy's.

'He's where you'll be going too if you don't answer the fucking question.'

Tracy was staring into Dmitri's eyes with a look somewhere between misery and murder.

'What've you done with him?'

Dmitri looked away from her to Cheslav. A small smile played around his lips as Cheslav stood very very still like a condemned man waiting for the firing squad.

'Let's just say he doesn't work for me anymore. In fact, let's just say he doesn't work anymore. Like a broken toy that can't be mended.'

Cheslav tried not to look at Tracy. She was still staring at Dmitri with that same look of mingled grief and hatred, and tears were silently running down her face and dripping from her chin.

'You fucking evil cunt,' she managed to say in a voice that trembled only a little.

She wanted to reach up and grab hold of that filthy fucking vodka-stinking face in front of hers and tear its eyes out. She wanted to pull it down towards her teeth and bite his fucking nose off. She wanted to tear the whole fucking face right off like a mask and stamp it into the dirt on the floor.

Instead, she went on gripping the edges of the chair beneath her. Now wasn't the time. It couldn't be done. Not here, not now – she knew that, she wasn't stupid.

But she would get the cunt. She knew that too. She would get the cunt when he was on his own and she would kill him.

She spat in his face and swore it to herself.

'Jesus,' said Dmitri flinching away from her spittle.

His hand didn't know which to do first, wipe his own face or crack hers. Instead he controlled it, took out his handkerchief, cleaned himself up. He would keep back the violence for now, not waste it on rage, wait until it could be used for a purpose.

'Please hold her arms,' he said to Cheslav.

'Go on, ya dickless dog,' said Tracy to Cheslav. 'Do yer fuckin' master's biddin'.'

Cheslav grasped her wrists behind her as gingerly as his meaty fists would allow, and felt sick about it. His mind went back to the grip on the Sri Lankan's ankles as he dangled him above the street hundreds of feet below, and the moment of unintentionally letting go.

'Now,' said Dmitri, looking down at her and twisting the rings on the fingers of his right hand one at a time, 'where the fuck can we find Stephen?'

17. Lost in Space

STEPHEN CROFT HAD his mother's surname because his parents had never married, and split up from each other almost before he was born. His father, originally from London, upped sticks and went back to his roots while the infant naturally remained with his mother in Leeds.

Later however, against all expectations, Stephen ended up spending a sizeable portion of his childhood living with his father and his father's new woman down south – while his mum was doing a stretch in prison that began just after his sixth birthday. When they let her out and he returned to Leeds, he was nearly ten. It wasn't quite the first seven years of a boy's life that the Jesuits claimed it took to mould the man, but it left a hefty impression on his personality, enough to leave him wondering whether he was a northerner or a southerner. His chief fear had been that the London accent he picked up from his Wandsworth years would get him beaten up when he moved back to school up north.

He remembered being told some bullshit story at the time to account for his mother's absence and his own upheaval. It wasn't hard to work out later what had really happened, though it would be years later before he found out why she'd been put away for so long: dealing heroin. In fact, they'd knocked two years off her sentence for good behaviour.

His elder brothers – Gary and Stuart, born to two different fathers, neither one of them the same as his and neither of which had married their mother either, or stayed with her for very long – had been ten and eight respectively when she went inside, and both of them were sent to live with their maternal grandparents in another part of Leeds. The reason Stephen got packed off down south was because his grandparents wouldn't have him, and the reason they wouldn't have him was because from the minute he was born, they knew his father was black.

When he came back up north, his new school mates didn't give a shit about his accent because they'd never heard anything different come out of his mouth, while those who were never gonna be mates anyway were more likely to use the colour of his skin rather than his Estuary twang as an excuse to pick a fight.

Now, at the age of seventeen, he'd just about reached the conclusion that the question of his identity didn't ultimately matter, at least not to him and not to anyone who counted. And those who it did bother – well if it bothered them that much, life had taught him how to deal with them.

Learning that his grandparents were racists was something harder to live with, but over the intervening years he'd managed, by having as little to do with them as possible. It made for a cheap Christmas list. Luckily, their prejudice had failed to rub off on his two half-brothers, neither of whom he had any beef with, although he didn't see much of them these days since Gary had flown the family nest three years back and Stuart had been away at college in Hull for the past couple of years.

He wondered now how long he should leave it before contacting one or both of them to tell them what was going on. Could they help? Would they help? And what would he say to them anyway? He didn't even know himself what was going on.

The guy who'd phoned him out of the blue – Don, a neighbour, decent bloke but not gifted in the imagination or sophistication departments – said his mum had gone off with some Russian after a ruckus down at the Lib, and by his account she hadn't gone of her own free will. Don had tried to contact Sanjeev too but hadn't been able to get hold of him. Neither had Stephen.

That meant the little Asian twerp must be hiding out somewhere, scared to show his face. Fucking coward.

There was nothing evil about Sanjeev, quite the opposite. He was one of these spiritual types, into non-violence and vegetarianism, and that was OK, fair play to him, but did he have to be so fucking spineless?

He wasn't right for his mum. Whatever the fucking Russkies promised him – OK, Ukrainians, he wasn't as naïve as Don about these guys – he should've turned them down. No amount of money was worth selling out to those people. And he knew his mum needed to stay well away from drugs, especially the dealing side of it. For fuck's sake, if sentences were that stiff for dealing, what must they be like for manufacturing the stuff?

When Stephen had found those pills that Sanjeev had brought home, he'd seen red. He hadn't really thought about the consequences. He just knew he had to get them as far away from his mum as possible. That was the impulse that told him to take them, get them the fuck out of the house. He didn't want to lose his mum for that long again.

It was only later that he thought about the ramifications of what he'd done – that the Ukrainians would want them back, and that they'd be coming after him to get them if they found out he had them. That was why he'd asked his best mate Damien to hold onto them for him – just until he could figure out what to do with them, what to do about the whole fucking mess. They'd never know Damien had them, or even that such a person existed.

But now the D-Man's parents knew, and that's why the two of them had ended up sleeping the night on the cramped floor space of Damien's girlfriend's bedroom after she had sneaked them into the house just before midnight.

It had been down to their good fortune that Chloe was still up when Damien had phoned her and begged her to help them, and that her dad was out of the house, still not home from the pub. It was nearer to one o'clock when the three of them heard the noises of him coming home drunk. After that, they had to talk in whispers, the three of them, Damien and Stevo stretched out fully clothed under a blanket side by side on the carpet while Chloe occupied the narrow single bed in her pyjamas. It wasn't that Chloe and Damien had never done anything, they had, but it didn't feel right to her, the idea of them sleeping together with Stevo in the room just a foot or two away, so she'd insisted on this arrangement as part of the deal.

As for Chloe's dad, he seemed to like Damien well enough, but that didn't mean he entirely approved of him in his daughter's life, and would certainly not have liked him and Stevo both staying overnight in her bedroom, or anywhere else in his house for that matter.

Fortunately, Chloe, being a few months older than Damien, had reached the age where she didn't have to care anymore what her father thought of her – at least not in any legally binding sense. The sooner she struck out on her own, the better. It was just a matter of time, and of course money, before she moved out and left him to do as he pleased on his own.

She happily acknowledged that she was probably as much an imposition on his freedom as he was on hers. But it was still his house, so she had to at least pretend to play by his rules. She knew he'd never enter her bedroom uninvited without damn good cause, like the house being on fire or something drastic, and if the boys left early enough in the morning, her dad would still be sleeping his beer off and wouldn't know that they'd ever been there.

They departed before eight, and Chloe got dressed and left with them, drawn into their problems now that they'd involved her out of desperation.

Stevo tried his mum's mobile again but it was Don who answered, still in possession of it and still none the wiser about where she was. Don wanted to call the police but Stevo managed to talk him out of it, persuading him to wait a little longer, to give him some more time to try to track her down himself.

Don wasn't pleased.

'You do know he 'ad a gun, this Russian bloke she went off with?'

'I know, Don,' said Stevo, 'but you know my mum. She knows a lot of heavy people who mix in some weird circles and she probably won't thank any of us for gettin' the police involved. Leave it with me a bit longer, eh?'

Don didn't like it one bit but he recognized that Tracy's kid had a head on him older than his years and agreed to cry off for now so long as Steve, as he called him, kept in touch. In turn, he'd phone Steve on his mobile if he heard from his mam.

After that, Stevo tried Sanjeev's number again. Same as last night, he got nothing – no message, not even a tone to say the call was getting through to anything.

Like he was lost in space.

'What about phoning the house?' Chloe suggested.

'Shit, man, I don't even know the number anymore. None of us uses it, we all use our mobiles. Imagine not knowing your own fuckin' phone number. We'd be better off gettin' it disconnected if it weren't for the internet connection, and it's only Sanjeev who uses that. Maybe I'd just better go home and see if either of them's back.'

'D'you want us to come with you?' said Damien.

'D-Man, what you should be doing right now is getting home yourself and making sure those pills are all right. If that's what this Ukrainian geezer was after from my mum and we ain't got those, then we ain't got nothing.'

This was the part that Damien wasn't looking forward to, but he knew that at some point he was going to have to confront his own mother and her own boyfriend.

'Come on,' said Chloe encouragingly. 'I'll come with you if you like. Kelly won't do anything with me there.'

'Shows how little you know Kelly,' said Damien. 'OK, but listen,' he said, turning to Stevo, 'keep us posted, OK? An' I'll let you know as soon as I find out the pills are all right.'

'Fair enough,' said Stevo. 'We'll hook up laters, yeah?'

For a second there was something in his voice, some uncertainty, some probing for reassurance, that made him sound like a little boy, lost and alone.

'Damn right,' said Damien. 'Just be careful, OK?'

18. Back Together Again

TRACY BLABBED.

Dmitri only had to smack her around a little before she told him everything.

She told him about how she'd first got to know Sanjeev Coomaraswamy nearly two years ago when she'd lost her eighteen-month-old daughter Ruby to cot death.

SIDS, he called it: Sudden Infant Death Syndrome. He'd worked in the health service before being laid off, and the way he allowed the cold acronymic technical term to trip off his tongue made her hate him at first.

But Sanjeev had a tender heart and a winning way about him. He would go to considerable trouble to console Tracy over her loss and to be there when she needed anything, and she soon found herself warming to him and his ministrations.

It wasn't long – a matter of days rather than weeks – before she caught herself thinking that he was actually quite cute, which soon led to her taking a proper look at him and surprising herself with the realisation that he was really a striking and handsome little bloke. She wondered what he might be like in bed. It wasn't that she hadn't done it with a darkie before, just look at Stephen's dad – though, course, he was a proper darkie. Her mum and dad would hate it if they knew, as would her elder brother Barry if he were still alive, but she'd stopped telling them about her love life years ago, unless it was to deliberately piss them off.

She told Dmitri about how she used to deal drugs on and off over the years – smack, pills, anything she could get her hands on as long as it had a sell-on value – and that that was how she'd first met Dmitri's lapdog, Cheslav, through some druggie contacts of hers that he was sniffing around at the time. She didn't know him or who he worked for but he was definitely there one time when she'd made a point of introducing Sanjeev to them because he was trained as a chemist and she thought they might know someone who could put some work his way.

She told him how Cheslav's ears had pricked up at that but she'd thought nothing of it at the time and had thought about it very little since.

She told him how since then Sanjeev had kept his business

to himself and how she hadn't asked him about it because the less she knew the better.

She told him how her youngest son, Stephen, didn't like Sanjeev because he was Asian, which was pretty fucking rich coming from a lad who was half black, but then Stephen had a funny attitude to race as a warped reaction to the prejudice he'd suffered himself at the hands of her own family. Even so, she knew what the real reason was. He didn't like Sanjeev not because of what he was but because of who he wasn't: he wasn't his father, and even though his father lived down south, he'd been close to him as a kid and wished he could be again. He didn't like Sanjeev because he couldn't accept that his father and her would never be an item; because he couldn't accept that something which was never gonna happen was never gonna happen.

She told him that was why he hated Sanjeev, and that was probably why he'd stolen the pills that Sanjeev was supposed to be working on – if she were to believe at all that he *was* working on them, that the pills actually existed, or that it was Stephen who stole them.

Tracy told Dmitri everything – except the things he wanted to hear.

By the end of it all, he was smacking her around just to shut her up.

Dmitri called Cheslav out of the room and they left her locked in on her own again.

'She doesn't know where the boy is. Either she doesn't know or she doesn't care. What kind of a mother is she?'

This was not Cheslav's reading of the situation. She must know who the boy's friends were, for instance, or what were the places he was likely to be found. Was the boss going soft? Or perhaps he just didn't want to admit that she'd defeated him.

Cheslav kept these thoughts to himself though. He knew what cruelties Dmitri was capable of and he didn't want to have to stand by while he watched the woman maimed or scarred for life.

'He's seventeen, boss,' he said, trying to field a spot of diplomatic consolation. 'At that age – teenagers – they don't like their parents to know where they are or what they're getting up to.'

'Damn it,' said Dmitri, 'I need those fucking pills. You're sure they're not in the house?'

'My guys have searched it from attic to cellar, boss. If the pills were there we would've found them.'

'But they're still watching the place?'

'Of course. When the boy shows up we'll know about it.'

'You mean *if* he shows up.'

Cheslav had deliberately said 'when' to instil Dmitri with a sense of certainty, hoping it would make things go easier for the woman. For Tracy.

'He'll show up, boss. He has nowhere else to go.'

'Cheslav, he's somewhere fucking else now.'

'I meant he has nowhere else to come back to. Think about it
– '

'Don't tell me to think!'

'He's a seventeen-year-old boy,' Cheslav pressed on bravely. 'A teenager. He needs his clothes, his trainers, his music, his personal care products. We know his possessions are still in the house. If he'd gone for good he would've taken them with him.'

'But if he's got my pills he won't need them,' Dmitri protested. 'Those pills are worth a fortune, and once he's discovered that, he can buy anything his little fucking heart desires.'

Cheslav remained quiet for a respectful length of time before stating quietly but firmly, 'He'll come back, boss. And when he does we will get him.'

Finally, Cheslav noticed, Dmitri seemed to take some small measure of reassurance from this.

'I know. I know you're right. I'm just impatient.' Then he added, 'But in the meantime, what do I do with her?' He tilted his head towards the back room. 'She knows too much.'

'She only knows we want her boy, she doesn't know why. She doesn't know about the pills,' said Cheslav hopefully.

'She knows he took something of mine. And what would she think that is? Uh? Does she think I'm angry because he took my fucking Phil Collins records? I don't think so. Do you? Anyway – she knows about Sanjeev.'

There was nothing Cheslav could reply to this. He swallowed on a dry throat and kept silent, already knowing the inevitable that was to follow.

'We'll have to get rid of her.'

Cheslav was looking at the floor. His eyes were swivelling, searching the ground for an answer – a strategy maybe.

'Is that going to be a problem?'

'No, boss, of course not. But it might be a waste. I'm certain she will know something. The boy is sure to have friends, a girlfriend maybe. There must be someone she knows about.'

'Yes, but I haven't got all fucking day,' said Dmitri. 'And besides, look at her. Look at my fucking hand. It hurts like hell.' He pushed a set of sore knuckles under Cheslav's nose. 'She's not going to tell us anything useful. You heard her in there. She could talk all day and still say nothing.'

'Let me work on her, boss. If she knows something, I'll find it out.'

Dmitri thought about this for a second then assented.

'OK. I'm sending a couple of boys round to take care of the Baikals anyway so you can let them in when they get here. They have their orders already, they know what to do with them. In the meantime, you can continue with your girlfriend in there. But don't waste the whole fucking day on it. And when you're done, get rid of her. All right?'

Cheslav stopped himself just in time from saying thank you.

'Yes, boss.'

'All right?' Dmitri said again, angling his head to look into Cheslav's eyes.

'All right, boss.'

'Have that driver of yours wait outside until you're finished here, then you can take her out of town. Use the quarry. That's where they put her precious Sanjeev. She'll like that. Back together again. And don't get blood on the car. Cost too much to get blood cleaned out of a car. The bastards charge a fortune and they never quite get all of it.'

With that, he turned and walked away, leaving Cheslav to it.

Cheslav had already decided what he was going to do before Dmitri had exited the warehouse. He hadn't finessed the details yet but he'd made his decision and he knew he needed to act on it immediately.

When he unlocked the door to the back room and stepped inside, Tracy was waiting to hit him with the chair again. He knew she would be, that was the kind of person he recognised that she was. No quitter. He raised one arm to protect himself and caught the leg of the chair in his other hand, kicking the door closed behind him and stepping back to stop her from running out.

'Stop,' he said.

She let go of the chair so that he was left holding it aloft in one hand. Then she launched herself at him, fists and fingers seeking to scratch and batter while her feet kicked at his shins.

Cheslav dropped the chair and protected himself as best he could without hitting back.

'Stop,' he said again. He didn't raise his voice. He stayed calm, willing some of his own calmness to transfer itself to her. 'I want to help.'

'Help? You mean help that cunt!'

'No. No. You.'

She left off, backing up away from him, breathing hard, exhausted from the effort it had taken her to attack him after the beating she'd taken from the other one.

Her face was a mess, bruised and swollen, but would look better once the blood and tears and snot were washed off. It didn't look to Cheslav's professional wrestler's eye as if anything was broken. And she was tough. That was one thing he'd learned over the last fifteen hours, if nothing else.

'We're getting out of here now.'

'Whaddaya mean?' she mumbled through puffy lips.

'I don't want anymore harm to come to you. If you come with me you'll live. At least a little longer than if you stay here.'

Tracy ran the back of a hand across her face, smearing the mess away from her eyes, then regarded him suspiciously.

'Why are you helping me?'

Cheslav felt his rib cage booming with guilt over what had happened to Sanjeev and he knew he couldn't give that question an honest answer without making her want to murder him. At least, he couldn't give it a comprehensive one. *It's complicated*, he wanted to tell her, but that might stimulate her curiosity, if not her mistrust. Better to say nothing than to taunt her with ambiguities, or reveal confidences that she would only despise.

'I've had enough,' he said finally. The answer came out unbidden in a moment of epiphany but he delivered it in a tone that cloaked his own surprise at the self-revelation. 'Come on. There isn't much time.'

He took her by the hand and she let him.

As they crossed the warehouse space towards the exit he looked at the crate of guns sitting in the middle of the floor. He knew how valuable they were to Dmitri, and wondered if he ought to take them with him as a bargaining chip for later. Taking the guns would only serve, though, to doubly ensure that Dmitri sent someone in pursuit after them. Also Cheslav didn't want to let on to the driver outside what he was doing just yet and there'd be no way to explain to him why he was taking the Baikals, so the logistics of it was all wrong. He had his own weapon holstered under his jacket and a ready supply of bullets. That would have to do for now if it came to a fire fight.

The next move relied on a gamble that Olek, the driver waiting outside, hadn't been put in the picture by Dmitri on his way out.

'When we get back in the car say nothing,' he told Tracy. 'Trust me.'

'Trust you?' she laughed, spraying red spittle. 'Then take me to the police.'

'I can't do that. Not yet. But I promise I'm going to get you out of this mess.'

He took from his pocket the blindfold she'd been forced to wear on the way here.

'Please,' he said, holding it up towards her. 'We must pretend that nothing has changed.'

'Jesus!' said Tracy, submitting to its being refitted. 'I can't fucking believe I'm letting you do this.'

He took her by the arm, led her outside and hustled her back to the car. He put her on the back seat then walked round the car and climbed in the other side next to her. As he settled in and shut the car door, the driver turned round towards him.

'What'd the boss say?' Olek asked.

'As far as you're concerned, I'm the boss,' said Cheslav. That was how it worked – a system of line management, the driver just another one of his donkeys – and he didn't need to explain it further. 'Take us back to the penthouse.'

Tracy sat patiently and stayed silent, not even raising a whimper at the pain. She didn't quite believe in Cheslav just yet but she was willing to wait and see. Well, under the circumstances, she didn't really have much of a choice, did she?

19. Fur Fax Ache

THEY PARKED UP in the penthouse's designated underground parking slot and Cheslav removed Tracy's blindfold.

'OK,' he said to the driver, 'you can go. I won't need you anymore today. Take the rest of the day off.'

'You sure?' said the driver. It seemed a bit strange to him but he wasn't about to grumble too much at getting paid a day's wages for being at home.

'I'm sure. But leave the car here. You can pick it up again from here tomorrow morning.'

It would mean taking a taxi home, or slumming it on a bus if he wanted to save money, but the driver grinned anyway. 'If you insist.'

Cheslav took possession of the car keys and watched the driver walk away. He locked the car with the remote on the key fob. Then he took a clean linen handkerchief from his jacket pocket and started fussing with it at Tracy's face.

'What the fuck're ya doin'?'

'Trying to clean you up a little.'

'Well fucking don't, all right? Here, give it here.'

She snatched the hanky away from him and scrunched it up to her mouth. It looked conspicuous but it managed to conceal some of the damage.

'No one's gonna fucking see me anyway,' she said.

'Come on,' said Cheslav, and they rode the elevator to the top of the building.

When they got to the apartment and he tried his key, he said, 'Oh shit.'

'What's up?'

'Let me do the talking.'

Instead of opening the door and walking straight in, he pulled the key back and rang the doorbell and they heard it chime smartly within.

A minute later the door was opened by a tall, slender, good-looking young woman. She had her long brunette hair wound up in a neat bun from which one strand was permitted to dangle chicly by her left ear. Tracy guessed she was in her mid-twenties, and what folk generally called people who looked like her – well-to-do. The designer outfit she was wearing probably cost more money than Tracy would see in a year.

As they stood in the doorway, she regarded the two of them as if they'd just dropped out of a dog's arse, steaming.

'Madeleine,' said Cheslav warily, by way of greeting.

The girl looked back at him with obvious recognition but out of a face that was used to retaining a catwalk blankness.

'What do you want?' she said in a foreign accent that was thicker than Cheslav's or Dmitri's, and different – not Russian or Ukrainian by the sound of it, though Tracy was no expert.

'I need to pick up some things,' said Cheslav, not walking past her but waiting to be invited in.

'For fuck's sake,' said the woman. It sounded like *Fur fax ache.* 'I've told Dmitri before. If he wants to use my apartment he should facking find me another.'

'Strictly speaking, it is his apartment.'

'So he pays the rent. So what are you doing here?'

'I've told you,' he said patiently. 'I just need to pick up some things.'

'So it's yours too now?' You could see the girl wasn't pleased. 'So who's she?' she said, jutting her chin in Tracy's direction.

Tracy clutched the bunched-up hanky more closely to her battered face, feeling exposed and uncomfortable and hating herself for it. She had no cause to feel embarrassed or belittled. She hadn't done this. This girl's precious fucking Dmitiri had done this. And who knows? One day he might do the same to her. She took the hanky away from her mouth, pulled her shoulders back and stared her straight in the eye.

'A friend,' said Cheslav before Tracy could say anything.

Tracy swallowed her anger.

'So what happened to her face?' said the girl, talking about her as if she wasn't there instead of addressing her directly.

Was she going to start every sentence with 'So', Tracy wondered.

'An accident. Madeleine, can we come in, please? It will only take a moment.'

Madeleine stepped back away from the doorway and Cheslav led the way into the apartment.

Tracy followed him in and the girl shut the door behind

them. Then she led both of them from the hallway to the main reception room.

'How was Milan?' Cheslav asked Madeleine. 'You just got back?'

This was Cheslav at the most conversational that Tracy had heard him. She knew it was because he felt uneasy, and wondered if the girl could sense this. If the girl knew Cheslav at all, she must know this wasn't like him.

The last thing they wanted was for her to get on the phone to Dmitri.

'In reverse order, yes, and it was hot, but not the weather.'

'Hot?' said Cheslav, still not understanding; all across Europe, the same winter was approaching head on.

'Ze fashions,' said Madeleine, letting her accent slip.

Tracy noticed an array of shopping bags lined up on the sofa, their contents still unpacked. All the bags sported top international brand logos that Tracy had only seen before in the advertising pages of glossy magazines.

'Do you want to clean up?'

It took a moment for Tracy to realise that the girl was talking to her.

'What?' she said.

'Your face.'

The girl indicated her bloodied face and the stained handkerchief with an expression of barely suppressed distaste, as if she was sucking on something she was meant to enjoy but hated it. She jerked a thumb in a slutty truck-stop pose.

'The bathroom's through there.'

Tracy stopped herself from saying yes, she knew where it was. She didn't think that would go down well with either the girl or Cheslav.

'Thanks. Thank you.'

'I don't want you getting blood on anything,' the girl added needlessly and pointedly.

Tracy went off to the bathroom without another word and without looking at Cheslav.

She bolted the door behind her, being doggedly careful not to put a mark on anything she touched, then sat down on the toilet and peed. That was all she needed to do right now, just a pee. Jesus, she was hungry. No wonder she didn't need a shit.

When had she last eaten? Yesterday teatime – about eighteen hours ago. Her stomach felt like her throat had been cut.

She flushed the loo and pulled her knickers up then went to the sink and looked at herself in the mirror above it.

Christ, she was a mess. Her first instinct was to cry, and she couldn't stop the tears welling up in her eyes. After a second, though, she got the sobbing under control and managed to pull herself together. The time for self-pity would be later, or never.

Last night's make-up was a faint tracery of skid-marks barely visible beneath the bleeding and the bruises. She ran the tap, cupped warm water in her hands and splashed it on her face. Then she wet the hanky and began the delicate process of dabbing away at the damage.

Both lips were split, the blood just starting to scab over but still weeping a little. Its savoury taste had been on her tongue and running down the back of her throat for hours. Both her eyes were swollen and were going to be surrounded by black for days to come, then yellow for weeks after that. Her nose, though sore and bloodied, was OK. At least the cunt had managed not to break it. She'd been given a broken nose before, she knew what it felt like and it wasn't this. The cuts around her eye sockets could probably use some stitches but even without, the scars would only be little ones, probably hardly noticeable after a year or two.

It was going to take a lot longer though to recover from the rest of the devastation of these last eighteen hours.

She thought about Sanjeev, her poor little Sanjeev, and felt the tears pricking at her eyes and nose once more.

Then before she could wallow properly in his loss, she thought of Stephen. Oh God, she couldn't bear to lose him too. Ruby had been bad enough. Now Sanjeev. If she lost Stephen as well, she might as well throw herself under a bus.

She struggled to push her gloom aside because it was of no use right now, then dried herself off with a wad of toilet paper – pink, quilted, top of the range – and tossed the mushy pulp that remained down the loo without bothering to flush it away.

Fuck that bitch.

Back in the living room, the two foreigners were standing around in a strained silence, not looking at one another. Cheslav was holding a vinyl Adidas sports bag that she guessed contained the belongings of his that he'd come to collect.

'OK?' he said to Tracy.

She just nodded. If she opened her mouth now she might not shut it again for a long time.

'We'll leave you alone then,' he said to Madeleine.

'Oh will you now? So, that's very kind of you. Thank you and goodbye.'

She chirped up again before they got to the door.

'Tell Dmitri—'

Cheslav turned and waited.

'Nothing,' she concluded. 'I'll tell him myself.'

They left without another word.

'You look better,' Cheslav said to Tracy as they went back down in the lift.

'She's nice,' said Tracy.

'Dmitri's – mistress. It's not my place to have an opinion about her.'

'That sounds like summat you've been taught to say.'

She thought she saw the ghost of a smile ripple across his mouth at that but he didn't say anything else until they were back in the car.

She sat beside him in the front passenger seat and watched him open his bag and take something out. As he flipped open the object and inspected it, she realised that it was a box of bullets. She tried to breathe normally and act nonchalantly while he took his gun – the one he'd been waving around in the Lib last night - out of its shoulder holster and loaded it with cartridges from the box. Then he put it away, replaced the box in the bag and started the engine.

'What now?' said Tracy

'Now we eat.'

For the first time in eighteen hours, she allowed herself to smile a little, even though it hurt.

'Thank fuck for that.'

20. Transformer

AFTER STEVO LEFT Damien and Chloe, the first thing he needed was something to eat. Man, he was starving, hadn't had a bite since yesterday teatime. He scraped the change out of his pockets and found enough there for a fry-up in a greasy spoon. He didn't care to wait until he got back to the house in case there was trouble there. He couldn't rely on the home environment any longer. He was on his own now, or so it looked like for the time being, and he would have to live on his own wits for a while.

Once he'd eaten, it was a long walk home after last night's wanderings, but he was damned if he was going to waste what little he had left on overpriced bus fares.

Consequently, it was late morning when he reached his neighbourhood, and the men that Cheslav had organised to watch Tracy's house would have had nothing to report to their superiors earlier than the time that Dmitri finished his business with Sanjeev's woman and left her beaten and ostensibly useless in the warehouse under Cheslav's supervision.

Not that they immediately spotted Stevo anyway. But he saw them. A mate he'd bumped into a few streets away had tipped him off about the car and the guys in it that'd been watching his old lady's house all night long. So forewarned, Stevo spent fifteen minutes scoping them out from behind far corners before he made his decision about how to approach his home.

There were two guys in the car parked out front in the road, a few doors down from their house. But through negligence, over-confidence or under-staffing, they didn't seem to have bothered to station anyone in the alley that ran along the back of the terrace, giving access to the back yards, full of washing hanging from revolving clothes-lines. It was possible there was someone hiding, but Stevo had managed to get a good look from two angles and to the best of his knowledge the back door wasn't under surveillance.

He figured on taking it steady, walking up casually, playing uninvolved, but knowing there were a couple of the bin yards that people hid their house keys in and kids used for burgling between here and there to duck into if he needed them.

Just when he'd plucked up the nerve and had stepped out of

hiding onto the cobbled path to his back yard, a figure walked out of a gate from between two billowing pale-blue cotton bed-sheets.

Stevo tried not to jump. Some old guy in a suit and tie who looked as out of place as a verruca-plaster in a jacuzzi. The guy was suddenly there out of nowhere, standing between him and his back door.

'Are you Stephen?' said the smartly-dressed old geezer in some slight but dodgy accent.

'No,' Stevo shouted loud enough for any neighbours or passersby to hear, 'you fucking nonce!'

By this time, the Ukrainian had him by the throat in a Transformer-sized power grip.

'I've been told to bring you with me.'

The way they were delivered, they were the seven most chilling words that Stevo had heard in his life so far.

'Oi!'

The voice came out of nowhere and was ringing with anger.

The next second it was the old Ukrainian geezer's head that was ringing as Don from down the street swiped it with the curved end of a crowbar.

The Ukrainian dropped Stevo then dropped to the ground, at which point the four lads off the estate – friends of Stevo's who'd come to back Don up – laced into him with boots and bats.

'Jesus, thanks, Don,' said Stevo, getting his wind back.

'Have you seen your mother?' said Don anxiously.

'No, not yet. But there's two of his mates in a car out the front.'

'Aye, I know.'

'Have you seen owt of Sanjeev?'

'No. He an't been home all night, I know that, an' I can't raise him on t' mobile.'

'Nah, me neither. I'm actually worried about him. But I've got to focus on finding Mum.'

'Could they be together?'

'I guess so. But if so, where the fuck are they? Sorry, Don.'

'Don't be daft. We all swear at times like this whether we like it or not.'

The lads left off battering the Ukrainian to assess the damage. The Ukrainian rolled a little on the ground, groaning but barely conscious.

'Check he an't gorra gun,' said Don. 'That other fucker last night had a gun.'

One of the youths removed a leather cosh from one pocket and a butterfly knife from another pocket in the Ukrainian's jacket.

'No guns, just these.'

'I've gotta take off before those others realise he's out of contact,' said Stevo.

'What the hell's it all about?' said Don, exasperated.

'I can't explain it now, Don. I gotta go, but keep my mum's phone and I'll stay in touch, yeah?'

Stevo nipped into his back yard and pulled his mountain bike out of the shed. He hadn't ridden it for months but it was in a serviceable state.

'OK, lads, cheers,' said Don to his young comrades. He didn't feel right about the severe pummelling the poor sod on the floor had taken, but after the way he'd seen these bastards behave, he did feel good about it. 'We'd better take off, all right?'

The gang dispersed, leaving the Ukrainian heavy lying in a bruised and rasping heap, while Stevo made his escape down the alley, then bouncing on his tyres down a flight of stairs through a narrow passage, where no car could follow.

21. Tupperware

WHEN KELLY GOT home from his meeting with Denny and Ilko – or 'Bilko', as he'd started thinking of him – he walked in on Casey entertaining her best friend in front of the telly in the back room. Roisin. That was it: the other girl's name.

'All right, Casey. All right, Roisin.'

He pronounced it how he'd heard it – *Rasharn* – knowing it was Irish and having no idea what it looked like written down.

'What yer watching?'

There was an onstage band playing on the screen.

'Happy Mondays.'

'They're a bit ancient for you, aren't they?'

'Our Damien got us into'em, din't he, Rash?'

An unfortunate nickname, Kelly thought, though the girl didn't seem to care, which was something of a miracle for a fourteen-year-old. Still, Casey was a bit like that, mature for her age, and she attracted like-minded friends.

'Have you seen Damien?'

'No, not since yesterday. He din't come back last night, did he? What's goin' on, Kelly?'

'It'll be neither nowt nor summat. If he gets in touch with you, though, will you let me know?'

'Is he in trouble?'

'Not from me.'

Kelly meant it now. This thing had gone beyond being angry at Damien.

'Listen, I'll leave ya to it, all right?'

All right. Mam's in t'front room.'

'Yeah, she's 'ere in t'kitchen now, so I'll shut this door.'

Kelly gave Bea a kiss on the cheek and put his arms around her.

'So what happened?' she said backing up to look him in the face.

Kelly shut the kitchen door so there'd be no chance of Casey and Roisin ear-wigging.

'Denny's introduced us to this bloke who's gunner 'elp us.'

'How is he?'

'Who?'

'Denny.'

Bea said his name with a certain swallowed bitterness, not necessarily bitter at Denny but bitter at the memories that he inhabited.

'He's OK. Same as always.'

'So who's this bloke?'

Kelly didn't want to give too much away. Any mention of Ukrainian names or whiff of Russian mafia would have her shitting herself; he didn't want to increase the worry she was already going through.

'He's a mate a Denny's. He's agreed to take the pills off us 'ands and stow 'em in a safe place.'

'Till when?'

'Till we decide what to do with 'em.'

'Well how d'you know you can trust this fella? What if he's gonna sell 'em to kids? I thought that's what this were all about.'

'He's not gonna do that. He's a social worker, for Christ's sake. It's his job working wi' kids in trouble. I'm not sayin' I trust him cos I don't know him, but I know that he cares, an' I believed him. He's willing to help, that's the main thing.'

'Does he know where Damien is?'

'H dun't know our Damien. I told you, he's just a mate a Denny's.'

'All right, if you know what yer doin'. Is he gonna be able to help find Damien?'

'Put it this way, whatever he does, it's not gonna do any harm. Have you heard from Damien anyway?'

'No. He's not rung, nothing. I wish he'd get in touch an' let us know he's all right.'

'Right,' said Kelly, 'where are them pills? I wanna get 'em out the house in case he comes back.'

'Kel, I promised him you wouldn't do owt – with the pills.'

'I'm not letting him keep 'em. Not in this house.'

'I know but—'

'I'm not gonna destroy 'em. If I'd wanted to do that I'da flushed 'em last night.'

'Well just make sure this mate a Denny's dun't either. You don't know whether that'd get our Damien into trouble. There might be gangs involved, or all sorts. Yer just don't know.'

'He won't destroy 'em. He'll look after 'em. I'll make sure.'

Bea led him upstairs to their bedroom, where she had the bag of pills stashed away in a bedside cupboard. She handed them over to him.

'Have we got summat better to put 'em in? You know, like a big tin or summat?'

'I might have a Tupperware container big enough.'

'Let's have a look at it.'

Bea hunted out the plastic box back downstairs in the kitchen. It had a clip-on lid and seemed airtight when shut. Kelly pushed the bag of pills down inside it, snapped the lid on and stuffed it into a black leather holdall.

'Right, I'm out of here.'

'All right. But keep yer—'

'I know. I'll keep me phone switched on.'

Bea watched Kelly go out the back door and listened to him rev the bike up and ride out onto the road.

Five minutes later, Damien walked through the front door with Chloe behind him.

22. The Green Tiger

DMITRI WAS DRIVING to a business meeting when he got the
news on the BlackBerry. It was one of Cheslav's men, the ones
watching Sanjeev's house. They were telling him that one of the
guys had been beaten up by a bunch of locals.

'They bashed him up pretty bad, boss. I think we need to
take him to the hospital.'

'And why are you telling me this? Have you told Cheslav?'

'He's not answering. I don't know where he is.'

Dmitri remembered he'd sent Cheslav out on that job,
transporting Sanjeev's bitch out to the quarry. He usually
answered his phone though. Still –

'OK,' he said, 'that means Cheslav is busy right now doing
something for me. Who's this guy who got hurt?'

'It's Marko, boss.'

'Marko? He's usually pretty tough. What's he doing letting
the locals jump him?'

'They musta took him by surprise. They used bats an' shit.
He's hurt bad.'

'What the fuck they do that for? What the fuck is going on
down there? Have you seen the boy?'

'Well that's the thing, boss. I think maybe Marko saw him
and the locals musta jumped in to protect him.'

'What d'you mean, think?' Dmitri roared down the phone.
'Did he see him or not? Just give me a fucking straight answer,
you fucking coward!'

'Sorry, boss. Marko mumbled something about the kid but
he can barely talk, he's that beat up.'

'OK, take care of him. But don't tell anyone anything at the
hospital. It was a random attack, you understand?'

'OK, boss, don't worry, we'll take care of it. D'you want
one of us to stay watching the house?'

'Yes, I fucking want one of you to stay watching the fucking
house. Look, keep trying Cheslav until he answers. I can't deal
with this now, I have important business. Cheslav is going to
have to deal with this so fucking get through to him. That's an
order.'

'Yes, boss.'

'Have you tried phoning the driver?'

'Driver, boss?'

'Cheslav's driver,' Dmitri said impatiently. 'What's his name?'

'You mean Olek?'

'If that's his fucking name then yes. Phone Olek. They should be together. Get him to put Cheslav on. And don't fucking bother me with this again until it's sorted out, you hear me?'

'No, boss. I mean yes, boss.'

He ended the call and swore at the device, swore at the car, swore at the road in front of him. Fuck, fuck, fuck. It'd be a good two or three hours before Cheslav was back to sort this mess out.

In the meantime, he couldn't worry himself with it. He had important people to meet at The Green Tiger.

The Gren Tiger was a lap-dancing club on Wellington Street that was run by a friend of his who employed mainly East European girls. Dmitri liked the atmosphere there and frequently chose it as a venue for conducting serious business. He could watch the Polish girls do their pole-dancing and stand his guest clients a table dance or two from his stable of favourite Ukrainian beauties, which always broke the ice and smoothed the path of negotiations.

He was meeting two men today and wanted to be in the club before they arrived so he could set everything up the way he wanted it. He got a private room, away from the central bar and stage area. He'd have to catch up with the Polish pole-dancers another time. Today, they needed quiet and privacy, and maybe a couple of the Ukrainian girls to come in later, when shop talk was over, if that was what they wanted.

By the time they arrived together, both in business suits, both middle-aged, tanned and sleek in their financial well being, Dmitri had a good Cabernet Sauvignon, a bottle of Scotch, a bottle of Medoff vodka and three bottles of Evian water with all the requisite glasses arranged on a table that still gave plenty of space for their laptops. Lastly, he switched his BlackBerry to silent.

The one wearing glasses and fidgeting nervously was Conservative Councillor Frank Naylor. The other, the one wearing a charcoal-grey three-piece suit and a charcoal-grey beard to match, was Melvin Goldthorpe, and he was Dmitri's father's lawyer.

'Both here at the same time,' Dmitri observed, trying to sound like he wasn't making something out of it and sounding like he was.

'I had a car collect Frank then pick me up on the way,' said Goldthorpe, wondering why he had to bother explaining this. He knew what Dmitri was like though. He'd been his father Yosyp's lawyer for years and had watched the son's development since he'd come over to this country as a young man with a respectable wartime military service record behind him, but still a young hothead to boot. And maybe Dmitri was a big man now in many ways, but he was still that young hothead, in Goldthorpe's eyes. He wasn't here though to bandy his opinion on Yosyp's only surviving son. He was here to carry out a treasured old client's wishes.

'Drink?' said Dmitri after they'd sat down. He gestured elaborately at the array on the table. 'Please, anything you like. I tried to cover all the bases.'

'Mineral water for me,' said the Councillor.

Goldthorpe looked a little disappointed and said, 'Yeah, me too.'

Dmitri snapped his fingers and a young girl appeared from some niche in the back as if from nowhere. She looked about eighteen – you couldn't really tell with teenagers these days – and wore her hair black and bobbed and vivid red lipstick on her mouth and very little else.

Naylor and Goldthorpe both noticed the shoes at the end of the black stockings. High-heeled stilettos. It was every fantasy they'd ever looked at in secret in a magazine and they sat there very still, loosening their collars, their eyes taking it all in and trying to give nothing away while they both thought of their wives.

'Natasha,' said Dmitri, slipping an arm around the girl's waste while she stood ready to take their orders. 'Don't you think she looks like a young Natasha Kinski? It was later, you know, that she changed her name to Nastassja,' he went on with all the authority of someone who doesn't know what they're talking about. 'An affectation, I always thought, but I forgive her. Who wouldn't?'

'I take your orders,' said Natasha in a heavy Slavonic

accent.

Councillor Naylor didn't know whether this was supposed to be a question, an offer, or a simple statement of the girl's professional function.

Goldthorpe had been through the routine before and said:

'Pour my friend and me a mineral water, please, Natasha.'

The girl leaned over the table and opened two Evian bottles and poured them out. Then without asking she reached for the vodka and filled a shot glass for Dmitri.

Naylor and Goldthorpe both watched what she was doing with close attention.

Dmitri meanwhile was watching them and enjoying the looks on their faces.

When Natasha had finished pouring the drinks, she moved away and seemed to vanish back into the shadows that had delivered her to them.

Goldthorpe and the Councillor didn't move for a long time. Dmitri could see they were both lost in the dream that had been snatched away from their presence. The girl, their youth, their freedom; their lost manhood. He raised his vodka glass and their attention clicked back to the present.

'Gentlemen, let's talk business.'

He downed the Medoff in one. First of the day – always good.

'As you know,' began Goldthorpe, 'your father wants you to invest with him in some of this new waterfront development – '

'Hardly new,' said the Councillor. 'It's been ongoing since the Eighties, when Maggie was in.'

He had to get an advertisement in early for the Tories. It was ingrained in his nature. He had to be careful what he said though too. He didn't trust these bastards but he thought he could do business with them, as long as it was kept at one remove from him, if not more.

'As a way of drawing you into the family business,' continued Goldthorpe, ignoring the Councillor's interruption.

'I am in the family business,' said Dmitri.

'Into the respectable area of the family business.'

Dmitri let that go for now. In here was the last place he wanted to cause a scene. He'd hate to get banned. He'd hate to have to kill his friend, the owner, for banning him. But

Goldthorpe better not shoot his mouth off in front of Naylor. He was a lawyer, for fuck's sake, he should know better.

Unless he did know better, which was what Dmitri was gambling on. His father may have gone soft and legitimate in his old age but he still had a sharp eye for a good lawyer. If Goldthorpe ever let him down he would be out of a job by now. He at least knew that much about his old man.

'What are the figures?' said Dmitri.

'Here,' said Goldthorpe, sliding his laptop across the table, 'take a look for yourself.'

'Five million,' said Dmitri. 'You want five million from me. And what do I get in return? Let's take a look.' He scrolled down the page. 'Ah yes, here it is. Anticipated slice of revenue to me worth thirty million over the first ten years.'

He paused and looked them both in the eye. Then he said, indolently:

'It's not a great deal of money.'

The Councillor looked away, pretending he hadn't heard that.

'The sums aren't negotiable,' said Goldthorpe.

Councillor Naylor grunted as a prelude to inserting a point of his own.

'You're actually quite right, Mr Maximov,' he said to Dmitri. 'If you do the sums, it's a low return when you consider the potential rents and sales on these properties. But the riverside's a slow, long-term development. Look at Airedale Point.'

'I know it,' said Dmitri, flashing on Madeleine's thighs up around his ears on the big bed up in the penthouse.

'There's still thousands of square feet of apartments and business premises standing empty. But you've got to look at the long game. It's a slow market now but the long-term forecasts show a potential and likely tenfold increase on that figure over the *next* ten years after the first ten-year period.'

'Three hundred million,' said Dmitri with a smile on his face, 'just in time for my retirement. Now there's a decent inheritance to have sitting around for my kids.'

'Does that mean yes?' said Goldthorpe.

'Let me get this straight. What does the Councillor here get out of it?'

'We put some contracts out to companies that serve the Councillor's interests,' said Goldthorpe, choosing his words carefully.

'And a small donation to the Tory Party wouldn't go amiss,' added Naylor, leaning towards Dmitri in a fawning manner. 'Anonymous, of course.'

'And remind me, what do we get from Councillor Naylor?'

'Councillor Naylor's voice carries a lot of weight with the planning committee.'

'I *am* the planning committee,' said Naylor, staring across at Dmitri with what for the first time looked like a pair of balls. 'I'm the one who can make sure all the right permits get signed.'

Dmitri poured himself another shot, not bothering to fetch Natasha to come and do it, to the two men's unexpressed disappointment.

Then he laughed.

'And my father calls this legitimate business.'

'Listen—' said Naylor, leaning forward aggressively this time.

It would've pissed Dmitri off if it hadn't been so funny. Like funny pathetic.

'Please, Frank,' intervened Goldthorpe, waving his hands between them, 'will you let me handle this?'

'If there's anything dodgy about this five mil then I don't know anything about it, you understand?' Naylor continued. 'In fact I'd be a lot happier if I knew it came from legitimate revenue.'

'Relax, Mr Councillor,' said Dmitri. 'Nothing will tie you to the money. Certainly nothing that I do. You know what I'm saying? If there's a fuck-up at your end, well that's your business. And then I'm not involved. It cuts both ways, see? That way neither of us fucks up. Right?'

'I wouldn't have expressed it in those exact terms, but yes,' said the Councillor, telling himself to calm down now, it was over. 'In that case, I think we can do business.'

'And what about my old man?' said Dmitri to Goldthorpe. 'Any strings attached?'

'No strings. At least, not yet.'

'That's refreshingly honest.'

'You know what your father's like.' *It cuts both ways,*

thought Goldthorpe. 'He'll make those decisions as and when, and that'll be between you and him.'

'OK. I think we have a deal. I'll get my lawyers to talk to you about the paperwork,' he told Goldthorpe. 'Mr Naylor.'

Naylor leaned over out of his chair and they shook hands. Then Dmitri shook hands with the lawyer.

'Isn't this one of those moments that calls for champagne?'

'Oh, I—'

Before the Councillor could object, Natasha reappeared, with a magnum in a bucket of ice supplementing what remained of her costume in covering her up. That shut him up.

'Natasha,' said Dmitri, 'are you going to dance for us? What d'you think, guys? Should Natasha dance for us?'

'I—' Now Naylor was at a loss for words while Natasha uncorked the champagne, the froth spilling out everywhere as she poured it with abandon into their waiting flutes.

'I'll only dance if you let my two friends join me,' said Natasha, putting down the champagne bottle and beckoning two equally lovely young girls out of the shadows.

The three of them took up their positions on a mini-stage in the corner of the room and loud music started up, some rubbish with a pounding drumbeat.

'To the waterfront,' said Dmitri, raising his glass as the show commenced.

The other two could hardly close their mouths and look his way to join in the toast. The expressions on their faces were a scream.

Afterwards, back in the car, Dmitri checked his BlackBerry and saw that he had two missed calls: one from the idiot who'd phoned him earlier about Marko and missing the kid, the other from Madeleine.

He got onto the first one straight away before starting the car. There was still money on the parking meter. He had time to make the call.

'I told you to speak to Cheslav,' he said before the guy had even said anything.

'But that's it, boss. I called the driver, Olek, like you said, and he said Cheslav let him go a couple of hours ago.'

'What d'you mean, let him go?'

'He told him to take the rest of the day off.'

'Where did he leave Cheslav?'

'At the penthouse, boss.'

Shit, thought Dmitri, did everybody fucking dogsbody on the payroll know about the penthouse?

'OK . . .'

He couldn't ask this goon if Cheslav had got the job done that he was sent to do. This whole business was involving too many people already. It wasn't just the mismanagement of manpower, it was the need to have only those who needed to know know.

'Keep watching Sanjeev's place. And stay awake. Take it in shifts. Just use some fucking initiative.'

'Yes, boss.'

The penthouse.

The call from Madeleine.

He called Madeleine.

'Hey, baby. How was the trip?'

'Never mind the facking trip, Dmitri. So what was that gorilla of yours doing in my apartment while I was gone?'

'Has he been there? Today?'

'Yes, he's been here, with some kind of whore by his side. Said he had things to pick up. So that means he stayed here, and that means you gave him a key.'

'Wait a minute, go back. What d'you mean, some kind of whore? A woman? Was he with a woman?'

'That's exactly what I'm saying? So has she slept in my apartment?'

'What did she look like?'

'Like she 'ad just been beaten up. Like someone 'as been knocking her around. Dmitri, have you been knocking someone around in my apartment?'

'Now come on, Madeleine, that's ridiculous. Take a look around. Does the place look like it's been used as slaughterhouse?'

'That's a nice way to put it, you ape,' said Madeleine.

'That's a nice thing to call your lover.'

'I'm serious, Dmitri. So don't give anyone my fucking keys.'

'Look,' he said, getting tired of this now, 'did they say where they were going?'

'No, they didn't say where they were going and I didn't bother to ask them, OK?'

'How was the woman?'

'I told you—'

'I mean, did she look scared, did she look threatened? Or did she look relaxed?'

'You wanna know the truth?' said Madeleine. 'She looked strong.'

'Madeleine, I have to go. There's something important I must deal with. We can talk more later.'

'So are you coming round?'

'We'll see. I'll try my best.'

'Well phone me, at least. Promise me you'll do that.'

'I promise. But I'll try to come over. I've missed you.'

'So show me.'

'I'll try.'

And he would – after he'd taken care of this new problem.

He made one last call, to Cheslav's phone. Predictably, he got nothing but a message from his voicemail service.

It was becoming clear now that Cheslav had failed to do the job he was supposed to be doing. The timeframe didn't allow it. And from what Madeleine had told him about the woman, it was definitely Tracy, and his reading of the situation as she described it told him she wasn't being held captive anymore.

That big dumb fuck! Dmitri knew it: he'd only gone and fallen in love with that tough little bitch!

Instead of shouting at the car, Dmitri kept it together.

OK, the last time he saw Cheslav today, he was left alone with Tracy – and a crate of guns . . .

Dmitri thought about phoning the guys who'd been due at the warehouse later to properly store the merchandise. But no. Keep it need to know. Don't get these little odd-job men involved, with their wagging tongues and there easily bought disloyalty. If anything had happened to the guns he would've heard about it by now. There would be a message waiting, and there was no such message.

OK, next thing.

Think.

He thought hard, but not for long.

He turned back to the BlackBerry and keyed in a number to

Blowback

Kiev. After five rings, a deep voice answered in Russian.
'Yes.'
'Plotnik. It's me, Dmitri.'
Dmitri spoke in Russian also, the language people used in public there, unless they were fanatics or visitors from the west of the country.
'I know,' came the reply.
'I need you to get on a plane and get over here. I've got a job for you.'
'I'll be on the next flight,' said the voice at the other end.
That was all. The line went dead and Dmitri started up the engine, not quite knowing where he was going next, but knowing that when Plotnik got here he would take care of it.
All of it.

23. Without Them

TRACY MADE A point of knowing her own mobile number off by heart, it was just easier to be able to reel it off if someone asked you for it. So she could phone Don as long as he still had her phone, and then he could warn Stephen.

She made the call from a public phone box while Cheslav stood outside on guard duty. Don answered it after only two rings.

'Don? It's Tracy.'

'Oh thank God,' she heard him say, his voice quivering with held-back emotion. 'Where are you?'

'Safe. I'm safe, all right?'

'Are you all right?'

'Yeah, I'm doin' OK. Listen, you've got to gerrin touch with our Stephen.'

'It's all right, I've seen him. He's all right. I still dunno what the hell's goin' on though.'

'Is he there? Is he at home?'

'No, he's out there somewhere lookin' for you.'

'Phone him, Don. Tell him I'm OK. Will you do that for us?'

'Course I will, love. But I wish you'd put me in t'picture.'

'I will, Don, when I get back.'

'No. Don't come back here. There's blokes watchin' your place. Them fuckin' Russians or whatever they are. We twatted one of 'em earlier on.'

'What?'

'He were tryin' to snatch your lad.'

'Listen, Don, tell Stephen we need to meet up.'

'When? Where?'

'Oh shit, I dunno. I can't think of anywhere off top a me 'ead. Hang on a minute.'

She shouldered the phone box door open and tapped Cheslav on the arm.

'What's your mobile number?'

Cheslav dictated it to her and she relayed it to Don.

'Who's that in t'background?' said Don. 'Is that that Russian fella from last night?'

'It's all right, Don, he's on our side.'

'Come again.'

'Just get Stephen to phone me on that number. Then we can figure out what to do together.'

Don said he would.

'What about Sanjeev?' he asked eventually.

Tracy's stomach fell away like a collapsing floor over a deep pit.

'Have you heard from 'im?'

'No, I an't, Don.'

She couldn't tell him. She couldn't risk Don getting the police involved. It was too late already. The only thing that ever did was make the problem far worse than it would've been without them.

'He'll be all right. Worry about that later. We'll figure out what to do. We'll talk it over.'

She hung up and exited the phone box.

'We should keep moving,' said Cheslav.

'Where?' she asked plaintively.

'Somewhere safe. Somewhere we can get some rest. We're going to need it.'

They returned to the car and took off.

Ten minutes later Cheslav's phone rang with a number he didn't recognise. He answered it cautiously.

'Hello.'

'Is my mum there?'

Cheslav handed the phone across to Tracy.

'Stephen?'

'Mum. You OK?'

'Yeah, I'm fine. Really.'

'What the fuck's going on, Mum?'

'Did you take something of Sanjeev's?'

She looked over at Cheslav, whose eyes were fixed on the road and the traffic.

'A bag a pills?'

'Oh shit, Mum. Look, I'm sorry, right? I just didn't want him leaving drugs around tempting you when – '

'I know, love,' she said, all the parental anger deflated out of her. 'I know. I just need to know.'

'I didn't imagine all this shit was gonna kick off. They've

113

been at the house an' everything. An' I can't find Sanjeev. I've tried, Mum, really.'

'I know, I know. Where are they now though?'

'I haven't got 'em. I gave 'em to somebody to look after. Now his stepdad's got hold of 'em, an' – '

He was rambling now, lost.

'All right, listen. Stephen, listen. We need to meet up. Where can we meet up?'

'I dunno, Mum. Let me find somewhere an' I'll get back to you. One other thing. I thought about phoning Gary an' Stu.'

'No,' Tracy said emphatically. 'Don't. I don't want 'em upset, there's no need for them to know anything yet.'

What she meant was, she didn't want any more members of her family migrating into the danger zone.

'Let me work on it, Mum. When I've found somewhere I'll get back to you on this number.'

'OK, love. But be careful. Stay away from the house.'

'I will.'

She handed the phone back to Cheslav, saying nothing.

He didn't ask her any questions about the call, just stayed silent, kept his eyes on the road. The strong silent type.

After several minutes she asked:

'Where are we going?'

'A place I know. Somewhere safe.'

'You said that. Where?'

'In the country,' he said. 'Little place I know there. We'll be there in an hour. Try to get some sleep. Sleep heals.'

'Sleep,' Tracy laughed. 'Fat chance a that.'

She forced her head back against the seat nonetheless and was quietly snoozing away before they even got out of the city.

24. Screaming for Pills

BEFORE KELLY MET up with Ilko to hand over the pills he
texted Denny.

Where are you?

He got one back immediately.

At home.

Can I come over?

Sure.

It was one of those crisp winter days of sunshine and blue
skies and being able to see your own breath. Kelly wore a scarf
slipped over his mouth and nose under the helmet and a pair of
wool-lined leather gloves over his hands as he biked along,
throttling it on the open stretches.

When he parked the bike outside Denny's block, he was
careful to take the holdall with the pills in it up to Denny's flat
with him.

Inside, the place was just as much a mess as it had been the
night before but somehow didn't look quite as bad in daylight, as
if all the junk, fag-ends and the debris of a dozen takeaways had
a breath of fresh air blowing through them.

It was late afternoon and a layered mist of green-grey smoke
glowed in the sunshine streaming in through the window: Denny
was sucking on a spliff, which Kelly declined this time when it
was offered to him. He wanted to get straight to the point.

'You took one a these pills, didn't ya? The one I left behind
last night.'

Denny was determined not to act guilty over it.

'So?'

'So what was it like? What happened?'

Denny smiled.

'Don't wanna try it for yourself?' he asked Kelly.

'Er, no.'

'Shit, Kel, it was weird. Fuckin' weird. I'm not sure how
else to describe it.'

'Well what happened? Did you have hallucinations? Was it
like acid?'

'Yes and no. I did hallucinate but it was different from acid.
A different kind a trip altogether.'

'In what way.'

'I felt like I was dyin'. OK, you get that on acid sometimes, but this was different. If you think you're dying on acid, it's a bad trip. On the DMT, though, it's like I knew I was gonna die but I didn't care. In fact, not even that. It's not that I didn't care. It's that I wanted it. It made me feel like, before I took it I knew what was gonna happen and taking it was a way of ensuring that it would. That I'd die. Dyin' felt like the purpose of takin' the pill. Does any a that make sense?'

'No.'

'Which is why you need to try it yerself if you wanna know what it's like.'

'Right, well maybe I'm not that desperate then,' said Kelly. 'Sounds fuckin' 'orrible.'

'No, it wasn't. I'd do it again like a shot.'

'That goes without sayin'. But it sounds sli–ght–ly dangerous to me. I mean, if it makes you wanna die, how d'you know it's not gonna make you kill yerself?'

'I just do,' said Denny. 'It's not like that.'

'I wonder how much he's chargin' a pop?'

'Who, Dmitri?'

'If that's who they belong to. If it's as moreish as you say it is, he must be losin' a tidy profit on this missin' bag.'

'You don't even know if there are any others. For all we know, these might be the prototypes.'

'Maybe it'd help if we could find the guy who made 'em.'

'I thought your lass's kid knew who it wa'.'

'Yeah, but he's still fuckin' AWOL, in't he?'

In one of those moments when the world seems too full of coincidences, Kelly's phone rang. It was Bea.

'He's back.'

'When?'

'Just after you set off. He's furious, Kel, about—'

'Is that 'im?' Kelly heard Damien saying in the background. 'Tell 'im I need 'em back right now!'

'He says this lad who he's lookin' after 'em for, his mother's gone missin', *and* the bloke who made 'em – that chemist bloke.'

Kelly pondered the situation for a moment.

'All right,' he said finally, a simple acknowledgement of the information he'd received, not an agreement to anything.

'Well are you gonna bring 'em back?'

'I'll have to think about it. Let me talk to this mate a Denny's first.'

'What's so important about his opinion?'

'I think he knows who they belong to. He might be able to see a way around all this.'

'But if this woman's disappeared, an' this chemist bloke, it must mean somebody's tryin' to find 'em. What if they come round here?'

'What's Damien said? Do they know he's got 'em?'

'Not from what he's said to me.'

'Listen, don't let him bugger off again. Keep 'im there till I get back, all right?'

'I'll try. He's here with Chloe. I think he brought her for moral support.'

Damien must've left the room. Either that or Chloe had managed to drag him away. That was good. It was good having Chloe there with him.

'Try an' talk to Chloe then. See if you can get her to keep 'im there. I'll get back as quick as I can.'

'Your Damien turned up then?' said Denny when Kelly had ended the conversation.

'Yeah. Screamin' for t'pills back.'

'What yer gonna do?'

'I'm gonna talk to Sergeant Bilko – I mean Ilko. Your sure he's all right, this guy? How well d'you know 'im?'

'He's a good bloke. I trust 'im.'

'There's a lot ridin' on this.'

'I know. I still trust him. We want some'dy on our side, don't we? Remember 'Amed?'

Oh yeah, Kelly remembered Hamed, the Iraqi ex-army captain who'd helped to get the terrifying Big Baz off their backs when he was out for revenge for what they'd done to one of his nephews. It was hard to keep in mind that the kid they beat up was the brother of the kid who'd apparently got Damien involved in this recent bother.

Denny attacked the kid in an all-night-garage robbery that the two of them pulled off with a couple of mates three years ago. The bad old days. They didn't know it was Big Baz's nephew, though admittedly Denny was at fault in hurting the kid for no good reason other than anger and showing off. But Big Baz, given the opportunity, would have crippled them all for life.

Hamed, a mercenary between jobs, had broken Baz's leg as a warning to leave them alone. Of course it all went shit-shaped in the end and Baz and a West Indian lad both ended up dead. Not that there weren't plenty who believed Baz deserved it. But hiring Captain Hamed was probably not the brightest move they could've made at the time.

If that was Denny's idea of somebody on their side then maybe he should think twice about Sergeant Bilko after all.

'Listen, before you hand 'em over to Ilko, Kel, d'yer mind if I take a couple for Ron?'

He meant for later on.

'Aw, fuck off, Denny. What yer like?'

'Come on, nobody's gonna miss two more pills from that lot. Or three, or five. Come on, you can spare us five. I've 'elped you out so far, an't I?'

'Fuckinell,' said Kelly, knowing he'd feel shit now if he didn't do it.

He opened the Tupperware box and the paper sack inside it and carefully counted out five of the little white caplets.

'Make it a round ten?' said Denny.

'Fuck off, Denny. That's your lot.'

Oh well, it was worth a chance.

Denny was still smiling as he slipped the pills into the penknife pocket at the hip of his jeans.

25. Dark Corners

DAMIEN WAS RANTING at his mother.

'You shoulda told 'im!'

'I did.'

'If we don't get 'em back they might kill Stevo's mum.'

'I know, an' Kelly knows. I've done all I can do. It's up to 'im now.'

'Well that's fuckin' great!'

'Come on, D.'

This was Chloe, trying to calm him down with consolation, her hand on his shoulder gently massaging the muscle there.

Bea wondered if that was all it was going to take. She suspected not.

Then Damien's phone went off.

Jesus, thought Bea, *is the world made of frigging mobile phones?* But then, how much worse would this situation be without them? At least nowadays you could get bad news straight away wherever you were, without the added misery of waiting in anticipation and dread.

'Stevo,' she heard Damien say, 'you all right, man?'

A long pause, then Damien palming the phone and telling them, 'His mam's been in touch, she's OK.' He put the phone back to his ear. 'Go on.'

Another pause, before Damien said, 'I'll ask 'er. 'Old on.'

He looked up at his mother.

'Can he come round here? They're watchin' 'is 'ouse, he an't got anywhere else to go.'

'Who's watchin' 'is 'ouse?' said Bea.

'I dunno. Blokes.'

'Fuckinell, Damien.'

She shut up a minute, breathing hard.

''Ang on, Stevo,' Damien said into the phone.

'Where's his mother?' said Bea.

'He dun't know yet. He reckons she's safe though.'

Damien spoke to Stevo again.

'He wants to meet up with her somewhere. Is it all right, Mum, if they come round 'ere? They've got nowhere else to go.'

Shit, thought Bea. She couldn't let them roam the streets,

hiding in dark corners. Her Damien was involved in all this, after all. She'd just have to deal with it. *They'd* just have to deal with it.

'Go on, then,' she said.

Bea prided herself on making good decisions. The only bad one that stood out in her memory was getting done for dealing back when she lived in Leeds 6, for which she did two years' community service; and even that was down to someone ratting her up, so really the bad decision had been in her choice of friends.

She'd been saved from another major mistake when she pointed a gun at Big Baz. Someone else shot him in the end, thankfully – though in a way she missed the grumpy old bastard: he was a friend for a lot longer than he was an enemy.

As for the rest, there were no regrets. She had good reason to trust her own judgement.

But about this decision, she had a bad feeling already.

Her heart sank a little further as she listened to Damien give out their address.

26. Blood and Magic

KELLY LEFT DENNY at home when he went to meet Ilko. He could see that Denny was itching to know what Ilko was going to do with the pills but not daring to bring the subject up now he'd managed to weasel five of the little buggers out of Kelly. He knew when to keep quiet, not to overplay his hand and go blotching his copy book for later. So Kelly left him contented for now, and keeping his nose out.

He had arranged to meet Ilko in the Royal Park pub not out of his own choice but Ilko's. It was one of the few pubs Ilko knew where he didn't have to feel on his guard. Kids that he worked with in the hostel went in there, and he had no bad business with any of them, or certainly none he couldn't handle. Most of them were just unlucky. They'd been forced to make some bad choices in life before they were old enough to be able to face those kinds of decisions. Growing up hard meant growing up tough, sure, and probably growing a big pair of balls as well, but that didn't always make it right. Most people where he came from wouldn't normally think this, but he'd always thought it, always felt different. The hard knocks that life and history had given his mother could in no way be seen to have some good come of them; that was what only a sentimental fool accepted, to make the yoke feel like it was lighter and chafing just a little less than the day before.

In addition, the Royal Park was a pub lively with students. Whatever happened, things were less likely to kick off big time the busier it was.

But it wouldn't have been Kelly's first choice because a lot of locals went in there as well, and not all of them would be people that Kelly wanted to see. Not that he had any grief with anyone that he could remember, just that the Royally was the past for him and he didn't want to slip back into it.

Parking the bike in the forecourt, he glanced over at the spot where Big Baz had had him up against the wall pummelling the shit out of him three years ago. He vaguely remembered seeing Denny all beaten up, but the sight he'd never forget was of Bea pointing Denny's gun at Big Baz.

That was the night it all changed. That was the moment that

changed everything, for him and for Bea. As frightening as it still was, he had to hold all the madness and the terror and the potential devastation and loss from that scene in his mind to keep things in perspective.

When he walked in, the place hadn't changed much. It had changed hands by the looks of it, and he idly wondered what had happened to Geoff, the old manager, and his two Rottweilers. He didn't recognise any of the bar staff, though it always did have a fast turnover of students looking for extra cash.

It was quiet for a Saturday afternoon and none of the faces there was anyone he'd seen before except for Ilko's, sitting in a corner in what used to be the music room back in the day when an old guy would play the piano, long since replaced by a flashy jukebox.

'Where's Denny?' said Ilko as Kelly sat down at the table facing him across it.

'He's not coming.'

Ilko just looked at him, waiting for more, sipping his orange and passion fruit J2O from the neck of the bottle.

'I thought it best not to bring 'im,' said Kelly. 'If he knows where you're gonna stash 'em, they won't be safe. I think you know what Denny's like. He wouldn't be able to help himself.'

Ilko looked at him for a minute longer but that was all Kelly had to give.

'Wise move,' he said at last. 'Denny's a nice boy – most of the time – but he's not a good boy. That takes a little more work.'

Kelly took this comment as an invitation to question him about how they knew one another.

'Has he been in prison? I mean recently. Cos I kinda got the impression you mighta been his social worker or summat.'

'No,' laughed Ilko, 'nothing like that. I know Denny was in prison when he was younger. He never told you about me?'

'Not until yesterday.'

'We are related. Distantly. Distantly by your definition, I guess.'

'Related?'

'His mother's sister-in-law is my cousin.'

'So you're his uncle or summat?'

'Not uncle, no. Maybe second cousins by marriage, something like that.'

'I never knew Denny's mother were Ukrainian.'

'Not his mother. His mother's sister-in-law. Denny's *uncle* married my cousin.'

Kelly gave up trying to figure it out before he got more confused.

'I met first Denny maybe seven years ago at a family wedding.'

Kelly tried to imagine Denny at a family wedding. In a suit. Yeah, right.

'It was just after I came over here. It helped, having family over here already, even though they are distant relations. We are used to distance in Ukraine. But family – blood – that's a strong tie and we take it seriously.'

Kelly tried to think of a place where family ties weren't taken seriously and couldn't come up with anywhere, but kept quiet about it.

'So what ya gonna do with the pills?' said Kelly, putting his hand on the straps of the holdall on the table between them.

'Like I said before, I know a place they won't look.'

'Where is it?'

'You don't need to know. Do you want to know?'

Ilko managed to make the question sound like a threat, but Kelly put it down to his clumsy intonation.

'I want to know that I'll get 'em back if I need 'em. I've told you what's at stake.'

'I know,' said Ilko. 'That was the deal we discussed. As long as we keep them off the streets.'

Kelly nodded a cautious agreement.

'Are they gonna be somewhere safe?'

'Why would I put them somewhere else?'

'I just don't want some wino stumblin' across 'em in some ginnel behind a bin, ya know what I'm sayin'?'

'No one will find them. No one will look for them there. Only I will know where they are.'

'And what if summat 'appens to you?'

'Then . . . poof!' – his hands magicked them away in the air – 'the pills are gone.'

27. Entertaining Visitors

IT WAS STILL long before dark when Kelly got home.

The minute he was in the house he was searching through it looking for Damien and it didn't take him long to find him. To find all of them, waiting for him in the front room.

Bea standing next to the window.

Damien sitting on the settee, Chloe beside him gripping his hand.

And another one, a young dark-skinned lad, sitting in his armchair. Not that he minded as long as he got an explanation.

He heard the telly playing to Casey and her mate next door. Then he heard the door to the back room open, and Casey was standing behind him in the hall.

'Kelly, remember what you promised.'

She was like an angel or a conscience at his shoulder, then she was gone, back to the Happy Mondays.

'Promised what?' said Bea.

'I said I wun't 'ave a go at Damien when he got back,' said Kelly, wishing Bea hadn't heard. Shit, now they'd all heard.

'What've you done wi' them pills?' said Damien maungily.

Chloe kept a hand on his shoulder.

''S all right, D, give 'im a chance.'

'I've done what your mate did,' said Kelly. 'I've given 'em to someone else to look after.'

'Mr—' Stevo rose out of the chair without knowing D-Man's old lady's old man's surname.

'Me name's Kelly.'

'I'm Stevo. I'm the guy that asked D-Ma— I mean, that asked Damien to look after those pills.'

'What did he call you?' said Kelly, looking at Damien. 'D-Man? What's that, is that like a tag or summat?'

'It's just a name,' said Damien.

'It's not a gang thing, is it?'

'I'm not in a fuckin' gang, all right?' Damien shouted. 'It's nowt to do wi' gangs.'

'Oh yeah. Well tell that to the fuckin' Ukrainians.'

Instantly, Kelly wished he'd kept his mouth shut. He didn't want to upset Bea, and now he'd gone and opened it. She didn't look surprised though.

'It's all right,' she said, 'I've heard all about it from Stephen here.'

'Mr Kelly, I'm sorry, all right? I thought I was doin' it for the right reasons. My mum got done for drugs when I was little an' I didn't want 'em in the house. That's why I asked Damien to look after 'em. Cos I trusted 'im. It was only to keep 'em out a my mum's reach. I was gonna find a way to give 'em back. Then the Ukrainians took my mum, an' I think they mighta taken Sanjeev too.'

'So it's safer not 'avin' 'em 'ere,' said Kelly. 'If they come, they can look. What they gonna find? It's better than if they found 'em 'ere.'

'I don't think the Ukrainians are gonna be satisfied with just lookin', do you, Mr Kelly?'

'Just Kelly, all right?'

He waited for the atmosphere to settle.

Bea stepped forward.

'Well there's summat else you might as well know about. Stephen's mother's on her way round.'

'I thought he just said they'd taken her.'

'She got away,' said Stevo. 'One of 'em helped her escape. The same one that took her in the first place.'

'What?' said Kelly.

'Yeah. It's crazy, innit? They're comin' round here, now. I 'ope that's all right, Mr Kelly.'

Kelly remembered what Ilko had said about family and blood. If all this was true, what had happened to this guy's loyalty, the one who was on his way round here now? And how could he be trusted?

'Bea,' he said. 'Word outside.'

'Don't you go blamin' Mam,' said Damien.

'Will ya take it easy?' said Kelly. 'I just want a word in private. I'm entitled to that, aren't I?'

'Just don't be 'avin' a go at her, that's all.'

Outside the front room in the hall with the door shut between them, Kelly put his arm around Bea's shoulder.

'You do know who Stevo's mum is, don't yer?'

'No, who is she?'

'Tracy Croft. Big Baz's sister.'

'Fuckinell,' Bea sighed, looking at her wit's end. 'This just keeps gettin' better an' better. I'm sorry, Kel.'

'Eh. It's not your fault.'

He gave her a kiss but before they could go back inside there was a knock at the back door. Surely, this couldn't be them already. Besides, only neighbours used the back door. Visitors usually went to the front door.

'Is that back door locked?'

'Yeah,' said Bea.

Then she looked up at him, scared.

'Go back in there. I'll see who it is.'

'Fuckinell, be careful, Kel.'

He approached the back door cautiously, trying to see something, anything, through the frosted glass.

'Who is it?'

'It's Stephen's mam,' a woman's voice replied. 'Is he there?'

Kelly was breathing a sigh of relief at something which a moment before he'd been in fear of in his imagination. He unlocked the door and ushered her in, followed by some massive guy in a suit who didn't look intimidating to Kelly *at* all.

'I'm really sorry about all this,' the woman started saying, and Kelly noticed the bruises on her face and the game job of covering them with make-up that had gone on. 'I'm Tracy an' this is – Chezz.'

'Jez?' said Kelly.

'Chezz,' said Tracy. 'You know, like that actor, Chazz Palminteri, but instead o' Chazz with an A, it's Chezz with an E.'

The door to the front room opened and Stevo emerged.

'Mum!'

He ran to the kitchen and threw his arms around her. She winced in pain and he backed up.

'Aw, Jesus, Mum, what did they do to you?'

He looked at the big suited geezer standing behind her and decided that size didn't matter in this case.

'Was it 'im?'

'No, Stephen' she said, taking hold of her boy. 'It wasn't him.'

She looked at Cheslav, whose eyes fell to the floor for a moment.

'Besides, it's not that bad. Nowt broken. I'll live.'

Tracy's eyes welled up then, thinking of Sanjeev, and Cheslav's gaze burned deeper into the linoleum. Poor Sanjeev. She couldn't tell her boy yet. For a million reasons, she just couldn't.

Bea and Damien and Chloe had spilled out into the hall like woodland animals watching the signs of a distant fire.

Then the door to the back room opened and Casey stepped out. She froze in the no man's land between the group in the kitchen and the group outside the front room, swept a glance at everyone around her, counted one, two, three, four, five, six, seven people, then said reluctantly:

'Does anyone want a cup a tea?'

28. Into the Valley

OTTO PLOTNIK FLEW Dutch KLM from Kiev to Leeds/Bradford Airport with a four-hour wait at Schiphol.

He had an unusual first name because, although his father had been a miner in the east of Ukraine, his mother was German by birth. His mother had fought against her own countrymen during the Great Revolutionary War against Hitler and the Nazis, not just for love of his father but for love of the country she loved, for love of a dream – for Ukraine.

He wondered if the Ukraine of today had featured in her dream, with its poverty, corruption and squabbling politicians. And still there were gangs of Nazis roaming the streets of Kiev.

Yet Plotnik liked Kiev. It was where he chose to spend his time when he didn't have business elsewhere. The poverty, the violence: with what he earned elsewhere, he could afford a lifestyle there that kept him comfortably above all of that, in a place where no one was going to bother him or worry themselves about his business.

But the winter. He would be glad to be away from the Ukrainian winter for a few days. Here in England, he barely needed a coat.

At Passport Control, the man spent too long looking at his passport, but Plotnik expected this. They weren't used to Ukrainians having visas into the UK at all, never mind one that was multiple entry. But it was authorised so they weren't going to waste time asking him pointless questions about it. *OK, it's weird but it checks out. Move on. Next.*

It was late, nearly midnight, but in Kiev now it was two a.m. Plotnik, travelling light, marched past the baggage carousel without stopping. Before he left the building, he paused to change the SIM card over in his mobile phone.

Then, outside, he phoned Dmitri Maximov.

'Plotnik,' said Dmitri.

'I'm here.'

'Go to the safe house,' said Dmitri. 'I'll meet you there in the morning.'

Plotnik hung up and walked over to the taxi rank. As he did so, he tilted his head up at the clear night of stars, and the moonlight threw a shadow into the valley of a scar that crossed his face.

Just as he thought: outdoors, it was a positively balmy night compared to Kiev.

29. Here's My Number

ALL THE BEDROOMS were taken by the household. Chloe was sleeping with Damien in his room up in the loft conversion, and tonight they'd rather do it without Stevo's company; Casey was reluctant to give up her bedroom, understandably, as were Kelly and Bea theirs. So the rest of the visitors were left to make what they could of the settees and cushions in the front and back rooms.

Cheslav said he would take the back room because if Dmitri's men came, they could come either way – the front door into the hall next to the front room or the back way through the kitchen, and the back room was in between the two so strategically it was the best place for him to remain on guard.

That meant that Tracy and Stephen took the front room together. She lay underneath a couple of TV blankets on the settee while Stephen used the floor, lying on a makeshift bed of cushions, coats and various soft furnishings.

Neither of them was complaining. Cheslav had wanted to take them both out of town to the country hotel that he and Tracy had been heading for before they were diverted back into Leeds, but Tracy and Stephen were both tired out and couldn't face the idea of the long drive through the night. They should wait here till morning then decide a common strategy, seeing as these people were involved now too. Cheslav wasn't happy about it but he conceded.

Tracy and Stephen, despite their exhaustion, talked late into the night over the events of the last few days. Tracy gave an edited account, as no doubt Stephen did too.

She told him how she'd introduced Sanjeev to Cheslav a while ago, leaving out the fact that she hadn't known his name at the time. She wanted to build a picture of Cheslav as someone she'd known for a while, to instil the boy's trust in him. She wasn't even sure she trusted him herself yet, but she believed him when he told her that Dmitri was going to kill her if he didn't get her out of there.

She told Stephen about what Dmitri had done to her but she didn't mention that it was Cheslav holding her down. When Stephen asked where he was during all this, she said he wasn't there. She invented Cheslav's discovery of her afterwards and played up her rescue by him.

She didn't tell him that Sanjeev was dead. She couldn't face that now, and she couldn't make him face it. She recognised that if Stephen hadn't meddled with Sanjeev's property Sanjeev would still be alive. She also acknowledged that Stephen thought he was acting in her interest. She couldn't blame the boy.

There was only one person responsible for what had happened over the last forty-eight hours and that was that cunt Dmitri. If anyone was going to pay, it was him. This was another thing she omitted from expressing to Stephen. She just held it to herself in her heart like a tenet.

The next morning Tracy woke up early, and despite her injuries felt refreshed after an uninterrupted night's sleep. Her face was still swollen and a mass of pain, but she knew that if she kept swallowing the Nurofens that Cheslav had bought for her, the pain would soon ease up.

Otherwise, she felt more awake and alert than normal. It struck her that yesterday was the first day she'd gone without alcohol all day in living memory. She hadn't even noticed. She'd forgotten what waking up without a hangover felt like.

The curtains were drawn against the morning light and she let Stephen sleep on as she tiptoed across the room and stepped over him. It was chilly being out from under the blankets but she was fully clothed, and in the hall she heard the central heating timer kick in.

She knocked softly on the door of the back room and it was opened immediately. Cheslav was standing there fully dressed in his suit and tie, looking exactly as he'd looked last night.

'Have you moved from that spot all night?'

'Good morning,' he said. 'How are you feeling today?'

'I need to take some a them painkillers.'

He followed her down to the kitchen where she poured herself a glass of water to swallow the tablets with.

'I need to see Don,' said Tracy, turning to see the effect on Cheslav.

'Don?'

'The bloke from the other night. The one I was sitting with in the club when you burst in.' She put on a guilty tone. 'He's got my mobile phone. I slipped it to 'im while you weren't lookin'.

Sorry.'

'Good thinking,' he said. 'It probably saved Stephen's life. For now.'

That put a shiver down her spine.

'I wish these radiators'd hurry up and heat up. 'S fuckin' freezin'.'

'Do you want my jacket?' said Cheslav, beginning to remove it.

'No, don't be daft. It looks better on you, you keep it. I'm just moanin' for summat to moan about. I wish I had a fag. D'you think they'll have some in here somewhere? D'you think they'd mind?'

Cheslav conducted a search of the kitchen and found a half-full ten pack of Benson & Hedges in the pocket of an apron hanging up by the cooker. He handed them over and produced a Zippo lighter from his own pocket.

The first drag was wonderful, felt like it was helping the painkillers to spread through her system. That was another thing she missed all day yesterday without realising it. A whole day without a drink or a cigarette. Definitely a first.

'I need to get me phone back, I feel 'opeless without it.'

'We shouldn't take the car.'

It was parked in the backstreet a few houses down from Kelly and Bea's kitchen door. Cheslav was taking a chance with the locals, but Kelly said it wasn't so bad round here.

It would be better not to have it here. They should have parked it somewhere in town and come here by minicab, but the problem of finding a place to leave it where it wouldn't get clamped overnight was overruled by Tracy's insistence on reaching Stephen as quickly as possible. He couldn't deny her the swift reunion with her son after all that'd happened and his part in it, even if it was stupid to keep the car.

At least, round the back, somewhere in the four-block maze of through terraces and cul-de-sacs, Cheslav didn't think it would be spotted unless they already knew where to look for it. But it would be better if they didn't parade it around the neighbourhood.

'I should go on me own.'

'No.'

'Look, am I still your fuckin' prisoner or what? Cos we

never really clarified this bit.'

'You're not my prisoner, but you're my responsibility.'

'No, I'm not. I can fuckin' take care of meself.'

'Maybe you can,' said Cheslav, 'for a while. You can do it for longer with me. Together maybe we can make a way out.'

'What do you mean, *make* a way out?'

'A way to put an end to being hunted.'

'Is that what we are from now on then? Hunted?'

'It's not nice but you have to face it. Without my help, what will you do?'

'What are you gonna do?'

'That's what we need to talk about, with these people. It's what you said last night.'

'I know,' Tracy admitted, 'but I still think I need to see Don on me own. The other night, in the Lib, his pride'll have been hurt. It's not a good idea you being there, rubbin' it in. It's not fair on Don.'

'Take a minicab,' said Cheslav. 'Use a local company. Meet somewhere far from your house. And come straight back.'

He produced a scrap of paper and wrote something on it.

'Here's my number. It's not in your phone. Call me when you get it back.'

Sanjeev had only been dead half the weekend and already another man was giving her his phone number. It didn't feel right but, under the circumstances . . .

'Let me call 'im from your phone,' she said, 'then the number'll be in it when I get it back off 'im.'

30. Safe House

DMITRI DROVE ROUND early Sunday morning to the safe house. This was the address Plotnik used when he was in the UK working for Dmitri, a semi-detached house tucked away somewhere nice. Plotnik didn't work for anyone else in the UK. In other countries maybe – that was his business and Dmitri never asked. They kept their business affairs on a mutual need-to-know basis. It worked well that way.

'Plotnik,' said Dmitri as the big man opened the door to let him in.

He hadn't gotten any better looking since they'd last met, but Dmitri wasn't hiring him for a photo-shoot.

Inside, Dmitri sat at a kitchen table while Plotnik pulled a bottle of vodka out of his travel bag. Khortytsa – straight off the plane from Kiev. Plotnik got a couple of shot glasses from a cupboard that would have been above most people's heads, put them on the table, cracked open the bottle and poured two measures. Then he sat down on a chair next to Dmitri and they raised their glasses toward one another.

'To Mother Ukraine. *Budmo!*'

'*Hey!*' Dmitri responded in the traditional fashion. They both thought it unlucky to cheer in anything other than Ukrainian, though on the phone they'd used Russian. Whatever their feelings and fortunes, Ukraine *was* the mother country, and should be toasted in her own tongue.

The vodka went down in one slug, smooth as milk.

'Welcome back,' Dmitri said.

'What am I doing here?' said Plotnik.

'A job. Search and destroy. Or rather, search, destroy and retrieve something.'

'Who? What?'

'Let me brief you,' said Dmitri, reaching for his case.

He told Plotnik everything.

He supplied the address where Sanjeev had lived with his bitch and her offspring, the house that was still being watched.

When he got to the part about Cheslav and the woman, he didn't expect Plotnik to betray any reaction and he wasn't disappointed, even though he and Cheslav had worked together

134

on a couple of occasions. At some level, they must've connected: a common bond of silence.

'The idiot thinks he's in love with her. I could see it coming.'

Plotnik declined to ask, if he'd been able to see it coming, why he didn't do anything about it. He wasn't here as a business consultant. He was here as a carpenter. He fixed things for people like Dmitri Maximov. Sometimes, with tools.

'What do you want?' said Plotnik when Dmitri had stopped talking.

'I want the pills back,' said Dmitri. 'That's number one. I want the woman dead. No one escapes that, once I've decided. It would make me look weak. The boy too. I want them both dead. Anyone else – you know what you're doing, use your imagination, play it by ear. But Cheslav – bring him to me, alive if you can. I'd like a few words with him myself.'

'Remove the watch from the woman's house.'

'Are you sure?'

'You don't pay me to be unsure. If I wasn't sure, I wouldn't say it. Remove it. They won't go back there while they know it's still being watched.'

Dmitri didn't question this decision. He was happy to leave all of this to Plotnik now and get on with attending to business.

He reached into his case again and used a linen handkerchief to lift out a handgun. He placed it on the table and Plotnik picked it up immediately, turning it over in front of his scarred nose, trying to squint at it with the eye that was affected by damage to nearby nerve tissue. The wars in Afghanistan and Chechnya had not been good to Plotnik's face.

The gun was one of the Baikals from the first batch that Dmitri had received yesterday. It had a silencer attached, if Plotnik chose to use it. The important thing was, it wouldn't be traced; not easily, and not quickly.

'Rounds,' said Plotnik.

Dmitri took a box of these too from the case, his bag of tricks, his bag of goodies.

'Do you need anything else?'

'Cash. And a car.'

'Of course,' said Dmitri, producing his last trick, his final goodies, a bundle of Sterling for immediate expenses and half

Plotnik's usual fee up front in US dollars, the balance payable upon proof of results. At twenty per cent of the worth to him of the recoverable merchandise, Dmitri considered it value for money.

Plotnik pushed the dollars into his own bag without counting them, though Dmitri knew he would do so before the conclusion of business.

'If you come with me now, I'll drive you to where you can pick up a vehicle. What about resources, men? I can assign a team.'

'When the time comes, I'll call you.'

Dmitri watched Plotnik stow the gun down the waistband of his trousers and two extra clips of ammo in his coat pockets. He retrieved a battered-looking copy of the *Leeds and Bradford AZ* street atlas from a kitchen drawer. Then he replaced the top on the vodka bottle and stashed that too in an inside pocket of his coat.

Dmitri waited until Plotnik had fastidiously rinsed the shot glasses under the tap and placed them upside down on the draining board.

Then they left the safe house together.

31. Alvin Stardust

IN BEA'S KITCHEN, Tracy found a local taxi firm's card pinned to a notice-board.

When she phoned Don he was still asleep, but she was anxious to do this now and couldn't wait till a later, more civilised hour. He agreed to meet her in town, on the Town Hall steps, just because it was the only place either of them could think of off the top of their muddled heads.

She got the Asian cab driver to park as close as possible and asked him if he could wait for ten minutes.

'It's your fare, love,' he said, 'you do what you want. Tell you what, give me the one way fare now and the rest when you come back.'

'Promise you'll wait, though.'

'We're all right here, police won't move us on this time on a Sunday.'

She fumbled the right change from her purse.

'Thanks a lot, love.'

It was still early, only eight by the Town Hall clock, and a glister of overnight frost was visible on the paving slabs. She walked round the front of the building and Don was already waiting, pacing the Town Hall steps between the lions.

'Jesus, Tracy, look at yer,' he said when she was standing next to him and he saw her face. 'Who the hell did that? Were it that Russian bloke? Cos I fuckin' swear—'

'Don, it weren't 'im, not who you're thinkin' of.'

She took him by the arm and filled him in on all the details. Again, she skipped over Cheslav's involvement in her beating, but apart from that she told him everything, the lot. He deserved to know. He was a good friend and she'd kept him in suspense long enough. At the end of it all, though, he didn't know what to say.

'How did Barbara take it,' she asked, ' – me draggin' you out a bed at half past seven on a Sunday morning?'

Barbara was Don's wife. He smiled, more a delicate grimace.

'She weren't too pleased.'

He moved closer to her.

'Listen, if there's anythin' I can do to 'elp – It dun't matter what Barbara thinks.'

'Don't say that, Don.'

'I mean it, Tracy. I'd do owt. You've only got to say the word, you know that.'

'You can give me me phone back.'

'Oh, yeah, right.'

He took it from his coat pocket and put it in her hand.

'I'm grateful, Don, for what yer did for our Stephen, I won't forget that in a long time. An' I will phone you if I need ya.'

'Well where are you gonna be?'

'I'll be at the other end a the phone. That's all I know for now. Listen, do us a favour, try an' keep an eye on t'house, make sure it dun't get burgled. Please.'

'Course I will, love. An' I'll let you know when them Russians bugger off.'

'Thanks, Don.'

'I can give you a lift. I came down in t'car.'

''S all right, I've got a taxi waiting.'

She stretched up and kissed him on the cheek, then turned around and walked away.

Poor Don. He was a good man but he wasn't her type. He looked a bit like Alvin Stardust. And he was married.

By the time she reached the taxi, she was thinking about Cheslav, and got a shock when she realised it. It was a double shock to think that he might be married, and a treble shock to think that she might care.

32. Weapons Count

CHESLAV WAITED FOR Tracy's return in Kelly and Bea's back room with the door shut. No one else was up yet and he preferred it that way. He didn't feel at ease with all these people.

It was a long time since he'd spent much time at all in the company of anyone other than the *bratva* – Dmitri and the men who worked for him. They worked long and irregular hours, remaining permanently on call, so relaxation was hard to fit in and maintaining an acceptable family life for any of them was virtually impossible.

Even just a relationship: Cheslav couldn't remember the last time he was with a woman – any attention he may have received from girls in The Green Tiger or the other bars and clubs where the boss liked to hang out didn't count.

He heard someone upstairs go to the toilet and sat with the curtains drawn, in the dark, waiting and staring ahead at the chair facing him, his senses alert. He heard the toilet flush and his eyes were drawn to the ceiling as he listened for the person to go back to their bedroom.

When he looked down again at the chair, Sanjeev was sitting on it. Like the last time, he looked the way he'd looked in life, the way he'd looked when he'd appeared to Cheslav in the penthouse, just hours after he'd died.

'I'm sorry,' Cheslav said, taking up the conversation from where it had left off two days before. 'I didn't mean to drop you.'

'I thought we got on all right together,' said Sanjeev.

'We did. But Dmitri insisted I dangle you from that balcony. I didn't do it because I wanted to.'

'What about Tracy?' said the ghost.

'What about her?'

'You like her.'

This time, it wasn't a question.

'Yes,' he admitted. 'I always liked her.'

'Will you take care of her?'

Before Cheslav could reply, there another noise upstairs. Cheslav's eyes instinctively flicked back to the ceiling. Someone was getting up. When he returned his gaze to Sanjeev the chair was as empty as it had been a moment ago.

He stood up and opened the curtains, letting the daylight pour in. Then he tidied up the place where he'd slept, hearing the sounds of someone coming downstairs. The rhythm of the footsteps was a light trip, probably a girl's.

He opened the door to the hall. The youngest girl, Casey, was in the kitchen, dressed in slacks and slippers and a T-shirt. She turned and smiled when she saw him.

'Hiya. What's yer name? I've forgotten it.'

He thought about it for a moment.

'Chezz,' he said, coughing into his fist. 'You're Casey.'

'Well remembered. D' you want a cup of coffee, Chezz?'

'Yes.' Then, when she gave him a look, 'Yes, please. That would be nice. Let me make it. You made all the tea yesterday.'

She grinned at him.

'That's sweet. Yer all right, though, I'll do it. I don't mind, honest.'

'You sure?'

'I'm sure.'

He sat at the kitchen table and watched her while she filled the kettle and prepared the mugs. They both heard footsteps on the back path, and Casey looked out through the window before a knock sounded on the kitchen door.

'It's your friend, Tracy.'

Casey let her in and put more coffee granules in another mug.

Cheslav stood up as Tracy came in.

'Did you get your phone?' he said.

'Yes, I did.'

'You didn't call me.'

'I forgot. I just got the taxi straight there an' back. There were barely time, it wan't worth it.'

'Which?'

'Which what?'

'You gave me four excuses. Which do you want me to believe?'

'All of 'em.'

'Was your friend OK? I hope I didn't hurt him.'

'Only 'is pride. He'll get over it. I think he took most of it out on that Ukrainian bloke yesterday.'

Cheslav couldn't help feeling bad about that.

'Which man was it? Did he know?'

'I doubt it. He never said owt.'

Casey served the coffees up and was just about to take hers out of the kitchen when Kelly emerged.

'I've just made coffee,' she said pre-emptively.

'Don't worry, I'll make me own, as usual. Mornin',' he said to Tracy and Cheslav. 'Been up long?'

'I've even been into town an' back. Got me phone back,' said Tracy holding it up like a trophy.

'Nice one,' said Kelly, reaching into the pocket of the apron by the cooker for a fag.

'I hope ya don't mind, I nicked one a them earlier.'

''S all right, they're Bea's anyway. D'you want another?'

'I'd love one.'

Kelly handed her the pack and dug a Clipper out of his jeans pocket to light them both with.

'You know, I'm sure I know you from somewhere,' said Tracy, looking askance at Kelly.

'Yeah?'

'Did you used to live in Leeds Six?'

'Close. Technically, it were Leeds Four, but I used to knock about Leeds Six all t'time.'

Well, Kelly thought, *I'm not gonna lie, am I?* She'd have cottoned on eventually.

'I mighta seen you in t'Royal Park pub. Did you know R Kid, Barry? Me brother. Baz, everyone used to call him. I used to call him Baz, I don't know why I'm callin' him Barry now just cos he's dead.'

'Yeah, I knew Baz. Actually, Bea knew him more than me. They were mates for a long time. She were sorry for what happened to him.'

'What d'you mean?'

'I mean I think she misses 'im,' said Kelly.

'She'll be in a minority then,' said Tracy. 'Obviously, 'e were me brother an' we were family an' 'e never hurt me, not on purpose, but I know he could be a right bad 'un. He had a temper on him if things din't go 'is way, 'an' 'e'd 'ad it rough all his life – that's why his temper came out. But he used to look out for us. He were still lookin' out for us when he got shot.'

Kelly wondered how much Tracy knew about that.

Obviously Baz wasn't around afterwards to tell anyone, so unless she'd got them from Denny, all the details of the incident were beyond her possible knowing. He held his tongue about the bodies that were found in Baz's cellar after he was killed – the two students, Michael Chapman and Simon Hollister. Their names were still burned into his memory to this day from all the media coverage, and he had no doubt that she knew them by heart as well. If she wanted to mention that, fine. Otherwise, best let it lie.

Kelly busied himself at the kettle, relieved when Bea came down.

'Fuckinell, it's early for a Sunday,' she said, rubbing an eye with the heel of a palm.

'We should be up,' said Cheslav. 'We need to make a plan.'

Tracy, sensing what was polite in someone else's house, said, 'OK, all in good time.'

'We don't have much time,' Cheslav replied.

His tone kept an evenness that mismatched the urgency of the words.

'What yer got in mind?' said Kelly, joining him at the table with his coffee.

'We should itemise the things we can use against Dmitri.'

'Itemise?'

'Make a list.'

'I know 'e's got a mistress,' said Tracy. 'Bet his wife won't like that.'

'That's one,' said Cheslav, extending a finger from his fist.

'Ilko,' said Kelly. 'He's on our side.'

Cheslav didn't know this Ilko that Kelly had described last night, but he sounded OK.

'Two,' he said, and a second finger sprang out.

'What do we know about his business, apart from the pills?' said Kelly.

Cheslav hesitated. His disloyalty to Dmitri of course had gone way too far already, but now it was about to leap forward a whole lot farther. From here, there wouldn't be the remotest chance of turning back.

'Yesterday he received a shipment of guns.'

'How do they help if *he's* got 'em?' said Kelly.

'I know where they are. That knowledge can help us.'

'You talkin' about informin' the police?'

'If it came to it,' said Cheslav.

'I don't like police,' said Kelly. 'I don't trust 'em to do their job properly.'

'Neither do I,' said Cheslav. 'Like I said, if it came to it.'

'Well let's hope it dun't.'

'It could help us in other ways we don't know about yet. So, three.' He added another finger. 'But there's more.'

Tracy and Bea were gathered round now, asking him what else.

'I know about his other business dealings.'

He paused, hesitated. He had to be open with these people if he wanted them to be able to properly consider their options.

'I know that he's thinking about going into a legitimate venture with his father.'

'His father? Is he a gangster as well?' said Kelly.

'Dmitri's father wants Dmitri to go straight, like he has. He's made enough money that he doesn't have to go out stealing anymore. He can use the dirty money he made in the past to make clean money now. He thinks Dmitri should do the same, get out while he's still on top.'

'An' I bet Dad definitely wun't approve if he found out what he were up to now,' said Bea.

'So the father,' said Cheslav. 'He is number four.'

'And don't forget that we've still got the thing that he's after, the pills. At least, they're a bargaining chip. So that's five.'

Tracy stepped forward and they shut up to listen.

'I know you said yer don't want police involved an' all that, which I totally agree with, but there is one other thing.'

Cheslav had a feeling about what she was going to say.

'We know that Dmitri killed Sanjeev.'

The others looked at her, two of them with horror, the third, Cheslav, with something like relief.

'He told me himself.' She looked around at them all, grateful that Casey had left the kitchen. 'I 'an't told our Stephen yet so I'd appreciate it if you kept it quiet.'

'Oh no, I'm sorry, love.'

Bea enveloped her in a hug and Tracy looked appreciative.

'So that's six,' said Kelly, looking at the five outspread digits of Cheslav's raised hand.

'What?'

'That's six.'

Cheslav was remembering the words of Sanjeev's ghost.

You let me down.

'Oh, yes,' he said, raising the thumb of his other hand to complete the sum. 'Six.'

'So what now?'

Cheslav thought for a moment before turning to Kelly.

'This friend of yours, Ilko. I'd like to meet him. If he's the only one who knows where the pills are then he has our fate in his hands. I'd at least like to put a face to the name.'

'I'll call him,' said Kelly. 'We need to fill 'im in on what's happenin' anyway.'

'If he answers, let me speak to him,' said Cheslav. 'If he's as useful as you say, we should make a plan with him too. We should arrange to meet.'

Kelly found Ilko's number and pressed the CALL button.

Meanwhile, Tracy's phone, which was still in her hand, suddenly beeped, making her jump. She looked at the screen.

'It's a text from Don,' she announced. 'Them blokes watchin' me 'ouse – they've finally fucked off.'

Cheslav gave her a look but didn't say anything yet, not knowing if this was good or bad. It could mean something or it could mean nothing. For now, they should stay cautious.

33. Little London

PLOTNIK QUESTIONED OLEK first.

With an unswerving instinct to follow an order, even though he knew it to be a waste of time, Cheslav's driver had gone back that morning to the parking bay under Airedale Point, from where Cheslav had told him, yesterday, that he could collect the car. Of course, it hadn't been there, as he'd expected it wouldn't, seeing as Cheslav, he now knew, had turned coat and fled with the woman that they'd picked up on Friday night.

Olek related all this to Plotnik faithfully but reluctantly. He liked Cheslav, he still couldn't believe that he would turn against the *bratva* – there had to be some misunderstanding at the bottom of it all.

Mistake or not, though, he knew Plotnik and he knew there'd only be one reason why Dmitri had called him in. Cheslav had been the nearest thing Dmitri had to a righthand man. If he'd had a falling out with Dmitri, then Dmitri would not want him running around potentially shooting his mouth off. That was what Plotnik was called in for in cases like this: to ensure that someone stayed quiet – for good.

If anyone was going to shoot a mouth off, it was going to be Plotnik doing it to Cheslav's.

Plotnik spoke to a number of other men from the *bratva*, guys who'd worked with Cheslav a lot and knew his routines. He learned the places where Cheslav liked to hang out, hoping to discern some pattern to his known habits that would help him to track him down. The men he spoke to expressed the same opinion as Olek. They all liked and respected Cheslav and none of them could believe that he would deliberately betray Dmitri and the organisation. Everybody knew who Plotnik was and what he did, though, and at the end of the day no one wanted to fuck with him, or even slightly piss him off.

Plotnik knew now that Cheslav had a flat in a part of the city called Cookridge. Apparently, it was little more than a lair, a place he visited occasionally to sleep, and little else besides. Even Dmitri didn't seem to think it was worth bothering with. But Plotnik decided to take a look at the place himself anyway. He might find something, he might not, but even what he failed to find there could provide important information – for instance, about whether Cheslav was armed or not.

The state of the place suggested that Cheslav hadn't been there for at least several days. It was cold, hadn't been heated recently, and the few items of food and drink abandoned in the fridge, including opened tins of baked beans and corned beef and a half-used carton of milk, were way past their best.

He turned the rest of the place over, searching it from top to bottom: no gun, no ammunition, no razor, no toothbrush, no money, no passport. Whenever he'd last been there, he'd left expecting to be absent for a while.

As to where he might be now, however, Plotnik could see no clue. What were those peculiar English expressions that seemed to fit the situation? Cheslav had 'gone to ground' and if he wanted to find him he would have to 'flush him out'. The absence of a passport was the most worrying thing: it would completely piss him off if he was forced to go chasing this fool somewhere outside the country.

After leaving Cheslav's flat Plotnik phoned Marko, the man on Cheslav's surveillance team who'd been attacked outside the house they'd been watching.

'Where are you?' he said.

'I'm out of the hospital, taking it easy at home.'

Plotnik got the address off him and said, 'I'll come see you there.'

The way Marko hummed and hawed, he could tell he wasn't happy about it, but he didn't give a shit about what made Marko happy or not.

He lived high up in a block of flats in the Little London district. The tower blocks here reminded Plotnik of the old Soviet blocks that occupied the outlying regions of Kiev, except that in Kiev they covered hundreds of square kilometres. Inside, the stairways were more brightly lit but hardly any more inviting, and although the lift worked, it really did stink of piss.

Marko was home alone. He answered the door gingerly, moving slowly from his injuries of the day before.

'They broke my collar-bone,' he said, indicating the sling cradling his forearm and his strapped-up shoulder, 'and a couple of ribs. Mild concussion too. The doctor in A and E said I was lucky not to lose my eye.'

Marko's right eye was a scarlet marble from where a blow had burst a blood vessel inside the eyeball. He made a drama of swallowing painkillers and generally making it known that if it came to being called on to do anything more than languish in front of a TV set, he was pretty definitively out of action.

'Did you see the boy?' asked Plotnik.

Marko gave him a description of the boy he'd accosted just before he was jumped. About five-foot-ten in height – Plotnik mentally converted that to about one metre seventy-seven – with a slim build and skin the colour of milky coffee. Hair black, as you'd expect, and plaited into tight rows – corn-rows, Marko thought they called them. You could see his scalp between them, like the furrows of a ploughed field. There was something about his eyes: Marko got the impression that they were lighter than you usually saw in black people.

'You didn't say he was black,' Plotnik interrupted.

'I mean Afro-Caribbean or whatever they call it in polite company. The boy's a half-caste. Maybe he has his mother's eyes. Not dark, not brown – maybe hazel. It all went too fast. The next second after the kid appeared I was being cracked across the skull with an iron bar.'

'Describe the approach to the back of the house.'

Marko described the footpath that ran like a lane along the back of the terrace, the alleys that the path connected with at either end, where it connected to the street out front where his fellow watchers had been stationed in the car and what other houses overlooked it.

'So where did your attacker come from?'

'I don't know. They must've come out of one of the houses.'

'Did you see your attacker?'

'It was more than one. I don't know how many they were, I didn't get a proper look. All I saw was baseball bats. I was busy trying to protect my head. By the time they stopped hitting me I was too out of it to see any of them.'

'Right,' said Plotnik.

'It was that first blow to the head,' said Marko, pressing his case with a noticeable tinge of emotion in his voice. 'If it hadn't been for that I could've done something, but it sent me straight to the ground.'

'OK. Get some rest. You did good.'

Even Plotnik was capable of dishing out insincere comfort when he saw it was being cried out for.

After leaving Marko's place he walked a hundred metres to a corner shop that he'd noticed on his way there. Inside the shop he headed straight for the fridge, a small cabinet at the back of the modest premises. On one of the shelves was a row of sandwiches packed in triangular plastic boxes – four packs of various fillings, ham and mustard, chicken salad, and two with cheese and tomato. He grabbed the lot, plus two small bottles of mineral water, and took them to the counter to pay for them.

The Asian woman shopkeeper bagged them up for him and he carried them back to his car. Then he squeezed himself into the driver's seat.

He spent five minutes with the A-Z planning his route to the house where Sanjeev and the Croft woman and her boy had all lived together, then he started the engine, released the handbrake, put it into first and drove away.

34. In Whitelocks

CHESLAV HAD BEEN vetting his phone calls ever since he'd
absconded with Tracy, but now he received his first text message
since then, and could see no harm in opening it. It was from
Olek, the driver. Cheslav hadn't thought about him since
yesterday when he'd told him to come and pick the car up this
morning. The message consisted of five words only:
Plotnik is looking for you.
An abyss opened up in the pit of Cheslav's stomach.

It was good of Olek to send him the warning. Cheslav knew
that by doing so he was risking his job and possibly his life. The
risk was small of course, and by deleting the message as soon as
he'd read it, Cheslav reduced the chance of him ever being found
out to virtually zero.

'What is it?' said Tracy as he put the phone back in his
pocket.

'Nothing important,' he lied. There was no point worrying
her about it yet, or the other man, Kelly.

The three of them were sitting in the cramped space of the
Whitelocks pub around a brass-topped table tucked behind the
entrance door, waiting for Ilko where Kelly had arranged by
phone for them to meet him. The place was busy with Sunday
drinkers and they were lucky to get seats, but the crowdedness
and its city-centre location were why they'd picked it. They felt
reasonably safe nestled in there.

Kelly was nursing a pint of bitter and Tracy a gin and tonic,
while Cheslav, wanting to stay off alcohol and fully alert, had a
Coke.

They had all driven in the car into town from Bea and
Kelly's place, then abandoned it in a multi-storey car park.
Sooner or later, someone would tow it away and trace it to its
owner, but that wasn't Cheslav, it belonged to the organisation,
and he wasn't sure whose name it was registered under. Maybe
Olek's, maybe someone else's – certainly not Dmitri's, though he
would be one of the first to hear about it as soon as it was found.

The walk from there to the rendezvous with Ilko
Pogrebinsky had not been far.

When Ilko arrived, he and Cheslav showed no signs of

recognising one another and when Kelly introduced them all, the two Ukrainians shook hands tentatively and nodded terse greetings.

Ilko had been told who Cheslav was and he didn't like the fact that this man had worked for Dmitri Maximov, even if he had switched sides.

Kelly filled Ilko in on what had been happening since they last met – the news of Sanjeev's death in particular, then the resurfacing of the missing young lads, Damien and Stephen, and their concern over the whereabouts of the pills.

'The pills are safe,' Ilko reassured him.

Their voices were indistinguishable to the surrounding press of drinkers in the low, comfortable hubbub of general chatter and laughter.

'Where?' said Cheslav.

'Somewhere safe,' said Ilko. 'When the time comes for you to know, I tell you, OK?'

Cheslav didn't ask again, just twitched his eyebrows in resignation.

'So what's the plan?' Ilko asked.

'Still the same,' said Kelly. 'Find a way to get Dmitri off us backs.'

'He won't stop while he is still alive,' said Cheslav. 'Not unless we can compromise him with someone who has power over him.'

'You're in his little gang,' said Ilko – a remark whose implication Cheslav chose to ignore – 'so who's higher up than Dmitri?'

'In the gang,' said Cheslav, deigning to use the term that Ilko had introduced, 'no one. We were thinking of someone outside.'

'It sounds like you make a plan after all. Who?'

'His father and his wife.'

'You think his wife has power over him?'

'Why shun't she?' said Tracy, joining in the men's talk. 'She's the mother of his kids.'

'And the father?' said Ilko, letting that one rest for now. 'Isn't he the big boss, after all?'

'Dmitri's father has turned legitimate,' said Cheslav. 'He and Dmitri have some common business interests though, and

Yosyp would not want this business to interfere with them.'

'What you suggest?' said Ilko. 'Threaten Dmitri to expose him to his father?'

Although he didn't show it, Cheslav was smirking to himself inside at the impoverished state of Ilko's English. He'd have thought that he'd been over here long enough to speak it correctly by now, though Cheslav had the advantage of having been here a lot longer, ever since he was a teenager.

'It might work,' he said. 'Dmitri probably stands to make a lot of money from a property deal and he needs his father's help to grease the wheels. He won't want to lose it. Dmitri likes lots of money.'

'We should try the wife first, though,' said Kelly, bringing the conversation back to the previous topic. 'I reckon if we fire a warning shot there, he might back off.'

'I agree wi' Kelly,' said Tracy.

Kelly handed her a cig and they both cheerfully lit up, reaching out to the ashtray in the middle of the table.

Cheslav in the meantime bore a new look of concern on his face.

'There's something else,' he said, realising he couldn't put this off after all. 'Dmitri has sent someone to track us down. A man who specialises in this kind of work.'

'Who?' said Tracy. 'You never told me about this.'

'I only just found out. A man called Plotnik.'

'What?' said Ilko.

'You know him?' said Cheslav.

'Plotnik, you said?'

Cheslav nodded.

'Not Otto Plotnik?'

'That's him.'

'The Carpenter,' said Ilko distractedly, almost whispering it to himself. He had a faraway look on his face now, and wherever he was, it didn't look like a nice place. 'He's here?'

'I just got word.'

'I thought he'd gone back to Kiev,' said Ilko.

''Ang on a minute,' said Kelly, 'who's this Plotnik?'

'A bad man,' said Ilko, and when Kelly looked at Cheslav, his face seemed to confirm what Ilko was saying. It was the first sign that the two Ukrainians were in agreement about something.

'Well what does 'e want?' said Tracy.

'He wants what Dmitri wants,' said Cheslav. 'The pills. And me.'

He didn't tell her the rest, which he could only guess, but with a depressingly high degree of confidence.

'So what do we do about 'im?' said Kelly. 'Does this mean rethinkin' our strategy?'

'We don't have another one, do we?' said Tracy.

She was worried now by the look on Cheslav's face since the mention of this Plotnik. If this bloke scared Cheslav then she couldn't begin to imagine what sort of monster he must be.

'Plotnik will back off if Dmitri orders him,' said Cheslav. 'He's a professional. He only does what he's paid to do.'

'Then threatening against Dmitri is your best bet,' said Ilko.

'I agree,' said Cheslav. 'But if we threaten Dmitri, we must make him know that we are willing to back it up.'

'What are you talking about?' said Ilko.

'There's the wife and the father, like I said, but there are also other things that are important to him.'

'Like what?' said Kelly. 'You mean the – ' He paused to look around, making sure no one really was listening. 'Them guns you mentioned?'

'Those, certainly. They're worth money to him, and as I said, he likes money. Then there are his children.'

'Now wait a minute,' said Tracy. She lowered her voice self-consciously. 'I don't wanna hurt anyone who's not tryin' to hurt us.'

Ilko too was looking decidedly uneasy at the mention of this.

That's what these people are like, he was thinking, *and this one is no different.*

'You know,' he said, 'the intelligent thing to do here is to go to the police.'

'No,' said Kelly, immediately quashing the idea. 'No police.'

Ilko said nothing, because in his heart of hearts he knew that, whatever Kelly's reasoning, he was probably right. Without proof linking Dmitri to the pills or to Sanjeev's death, the police would ultimately be able to do nothing.

As for Dmitri's attack dog, any involvement of the police would only register with him as a minor annoyance. Certainly, no amount of British bobbies, with their cute little truncheons and 21st-century concerns about political correctness, was going to stop a man like Otto Plotnik . . .

35. War Rugs

OF COURSE, THEY were never going to win in Afghanistan. History should have taught them that quite easily. But it was never about winning, was it? It was about posturing, positioning and powerplay.

The USSR had to be seen to be supporting Afghanistan's socialist-leaning government in its civil war with the Mujahideen just as surely as the USA, through the medium of its Central Intelligence Agency, had to mount Operation Cyclone, the arming of the anti-communist rebels, who at that time included Osama Bin Laden, the guy they were now holding responsible for last year's attacks in the United States and the destruction of the World Trade Centre in New York.

In fact, the CIA was already active in Afghanistan six months prior to the Soviets' presence; and, despite having officially retreated from that country in 1989, the Russians were still pouring in arms and funding two years later, right up until the collapse of the Soviet Union in 1991.

It was a mess that they should never have gotten involved in, not least because the USA had secretly *wanted* the USSR to invade Afghanistan: the Americans had lost men, money and face in Vietnam, so how sweet it would be for them to watch their arch enemy do the same in its own back yard.

For their part, it was something the Soviets couldn't resist, a reflexive act of second nature, having already a long history of aiding the Afghans against the onslaught of western imperialism.

Now, the Americans and the Brits had gone in again, but this time there were no Soviets left to oppose them, only the ever-resilient Afghanis – so the amnesiac west could now have its 21st-century repeat of Vietnam all to itself.

Back then, in February 1986, Sergeant Ilko Pogrebinsky was there as part of an offensive against the Mujahideen's Zhawar base located in a network of caves in a mountain pass a hundred kilometres south of Kabul and fifteen kilometres from the Pakistan border. It was the second offensive against the base and would come to be known as the Second Battle of Zhawar. The first had been staged five months earlier by the 12th and 25th Divisions of the DRA – the Afghani government forces – with the support of Soviet air strikes, and they'd spent forty-two days getting their arses kicked.

This time, for good measure, the Soviets were sending in 2,200 ground troops.

Ilko was one of them.

So was Otto Plotnik.

To be honest, the Soviet troops, including the Ukrainians, participated in little direct combat, being there on what was essentially a security mission. Gorby had already announced his intention to withdraw all personnel, so their initial brief was to just guard and facilitate the DRA's installations and lines of supply and communication. Most of it was therefore donkey work – digging trenches and tunnels, erecting storehouses, transporting munitions up to the front line.

Ilko and the rest of them, including Plotnik, were barely more than glorified navvies, shovelling shit around in the freezing wind and sleet of the mountain passes, keeping one eye on the distant snow-capped peaks and hoping not to get targeted by some cadre of skulking peasants with a set of binoculars and a rocket launcher.

When they weren't breaking their backs, they spent the rest of the time languishing among the rubble and stray dogs of Gardez, trying to distil something that tasted like vodka, while Trofimenko, the general in charge, dithered around and generally fucked things up.

Later, after a string of fiascos and the loss of two dozen DRA helicopters, General Varrenikov would take the reins and their lads would be sent in to get their hands properly dirty and bloody some Mujahideen noses.

But it was that interim period that gave rise to Ilko's run-in with Plotnik, and his insight into the kind of man that they were dealing with here and now, five thousand miles away and fifteen years later.

Bored and miserable one day after the hooch had run dry, a group of lads in Ilko's squad were talking about war rugs and how prized they'd heard such items could be back in the peacetime world beyond the war zone. These were Persian-style carpets woven by local craftsmen and craftswomen using traditional techniques, but incorporating designs that reflected the conditions of war. A couple of the guys had seen examples brought back into the USSR by soldiers who'd been in Afghanistan on previous tours of duty and who claimed they could fetch high prices on the international black market. The images woven into the fabrics could be anything – weapons, helicopters, combatants, strategic maps – as long as they represented martial phenomena.

After a little asking around in Gardez, they heard where they could take a look at some, get to see them being made and possibly buy cheap at the source. Before they had time to talk themselves out of it, Ilko commandeered a GAZ-69 and they drove out to the recommended village.

The place was called something like Sekan Dara and it wasn't on any map they were able to get hold of, but somehow they got there. There was a high visibility of bearded and turbaned men with guns, but the guns were Russian Kalashnikovs, suggesting that the local warlord was a friendly, and the natives were amicable enough to point them in the right direction.

Pretty soon the four or five of them, however many they were at the time, had squeezed into one of the local one-storey houses and were gathered around a pile of rugs, while a child peeked shyly from a dark doorway and the man of the house squatted by the pleasantly smoky aroma of a dung fire.

The top rug that they were looking at depicted a T-62 tank. The details were crude but the overall shape and proportions were accurate and the execution was colourful and vivid. One of Ilko's lads – young Pavlov, he seemed to remember, all the way from Vladivostok – was smitten by the romantic idea of making his fortune in some unspecified future deal and was in the process of negotiating a hypothetical price with the Afghani man sitting on the floor when a tide of angry voices and barking dogs began to swell in the street outside and it all kicked off.

When they ran outside they thought at first that the road was clouded with dust raised by the convoy of motor vehicles they could see rolling into the village. Before it struck them that it couldn't be dust raised from ground that was cold and rain-muddy, the unmistakable smell of smoke grenades was filling their nostrils and armed, uniformed men were leaping from the incoming vehicles like fleas from a dead dog.

People were running everywhere – not just men but women

too, fleeing their homes as though driven out by bees. Men were shouting and women and children were screaming; screaming each other's names, screaming meaningless noises, screaming the sounds of anguish and outrage.

It wasn't long before the first gunshot rang out, and it wasn't the last. Other weapons responded in kind. Bullets struck up a hostile conversation, quickly descending into the firecracker squabble of open conflict. Ilko tried to see who was shooting who. He made out men in khaki uniforms running among the villagers, their own Afghani allies, but to what purpose it was impossible to say. His own sidearm was out now, gripped in his right hand ready for self-defence, but the DRA troops marauding with rifles and machine guns seemed only intent on destruction and chaos.

Something exploded close behind him – a shell, a grenade? – and a hail of stones and rocky shrapnel peppered his back as part of the wall of the house they'd just come out of disintegrated in the blast. His thick jerkin saved him from being badly lacerated but the whump of the explosion pushed him to the ground.

He found himself scrabbling around in the dirt on his hands and knees, managing to keep hold of his pistol and looking round frantically to see what had happened to his men. It seemed that they'd quickly fanned out and away from the house, and so had escaped the results of the blast more than he had. All of them were still on their feet, their guns raised but not firing yet. One of them, Private Mishkin as he recalled, scuttled across to him and grabbed his arm to lift him to his feet.

'I'm OK,' he told Mishkin, regaining his balance and his senses. 'What the fuck's going on?'

'Dunno, Sarge.'

Ilko looked around, trying to make sense of the carnage unfolding through the smoke and din.

'Take cover. Keep sight of the others. Regroup at the vehicle when it's safe.'

Mishkin moved away, ducking instinctively at the sound of more gunfire.

Meanwhile, an Afghani civilian, unarmed, came running up to Ilko shouting something at him that he couldn't understand and pointing to a donkey trotting comically up the broken street like a speeded-up creature in a silent movie. It was pulling a cart behind it and the cart was on fire and it became clear that the donkey was futilely running away from the pursuing flames.

Ilko pushed away the Afghani man clawing at his arm and ran across the street, diving for cover behind a low wall of baked mud. He stuck his head out cautiously to see what was happening, trying to locate the position of the attacking rebels, and saw only uniformed DRA overturning stalls, smashing in the windows of huts and stuffing their backpacks with food, goods, money, anything they could grab.

He witnessed one soldier ram his rifle butt into the face of a villager – a young man barely able to grow his beard yet, who crumpled to the ground bleeding and spitting out teeth – then, struggling to understand what he was seeing, he caught sight of a man in Soviet uniform, no one he recognised but one of his own nonetheless, running out of a yard with a big grin on his face and his fist wrapped around the neck of a live chicken. While the bird squawked to the limit of its ability and flapped its wings wildly, one of the locals, presumably its owner, remonstrated with the soldier to let it go, seeming to ignore the rest of the commotion going on all around him. As the two of them employed the unhappy poultry in a tug of war, the Russian soldier lifted his other hand in a fist, but before he could punch the Afghani, he was bowled off his feet from behind by a goat running into him and head-butting his legs from under him. As he went arse over elbow he let go of the chicken and the owner ran off with it while he had the chance.

Ilko calmed his breathing and got his thoughts under control. He didn't know why this was happening, he had heard nothing of any combat manoeuvres in this sector, but *what* was happening was now becoming obvious. This was no military operation – it was sheer looting and pillaging. The DRA seemed to be doing most of the damage but some Russian men were involved too, as it was becoming increasingly clear to him.

He saw two Soviet soldiers dragging loaded sacks of something or other out of a barn while two DRA standing by in collusion were fending off a knot of protesting villagers with fixed bayonets. Other soldiers, mostly DRA but with some Soviets mixed in among them, were tossing around smoke grenades and brawling with the local citizenry.

An Mi-24 assault helicopter clattered overhead somewhere

and smoke was wafted far and wide in its downdraught. Ilko could see no profit in staying put. Using the spreading smoke for cover, he left the shelter of the low wall and scrambled in the direction of where he thought they had left the Land Rover.

In passing the doorway of a hovel, he heard desperate, hysterical screaming coming from the darkness inside. It was a female, certainly, and he was unable to resist being drawn towards the noise of intense distress when he knew that there was someone who needed his help.

When he stepped inside the low-roofed house, he couldn't see a thing at first. The windows were built small to help keep the interior cool in summer and warn in winter, and the movement from outside to in threw Ilko into such immediate gloom that, from the evidence of his eyes, he thought the room was empty. The screaming, though, which had now intensified, could only be coming from in here.

As his sight got accustomed to the meagre light, a shape emerged out of a corner where a sleeping mat had been thrown on the floor. It was a bulky shape that resolved itself into the figure of a man – a huge bull of a man – bent over with his back to the doorway in which Ilko stood.

None of it made any sense to Ilko at first. He couldn't make out what the man was doing crouched on the floor with his head buried in the corner like that. Was he hiding? Was he praying towards Mecca? He looked unformed though, the more Ilko studied him. And why was he screaming like a girl?

The scenario took on the sinister appearance of a piece of surrealist theatre. Then he noticed that the man had his trousers down around his ankles, ruched like canvas manacles at the top of his army boots. He appeared to be struggling with something, like somebody filleting a live fish, and when Ilko saw two brown naked feet kicking out at his flanks, he realised what was going on and, despite the winter temperature, a wave of cold sweat washed over his skin.

Ilko lifted his pistol hand and edged into the room. He could hear the soldier's grunts of effort now as he worked at keeping his victim pinned down still enough to achieve his objective. In the distraction of the act, he'd laid his gun on the floor a couple of metres away from him. Ilko moved quietly towards it, skirting round to the man's right, and as he did so he got a proper look at the person pinioned beneath the brute.

She was too young to wear the full *chadri* yet, and the way her *burqa* had been tugged down around her waist revealed the undeveloped chest of a girl perhaps just on the brink of her teenage years. Her dress was little more than a hoop of cloth around her middle, the bottom of it pushed up above her lean thighs, which were pumping and twisting in the struggle to prevent the soldier from penetrating her. The girl's eyes were swimming in tears as she screamed straight into the face of her attacker, and Ilko prayed that she wouldn't see him and give away his presence too soon.

Carefully, he put a foot down on the man's gun and hoofed it away across the floor, at the same time pushing the barrel of his pistol behind the man's ear, hard up against the bump of his prominent mastoid. The man's limbs froze, his body poised motionlessly over the squirming girl, and Ilko saw for the first time the insignia of a corporal on his uniform.

'That's enough,' Ilko said in Russian. 'Hands behind your head. Kneel up now.'

He backed up so that the pistol stayed out of reach as the corporal obeyed.

With his fingers laced behind his head now, he twisted his torso halfway round to see the person who had just spoilt his fun.

Ilko thought he saw a flicker of recognition cross the man's face. As the corporal knelt upright, Ilko glimpsed his cock shrinking between his naked legs and tried not to let his eyes dwell there. He looked into the man's face – even kneeling down, the rapist was nearly at the same eye level – and a memory of a platoon of engineers he'd worked with fortifying a supply dump some weeks back came to mind. This giant had been one of them, he was certain. If he remembered rightly, the man was a fellow Ukrainian.

With his gun still pointed at him, Ilko stepped away a few paces and picked up the man's rifle while the girl scuttled away from her attacker, pulling her clothes together into some semblance of decency.

'Get out,' Ilko said to her. 'Go.'

She didn't understand the words but she didn't need to – she got the meaning immediately. The way the girl fled straight out into the street suggested there was no one else in the house. Ilko decided to check anyway.

He reversed his way to the doorway through to the next room, and glanced swiftly inside. It was a small cooking space, the only other room in the house as far as he could make out. Satisfied that it was unoccupied, that no one else was in danger from the intruder, he re-crossed the room, never taking his eyes from the kneeling giant, who returned his stare with a blank expression and a wordlessness that were more chilling than any threat or angry gesture could have been.

The man was still staring at him with his pants around his ankles and his dick shrivelling up in the icy draught from the street when Ilko unloaded the cartridge shells from the magazine of his rifle onto the floor, dropped the weapon to the ground, then turned around and walked away.

Sekan Dara, it would turn out, was not the only village to suffer. Others encountered the same fate: Kot Kalay, Chine Kalay, Seto Kalay. Later it would be justified as part of the push to secure the Naray Pass and gain access to the Khost valley, giving Soviet engineers a crack at destroying the rebel caves with seismic mines. At the time, on the ground, however, it was little more than the mindless and wanton destruction of innocent communities.

One of those same Soviet engineers, who would later be lauded as heroes, was the corporal that Ilko's coincidental presence had prevented from committing rape that day.

That man was Otto Plotnik.

36. Ifs and Buts

BEA STRUGGLED TO come up with an argument that would win the day, but probably failed chiefly because she could see too much sense in the opposing case. She tried to reason that it was too soon for Stephen to return home, even if they had been informed that the men watching the house had disappeared. Stephen, on the other hand, pointed out that tomorrow was a school day, there was stuff he needed to get hold of – his books, his school bag, clean underwear, his school uniform. They couldn't go on living in self-imposed exile forever.

Bea couldn't help thinking about what Tracy had told them that morning about Sanjeev's murder, but of course, she'd promised not to mention this to Stephen. Besides, the lad was right: it was impractical to think they could stay away indefinitely.

'At least phone yer mother an' see what she thinks first,' she told him.

Tracy was still out with Kelly and Chezz meeting the other Ukrainian fella.

Stephen made the call but got no reply.

'Her battery'll be flat,' said Stevo. 'It always is. She won't have charged it since Friday or before then.'

Bea tried Kelly's mobile and got a message that the phone she was trying to reach was switched off. Jesus. How many times had she fucking told him?

It never occurred to Stevo that he had Cheslav's number logged in his phone from when he'd called his mother yesterday. If he'd made the connection in his mind, he could've got through to them and the big Ukrainian would have advised him against it. But he didn't.

Ifs and buts, ifs and buts . . .

'We'll come with you,' Damien offered; Chloe readily agreed.

Bea wasn't convinced that Chloe knew what the hell was going on or the seriousness of it all, and she liked this idea even less. Apart from anything else, it would mean that she'd be left here on her own.

They argued back and forth like this for half an hour, during which the others still didn't return or get in touch.

Finally, Stevo decided that he was going and that was that.

Bea wasn't his mother, she'd never even met the lad before yesterday, so ultimately she had no say in the matter. Not that that would've made any difference, because Damien was equally insistent that he was going to go with him.

'Look,' said Chloe to Bea, 'I'll stay here and keep you company. But if you're not back in an hour,' she added, turning to the two boys, 'we're calling the police.'

Bea knew Kelly wouldn't like it but this time she agreed with Chloe.

Damien got his bike from where it was chained up in the back yard and the two of them prepared to set off.

'One hour,' Bea reminded them from the back doorstep.

If Kelly wanted to piss and moan about it, she'd deal with that later.

37. Harvey Nicks

THEY USED ILKO'S phone because Tracy's mobile was out of juice, and there was a risk that if they used Cheslav's the number might be recognised by Dmitri's wife, or identified in her phone's call memory, since his having her number stored in his phone in the first place meant he must have had cause to use it at some point, though exactly when, he could no longer remember.

Donna was with her husband when she got the anonymous text message. She'd arranged to meet him in town so that he could take her shopping in Harvey Nicks before it closed at five. Early Sunday closing hours could be a nuisance but at least they fitted in with her plan to eat with the children around six. She liked to get them bathed and in bed at a reasonable time on a Sunday before the start of the school week the next day. By the time they got home, Iris, the weekend maid, would have dinner ready before she clocked off, by which time Lillian, the au pair, would be back to settle the kids down in bed before they went in to kiss them good night.

The winter holiday season was coming up and Donna needed to shop for that. It was a rare event if Jimmy came away with them – usually, at this time of year, it was just her and the kids, with maybe one or more of her female friends in tow, taken along for adult company.

Last year, and the year before that, come to think of it, she'd taken a skiing vacation in Val d'Isère with Caroline, one of Jimmy's business associates' wives who she was thick with, and Caroline's nine-year-old daughter Tiffany. Tiffany, being slightly above the age group of her own two, had conveniently assumed a juvenile mothering role that allowed the two adults a little breathing space, and during the daytime professional minders had supervised and tutored all three of the children on the junior slopes while Donna and Caroline had worked on their off-piste skills and their gin and tonics.

This winter, however, Donna was taking Charlotte and Joshua to visit their auntie – her elder sister Lisa – in Hawaii, where she'd been living these past six years with her American businessman husband. It was going to be her first time out there, moving in a well-to-do circle of beautiful people, and she was trying to shop appropriately for it now.

So far, she had picked out an Alexander McQueen dress at £650, a £600 handbag by Stella McCartney, a Heidi Klein bikini for £180 and a pair of Patrick Cox's ankle strap sandals retailing at a modest £150.

Dmitri stood by looking suitably bored while his mind totted up the mental arithmetic.

When Donna's phone pinged with a text and she pulled it out of her handbag to read, Dmitri noticed the puzzled look on her face.

'What is it?' he asked.

'This is weird.'

She read it out loud to him.

'"Have you ever thought of buying an apartment in Airedale Point?" Doesn't say who it's from though.'

If Dmitri had been eating or drinking anything at that moment, he might well have choked on it. As it was, he just maintained an ominous silence. A silence which was broken by the conspicuous sound of his BlackBerry also receiving a text.

He dug it from his pocket and opened the message.

If you don't want Donna to meet Madeleine, back off now.

The sender was identified as Cheslav.

'Jimmy?'

Donna was regarding him with mild, amused curiosity at whatever was registering on his face.

'I've got the same thing,' he said. 'It must be some marketing thing.'

'That's weird though, that it doesn't say who it's from.'

'No, neither does mine. You know how these things are, though. They make it a mystery at first to draw you in. It's just clever advertising.'

'Well why target us? Airedale Point – isn't that some new building downtown?'

'Yes,' he said, knowing how disingenuous it would sound if he pretended not to have heard of it. 'It's all part of the riverside development. You know I'm doing some business down there with my father. That'll be why they're sending it to us. We must've found our way onto some young gun's distribution list.'

He tried to make it sound convincingly nonchalant while thinking that she wasn't so stupid as to not see straight through him.

'That's terrible,' said Donna. 'I hope we're not going to be getting junk messages and nuisance calls from now on. How the hell did they get *my* number anyway?'

'Don't worry,' said Dmitri, 'I'll sort it out.'

'Well please do.'

'I *said* I will,' he stated irritably.

'OK,' said Donna, looking around just to remind him where they were, 'no need to take my head off.'

Dmitri could see this turning into a row of attrition and a moody evening ahead if he wasn't careful. He couldn't help himself though. Who knew what that crazy bastard Cheslav would do next? He needed to get out of this fucking store and get in touch with Plotnik quickly, and Donna looked nowhere near done yet.

His phone began to ring and he looked at the screen apprehensively to see who it was now. This time it was his father trying to get through to him.

Shit. Whatever it was, he wasn't prepared to broach it here and now in front of Donna and a store full of uptight assholes with maxed-out credit cards, minimal sense and dubious taste.

He pushed the button to put it through to the answering service, and the ringtone cut out.

'Who's that now?' asked Donna.

'No one. Business. Nothing important. Are we done here?'

'I need to buy accessories.'

'Well fucking do it and let's go.'

'Jimmy!'

She looked around again, bug-eyed, subduing her own voice.

'What the fuck is wrong with you?'

'I'm sorry. I'm sorry, OK?'

He was making hand gestures that were supposed to be conciliatory but looked more like karate instruction.

'What the hell are accessories and where do we find them?'

'Forget it,' Donna hissed tetchily. 'Let's just pay for these and go. Suddenly, I'm not in the mood anymore.'

'Donna. I'm sorry.'

The words mimicked apology while the tone dished out blame.

'Save it, Jimmy, all right? Just save it.'

166

That was fine by him.

By the time they arrived home, the atmosphere between the two of them had accumulated to a thunderhead, and as Donna strode off towards the house, clutching her shopping bags like body armour around her, Dmitri hung back in the car so that he could finally make some phone calls in confidentiality.

First, he phoned Plotnik, to no avail. The Carpenter had his phone switched off. Dmitri assumed there was a good reason for that, but it was fucking inconvenient.

He cut the annoying message off with a vocalised curse.

Then he decided that he might as well get the worst over with and return his father's call.

'Why am I getting anonymous texts about you?' said his father, coming straight to the point.

Yosyp Maximov, like his son, was not a man to waste words.

'What texts?'

'I'm not going to spell them out over the phone,' his father said. 'It seems to me, though, that someone is trying to screw up this development contract for you. And from what these messages imply, the one trying to screw it up is you.'

Dmitri, still sitting behind the steering wheel, rolled his eyes angrily at the windscreen.

'I've told you everything is above board, haven't I? Or I've told Goldthorpe. He's seen the paperwork. He'll tell you it's all clean.'

'I'm not talking about the paperwork, Dmitri. I'm talking about you and these other – projects of yours. If you want in, you're going to have to stop drawing attention to yourself like this.'

'Like what? What fairy stories have you been listening to, Father?'

'Fairy stories.'

There was a hint of humour to Yosyp's voice now.

'You ever hear of a story,' he went on, 'by Agatha Christie? Called *Ten Little Niggers*? Well I heard a story about ten little somethings and I don't like it. You understand?'

Shit. Fucking Cheslav again. He must have told the old man about the arrival of the shipment of Baikals. What else had he told him about? More to the point, what else *could* he tell him about if he truly wanted to sour the riverside property deal?

'Listen, don't stress yourself about it,' said Dmitri. 'That business is already over and done with,' he lied. 'Nothing's going to interfere with our business from now on, OK?'

'Don't bullshit me, Son,' said Yosyp. 'I may be getting on but I won't be bullshitted, especially not by my own children. You make sure you take care of this. And be discreet about it. I don't want to see your name or mine in the newspapers, and I don't want to get anymore damn text messages, you understand?'

'Father, stop worrying. I told you, leave it to me. This is the last you'll hear about it.'

'It better be. And give my love to Donna and the grandchildren.'

His father ended the call abruptly and Dmitri thought, *You can shove your love up your ass.*

He sat there a moment longer with his thoughts stewing and boiling and finally festering.

Fuck it. He was fucked if he was going to lose out on the deal with the guns, no matter what his fucking father thought or said or did.

Acquiescing to Cheslav's demands for him to 'back off' was looking more and more attractive in the short term, if only he could get through to Plotnik.

In the meantime, a quick sale of the Baikals would seem to be the most propitious course of action, no matter how much he resented having his hand forced by someone who until yesterday was nothing more than a glorified goddamned lackey.

He didn't want to take too long to make up his mind. Apart from anything else, Donna would be in the house now imagining that he was out here still brooding about fucking Harvey Nichols and accessories.

He hunted down the number of Davy Wainwright, one of the Wainwright twins, potential buyers in Manchester. He could prolong the event in a bidding war or he could aim for a swift and sufficiently lucrative sale to these two young maniacs, who he knew were keen and ready to buy. After the conversation he'd just had with his father, the sooner he got the guns out of his warehouse and over the Pennines, the better.

Dmitri pulled up the number and hit the DIAL button.

38. Trapdoor Spider

PLOTNIK WAITED.

Plotnik was good at waiting. During his military service he'd never been a sniper, but he always thought it was something he'd be good at. He was good with tools – and what was a sniper rifle but a high-precision tool? – and he was good at waiting.

Like a trapdoor spider is good at waiting: for its prey.

The first thing he did was turn off his mobile phone: no giveaway, no distraction. After that, he took the time to eat his sandwiches, and stuffed the empty packaging into an overflowing pedal bin that he found in a cupboard under the kitchen sink.

Then he positioned himself sitting on the floor in the front room in a space between the end of a settee and a blank wall, with all the provisions for waiting ranged in front of him on the carpet: his bottled water, the remains of his vodka, a glass that he'd borrowed off of the draining board next to the sink, and the gun that Dmitri had provided.

The curtains were drawn, so the light in the room was dim, but he left them as they were because that was the way he'd found them. To the outside world, there was no sign that anything about the house had altered since the departure of Dmitri's watchers early that morning. There was a small chink where one drape was pleated back at a corner, but he left that too. In the position that he'd taken up, anyone looking in through that gap from outside would be unable to see him.

While he waited, a residual smell of stale cigarettes in the room reminded him of the days when he loved to smoke.

It was darker still by the time the noise of a key in the front door announced someone's arrival. He had patiently watched the faint imprint of daylight visible through the material of the curtains fade towards twilight, while he sipped a little vodka from the glass and chased it with a swallow of water just to maintain an edge of alertness, repeating the operation three or four times during the afternoon as the light outside gradually diminished. Now he carefully laid the glass and the bottles to one side and tripped the safety catch off the pistol, hearing two voices conversing in the hall beyond the living room door without being able to make out what they were saying to one another.

Young voices, male; boys, by the sound of it. He stood up silently and tiptoed across the room to position himself behind the living room door, reassured now by the clunk of the front door closing behind them.

'It doesn't look like Sanjeev's been back,' said the boy entering the living room first.

Plotnik, seeing the colouring of the boy's skin, assumed this was the one Dmitri was looking for, Stephen, the one believed to have stolen his experimental batch of DMT.

The lad looked tall and athletic for his age but represented about forty per cent of Plotnik's own body mass. Before he was even fully in the room, Plotnik side-stepped out from behind the door, grabbed him by the throat with one hand and pointed the muzzle of the gun at his head with other.

He was standing behind him now and they were both facing through the doorway at the startled expression on the face of the other boy who'd been about to come in behind him. A white boy of similar age and size, though the coloured kid had an inch or two in height on him.

Before he could think about making a dash for it, Plotnik caught his eye and gestured what would happen if he tried.

'I'll kill him,' he said just to make doubly sure the message had gotten across. The white boy's eyes toggled between Plotnik's and his hostage's, caught between hostility and helplessness, but his body stayed frozen.

'In here.'

As Plotnik reversed to make way, keeping a firm but not yet fatal grip on Stephen's windpipe, he waved the other kid forward into the room with his gun hand.

'Close the door behind you. Sit down over there.'

He indicated the settee. The white boy did as he was told. When he was seated with his hands clasped on top of his head, Plotnik let go of the coloured kid.

Stephen toppled forward onto his knees on the floor, both hands going to his neck as he coughed and spluttered and fought to get his breath back.

'On there, next to him,' said Plotnik.

He gripped the boy's arm and shoved him roughly towards the settee. The kid turned around and sat down next to his friend, adopting the same hands-on-head posture without needing to be told. Even in the murky light of all that remained of the day, he could see the tears on the boy's face, not from fear but from the physical stress of near strangulation.

Plotnik was aware that when they'd entered the house, they'd failed to switch on a light in the hall. Whether that had been a matter of deliberate caution on their part or simply a broken light bulb wasn't important. It made him reluctant, though, to switch on the living room light, and as there were probably only minutes of useful visibility left to him, that meant he had to decide what to do with them and do it quickly.

'Did anyone see you arrive at the house?' said Plotnik, directing the question at Stephen because he knew that he was the one who lived here and who would have noticed if any neighbours had been watching.

'Yes, they did.'

The response was too quick, too loud, too eager. Plotnik knew he was lying.

The near darkness helped him but he moved so fast that neither of them would've seen it coming anyway or could've done anything about it.

He darted forward and smashed the butt of the pistol against the side of the head of the white boy. The boy's arms flopped from his head to his sides and he keeled over onto the arm of the settee, unconscious.

The coloured boy half turned to his friend, concern radiating from him in the darkness, but he kept his hands where they were. Plotnik used what was left of the dying light to hook back his attention with the barrel of the gun against his jaw.

'Again,' he said. 'The truth.'

'No,' the boy shouted, an angry response to the punishment that had been dished out to his friend. 'No,' he said again, more calmly, 'I don't think so.'

'Better,' said Plotnik, and reached out to touch the boy's collar bone. His fingers dug underneath it, locating the relevant nerve cluster, and the boy fell asleep.

Working quickly, he took a bundle of plastic cable ties out of his pocket and used them to bind the hands of both the unconscious youths.

Then he gathered up his bottles of water and vodka before slipping out of the back door of the house and through the back yard.

It took him five minutes to walk to his car and drive it up to the front of the house. The street lights had just come on, still glowing a pale pink before they would come up to full brightness.

He went back inside, this time through the front door, which the boys had left unlocked when they had come in. To belay neighbourly suspicion, he picked up their mountain bikes one by one and dragged them inside.

After that it only took him another five minutes before he came back out, carrying one of his victims under each arm.

The last thing he did in there was to remember to wash up the glass he'd been using and leave it neatly upturned on the draining board.

39. Catch Phrase

'What the fu—'

'Don't fuckin' start, Kelly, cos I'm not 'avin' it.'

It was Bea's catch phrase, and Kelly's cue to zip it, to stitch his lips, to fit his top row and his bottom row of teeth together and keep them clamped.

'I told 'em not to go – '

Bea turned imploringly to Chloe.

'Didn't I tell 'em not to go, Chloe?'

'Yeh, you did, but they wun't' ave it, would they?'

Bea and Chloe were covering one another's backs now, the excuses flying between them like don't-blame-us tennis.

'No, they wun't. I knew you'd go off the deep end – I told 'em – '

'Then why din't you phone me?' said Kelly.

'Cos you 'ad yer fuckin' phone switched off, din't yer?'

Kelly's mouth hung open gormlessly.

'As per fuckin' usual,' Bea continued, driving it home like a truism. 'How many times 'ave I fuckin' told ya? Keep yer fuckin' phone switched on. How many times do I 'ave to friggin' remind yer?'

Kelly said nothing, feeling like that fucking sentence would be written on his grave stone: *Keep your fucking phone switched on.*

Mobile phones were supposed to make life easier, and it was true that they were convenient for making arrangements on the wing, as it were, but he was sure that in the world before they were around he used to get shouted at a fuck of a lot less, and he would gladly have swapped the fucking thing for a quieter existence.

Bea turned to Chloe.

'Sorry for all t'swearin', love.'

Chloe didn't quite know where to look or who to feel most sorry for.

'No, don't worry.'

Tracy looked guilty too, and decided it would be better to 'fess up straight away, unprompted.

'Mine were outta power. I shoulda charged it up this

mornin'. Fuck, I 'ope our Stephen's all right. I' ope they're both all right,' she added quickly.

'How long've they been gone?' said Kelly.

'Two hours now. An' they said they'd be no more than an hour.'

'Have you tried phonin' your Damien?' said Tracy.

'Course I 'ave,' Bea snapped, and immediately felt bad, remembering what the poor woman had been through this weekend. 'Sorry, it's not your fault. He's not answerin' though.'

'Right,' said Cheslav. 'I'm going to phone Dmitri. We need to act now before he hurts them. Or before this other man, Plotnik, hurts them.'

'What we gonna say to 'im?' said Kelly.

'We've discussed this already. We offer him the pills, but now it's in exchange for your boys. We need to inform Ilko of this development, get him ready to give up the location.'

Tracy bristled at his calling the disappearance of her child a 'development', but kept it to herself.

Bea, however, was in a more vocal mood altogether.

'Well I think it's about time we called the police. This 'as bloody gone far enough. I think we're gettin' in over us 'eads.'

Kelly opened his mouth but thought better of it: nothing came out but his disgruntlement with the idea was written all over his brow.

Cheslav stepped into the breach.

'I'm not sure that's a good idea. Dmitri and his father are rich and powerful people. I can tell you for certain that Dmitri has friends who are highly placed in the West Yorkshire police force.'

Now it was Bea's turn to open her mouth and say nothing. She heard what he was saying but she wasn't happy about it and she was still unconvinced that keeping the police out of it was the best decision anymore.

'He's got a point, Bea,' said Kelly.

Bea just glowered back at him . . . as if any of this was his fucking fault!

A couple of moments passed in silence as they all seethed in a stew of aimless recrimination. Beneath the hell of holding each other to account, each of them was aware that the one person they should be blaming wasn't anyone in the room.

'Make the call,' said Tracy eventually, speaking for them all.

Cheslav phoned Ilko first, explaining what had happened since they had seen him earlier. He asked him where the pills were and Ilko gave him the location, saying that was where they should set the meeting.

Then he phoned Dmitri.

'I was wondering when you would be in touch,' said Dmitri, barely able to suppress a sneer from his voice. 'What the fuck do you think you are playing at? You had it all and you've thrown it away, for what? Some council estate whore with a welcome sign tattooed over her cunt.'

Cheslav refused to rise to any provocation.

'Where are the two boys?'

'What two boys?' said Dmitri.

'Cut the bullshit. You know who I mean.'

'If you're talking about that bitch's offspring Stephen, the one who stole my drugs, then OK, but I still don't know where he is and I don't know anything about any other boy.'

'You sent Plotnik,' said Cheslav.

'Who told you that?' said Dmitri, suddenly finding himself on the back foot.

'Never mind. But if he has them, you'd better pray he hasn't touched them.'

'Or what?'

'You mean your wife didn't tell you about the text she got?' said Cheslav. 'If you want, I can arrange an introduction to Madeleine, and you wouldn't be able to do a thing about it.'

There was a moment's silence at the other end of the line.

'Let me speak to Plotnik. If he has your boys, we'll set up a swap. The boys for my DMT.'

'You read my mind.'

'I'll get back to you soon. I hope you're going to take my call this time.'

Cheslav hung up and turned to the others, deciding the best thing was to keep it simple.

'We're on,' he said.

40. Carpentry

WHEN STEVO CAME round he couldn't move his arms.

That was the first thing he noticed. Not that he couldn't move them exactly; he could lift them up and down in front of him, he just couldn't move them apart.

The second thing he noticed was that he didn't know where he was.

When he opened his eyes, they instinctively blinked shut again for a moment against the light.

The last thing he remembered was being in darkness. Him and Damien sitting in the dismal light of dusk in his own front room, while a very large man held them both at gun point.

Shit: Damien.

The man had cracked him in the temple with the butt of the gun.

Shit, man, shit like that could kill you. Or give you permanent brain damage. Fuck.

He opened his eyes again, forcing them to deal with the bright light.

Where the fuck was he?

The walls were white – blank and white. Painted; clean-looking; unmarked. The texture of the light was hard and flat, like overhead strip-lighting.

This sure as shit wasn't his home anymore.

Then the music started.

That was the third thing he noticed.

He didn't know where it was coming from but it was awful. Some treacly, maudlin rubbish that belonged on one of those radio stations that played shit from about a zillion years ago. A melancholy oboe tootled a depressing melody and a sickly woman's voice quivered terrible Hallmark-style words over the top of it.

We've only just begun – to live . . .

The Carpenters – that was it. He recognised it now from God knew where. Some sick fucking adult must've played it to him somewhere down the line: white granny music.

Stevo heard a groan from behind him and tried to turn around towards it, only to realise that it wasn't just the motion of his arms that was restricted. His right ankle was trapped, as though caught on something.

Squinting against the light, he saw that he was lying on bare wooden floorboards, that his hands were locked together at the wrists by a plastic cable tie, and that a second and third tie, one bound tightly around his ankle and the other looped through it, had been used to attach his foot to a radiator pipe that ran close to the ground next to a skirting board. He gave a few experimental tugs but he knew how tough these cables were and what a painful waste of time trying to pull them apart was. The only way to get free was to cut them off.

He gained enough leverage with his arms and his free foot to half twist himself over.

Damien was lying next to him, similarly bound, and just this minute regaining consciousness. He had a massive bruise up the side of his head but, miraculously, the skin hadn't split and there was no external bleeding.

Karen Carpenter warbled on.

So many roads to choose . . .

'D-Man.'

He watched Damien's eyelids creep open and flutter against the intrusion of the light.

He didn't know whether it was day or night. There appeared to be a window set in the wall across the room but a white roller blind was drawn down over it and it was hard to tell whether there was dark or light beyond.

There was an open door across the room but the oblique view through it seemed to give onto a hall or corridor as featurelessly decorated as the room they were in, offering no answer to any of the questions springing to his mind.

He didn't know how long he'd been unconscious but somehow it didn't feel like a whole night had passed, so he guessed it must still be the same night outside.

He wondered how long it'd been since they'd left Damien's place and whether anyone would be missing them yet. It wasn't much of a straw to grasp at – if he didn't know where the fuck they were then how would anybody else? Shit, though, it was better than nothing. Maybe Damien's old lady's old man would get off his high horse and call the fucking police now, get them on the case.

And when the evening comes, we smile . . .

'What the fuck's that?' mumbled Damien, twisting towards his friend and giving his own limbs an exploratory squirm.

'The Carpenters,' said Stevo. 'Must be a torture thing.'

'Fuck, man, don't say that. Not even as a joke.'

Stevo remembered what they'd done to his mother and realised how suddenly right Damien was.

The room they were in was virtually empty. It was like a room in a newly built house that no one had bought yet. The floor was uncarpeted, the walls naked, devoid of wallpaper, pictures, anything personal. The radiator fed by the pipe they were both tied to was painted as white and impersonal as the walls. The only piece of furniture was an arch-backed black wicker-work chair positioned a few feet away in the middle of the floor space, just beyond their reach.

The absence of cupboard space or a sink unit suggested it wasn't a kitchen. Other than that, they were clueless; it could be a reception room, a dining room, a bedroom. Its size gave nothing away. Not that it mattered anyway. As far as they were concerned, it was simply a prison chamber.

'How's the head?' said Stevo, struggling and managing to wriggle himself up into a sitting position.

'Hurts like hell,' said Damien. 'Like the world's worst fuckin' 'angover.'

Damien too succeeded in pushing himself up till he was sitting propped against the wall. In the glare of the artificial light, his face looked grey, and Stevo decided that couldn't be good.

'How did we get 'ere?'

'I ain't got a clue, mate. He put me out as well. It was like some fuckin' Vulcan death grip or summing. My arm still feels paralysed.'

'Yer jokin'!'

'I wish I was. I'd settle for just dreaming. If I woke up now and found out this was all just a dream I'd – '

'You'd what?'

'I dunno. Start goin' to church or summing.'

'Jesus, Stevo, come on, man, get a grip.'

They both laughed at that, but each sensed the bleakness of it, a forced laugh to stave off the crying.

'Is he still 'ere?' Damien asked.

'I dunno. I only woke up about a minute before you did. I ain't seen him. I didn't even get a good look at him when he nabbed us at my place.'

'Fuck, man, you were lucky then. When he had you by t'throat – it were like fuckin' Frankenstein's monster. Fuckin' ugly bastard.'

'Oh fuck . . .'

There could've been no clearer expression of Stevo's desperation – an expletive teetering on the brink of tears.

'I still can't see properly,' said Damien. 'Can you see anything that might cut these ties?'

'D-Man, there's nothin'. Nothin' except a chair. And that fuckin' music.'

The Carpenters song had faded out a couple of moments ago, but now it ground up again from its invisible source, cranking out of the speakers in repeat mode.

We've only just begun . . .

'Shit,' said Stevo, as a new thought occurred to him.

Damien knew it was gonna be something dreadful.

'What is it?'

'This music. I'm sure it started after I woke up.'

'So?'

'That means somebody must've switched it on. That means he's still here somewhere.'

'Oh shit.'

As if just saying it would bring him forth, the two of them became aware of a shadow growing against the bit of wall that they could see through the doorway, and a loose floorboard was heard to creak and clap beneath a heavy tread.

Both Stevo and Damien realised that they were holding their breath.

A giant figure in a long coat lumbered into the room and for the first time they got a good look at his scarred face in the full, unforgiving glare of the fluorescent illumination.

Plotnik paused in the doorway. If he did it purely for dramatic effect, it was working on them. His long arms dropped straight down along his flanks and at the end of one of them was suspended a large metallic-blue tool box. He stepped inside and set it down on the floor with a heavy rattle of the contents within. Its presence was like a fourth person in the otherwise echoing emptiness of the room.

Stevo and Damien couldn't speak to him but neither could they take their eyes off him as the giant stood over them, looking down wordlessly at them. For some moments he stood there, saying nothing. Then he turned around and walked out of the room.

Their eyes went straight to the tool box, then to one another. They didn't need words to share what they were both thinking – that within that box were the means to cut their bonds. That box right there, left just beyond their reach.

Neither of them made any connection yet between the concept of a tool box and the music that was playing.

Sharing horizons that are new to us . . .

Before either of them had time to make the vain effort to stretch out towards it, Monster-Face returned, this time holding something else.

The object wasn't immediately recognisable to them – all they could see was that it was something made of wood. It looked like something rough and home-made, about a foot square, strips and wedges of wood fitted together to form something like a miniature raft with a handle or spindle attached to one side, the kind of thing – model – you might build as a kid, or put together in woodwork class and be obliged to call it design and technology.

It was only after he'd put it down on the floor beside the tool box that the two of them noticed what he was carrying in his other hand. Their imaginations had been so running riot on the purpose of the wooden block that only now were they allowed to unleash their full potential of horror with regard to the polythene sheet that he proceeded to unfurl and spread out on the floor at their feet.

Stevo was the first to speak to him. He was the one who'd gotten them into this mess, it was his responsibility to try to get them out of it, and the only way available to him, it seemed, was through talk.

'Jus' tell us what you want. Jus' tell us. We can talk it out.'

Plotnik took no notice. Plotnik continued with his business, unrolling the plastic sheeting and smoothing it out to protect the floorboards, lifting the legs of the youths to push it underneath them as if they were nothing more than items of furniture. The black chair wasn't the only furniture in the room. Stevo and Damien – they were furniture too.

He spread it out with both hands, pushing out the edges of the sheet like swimming the breast stroke, smoothing out the creases with all the painstaking effort of preparing for a perfect picnic on the grass.

When he'd finished doing that he brought the wooden contraption and put it down squarely between the boys' feet. It looked to them like some kind of home-made vise, with a wooden handle that turned around to bring two opposing sides closer together.

While they watched speechlessly, the big Ukrainian opened out the wing-like drawers of the tool box and pulled an electric screwdriver out of the central section. Then he proceeded to drive a couple of screws through the floor of the vise-like object, securing it to the floorboard beneath it.

The noise of the drill unnerved them both more, to the nth power, than they were already unnerved. While he was bent at the task, they could probably have both kicked him in the head with their feet that weren't tethered. Even assuming that that would've had any effect on him, though, the tool box was still out of reach and the drill, which might have been some help in cutting through their bonds, would probably have dropped to the floor too far away and they would've had to just wait there in the condition they were already in until he woke up, deeply pissed off at them, and it all happened in such a distracting manner that neither of them thought of the idea in the first place until it was already too late. In any case, it looked like the kind of head that could take a lot of punishment before it began to notice it was being knocked about. A boxer's head, if there was a weight category in boxing big enough for this guy.

Plotnik leaned back from fixing the vise in place and looked at his two captives, from one to the other. Although he said nothing, the boys could see him playing a mental eeny-meeny-miny-moe, while the plaintive introductory notes of the Carpenters song started up once more.

We've only just begun – to live . . .

Plotnik's face expressed no pleasure in the music, nor any compunction about what he was intending to do. It was a thoroughly expressionless face, showing only a factual interest in the manipulation of the objects under his control. The screwdriver as he replaced it in the bowels of the tool chest. The jaws of the vise as he tested the smoothness of their motion. Stephen's foot as he took hold of it and removed its training shoe and sock.

'Whoa, whoa, whoa,' said Stevo, 'what you doin'?'

Still,Plotnik paid no attention to anything they said.

'Leave him alone.'

'Get off my foot, man.'

'What the fuck d'yer want?'

'Yeah, jus' tell us. Whaddya wanna know?'

Stevo wriggled and kicked but it was pointless. The big man was way too strong. He jammed Stevo's naked foot down in the vise and started turning the handle.

'No, no, stop, please!'

'Please,' screamed Damien, 'don't!'

Both of them thought he was going to keep turning until he'd crushed the bones in the foot. Stevo braced himself against the pain as the vise tightened against the sides of his foot, squeezing, squeezing.

'Aah! Aah! Please! Please!'

Then he stopped.

Before any real pain set in, the Ukrainian stopped turning the handle. Stevo's foot was wegded in, locked tight, immovable, but at least nothing was broken yet.

Again, Plotnik leaned back on his haunches, looking disinterestedly at the work he'd accomplished. He pushed himself up off the floor and settled his bulk in the wicker chair.

The two boys looked up at him from the floor, their faces and voices brimming with anxiety.

'What the fuck do you want?'

'Do you even understand English? Jus' tell us what you want.'

Plotnik raised a hand and they both shut up.

'Where are the pills?' he said.

'We can get you the pills,' said Stevo eagerly, as though he'd finally seen the sign that pointed the way out of a nightmare.

'No,' said Plotnik. 'Listen to the question. *Where are* the pills?'

'We haven't got them,' said Damien, hoping a modified

182

answer would do the trick.

'We can find out where they are for you though,' Stevo added, flushed with the conviction that if they explained themselves clearly enough they could all still be friends here.

Plotnik eased himself out of the chair and down onto his knees on the floorboards at the boys' feet once more. He leaned over and peered into the tool chest, taking his time to select the appropriate implements for the job at hand. Finally, satisfied with his choice, he reached inside and took out first a hammer, then a chisel.

So much of life ahead . . .

'Aw no, man, please!'

'Don't. Please don't.'

There was nothing Stevo could do except kick at the big man with his free foot, so Plotnik grabbed hold of the thrashing leg and pinned it to the floor under his own knee while keeping out of range of the other boy's foot. Thus unencumbered, he fitted the bladed tip of the chisel snugly in behind the joint of the little toe of the foot trapped in the vise.

We start out walking and learn to run . . .

There was no more questioning now. The time for words was over. Not even *This little piggy went to market.*

He raised the hammer just as high as he judged necessary, no more than a foot or so, and brought it down once on the head of the chisel.

Stevo screamed and the toe slid off like a piece of chipolata.

After that, Plotnik gave the boys a couple of minutes while they both screamed and cried and slobbered and shook with pain and fear and tried to huddle protectively towards one another, like a couple of chicks when the hungry fox's muzzle nudges over the edge of the nest.

Snot oozed from both their noses.

Blood oozed from the amputation, making a sticky bond between the boy's foot and the wooden vise.

'Where are the pills?' he asked again.

Stevo was too busy crying and heaving for breath to be able to speak.

'We d-don't know where they are,' said Damien through his sobs. 'Honest . . . Uh-huh . . . Somebody t-took 'em from us . . . Huh . . . But we can get 'em b-back. Huh-huh. Jus' let us make a

– a phone call, that's all. You'll 'ave 'em straight away, I pro— I promise.'

'Not good enough.'

Somewhere in the crazed, lost distance there was a silence, then the haunting melody and the now familiar lilt rising again as Plotnik took up his tools, ready to resume work.

We've only just begun . . .

Then another, louder sound drowned out the end of the line.

Ding-dong.

Plotnik clattered the hammer and chisel away in the tool box, closing it up and making sure it was out of his captives' reach. Then he left the room, shutting them away from sight, and went to answer the front door.

It was Dmitri on the doorstep.

He wasted no time stepping inside past Plotnik, who closed the door behind him.

'I've been trying to call you. You should keep your fucking phone on. What's that?'

Two people were screaming for help from the room next door. He ignored them and waited while Plotnik gave him a synopsis of the day's events.

'Shit,' said Dmitri. 'OK. You did good. But now we have to make a trade. These kids for the pills. I've spoken to Cheslav and he's told us where to meet. I want you to go along. Make sure you get the pills. When you've got them, you can release the hostages.'

'Release them?'

Plotnik rarely expressed surprise but this was one occasion that called it forth.

'Yes, you heard me. If they die, it'll fuck things up, but if I let them go, it'll mend some bridges for me.'

'If you're sure,' said Plotnik.

'I'm sure,' said Dmitri. 'Can anyone hear them?' he asked, frowning and jerking a thumb at the racket the captives were making.

'Only us.'

'One more thing. I still want Cheslav. He's a loose cannon who knows too much. I can't have him running around holding threats over me indefinitely. He needs to be taken care of. You can let these noisy fuckers go but I want Cheslav shut up for good. Understand?'

'You want the pills and you want him dead. Achieving both should not be impossible. But I'll need a couple of men on hand to release the hostages as soon as I give them the word.'

'No problem. I'll have two men sent here.'

Dmitri indicated towards the sound of the boys in the other room.

'Have them fixed up and ready. Then phone Cheslav. He'll tell you where and when. Plotnik.'

'What?'

'Get the pills, OK?'

'I will.'

Dmitri turned away and was about to go out the front door when he stopped and turned around.

'Is this the Carpenters?'

'Yes.'

'Is it on tape or CD?'

'CD.'

'Could I borrow it? I can burn a copy and give you it straight back tomorrow.'

'Sure,' said Plotnik. 'No problem.'

Dmitri smiled and hummed the tune to himself as he left.

41. The Hetman's Daughter

'WHO'S THIS THEN?' said Kelly, looking at the mausoleum.

The question annoyed Ilko slightly. Couldn't Kelly read? The information was plain to see in front of his face, right there on the wall of the tomb, engraved in a panel just above the broken window of latticed stonework. It may be night time but there was a three-quarter moon right over them in a winter-clear sky full of stars and enough residual light from the path near by to make the words out clearly.

CAROLINE DOYLE
NEE
CARLOTTA SKOROPADSKY
BORN IN UKRAINE
1918
DIED IN LEEDS
23RD AUGUST 1950
AGED 32 YEARS

'She was the daughter of the last Hetman,' said Ilko.

'Hitman?' said Kelly. 'Ya mean like this geezer we're supposed to be meetin'?'

'Not hitman,' said Ilko. '*Het*man.'

He struggled to differentiate the two vowel sounds, wondering if he'd made himself clear.

'Het,' he added, 'with an *e*.'

'What the f— What the 'ell's an 'etman?'

'Something forgotten, from long ago,' Ilko said rather poetically, and wondered what he was doing here explaining his distant heritage to this ignorant Yorkshireman.

'Cossack royalty,' said Cheslav.

Ilko wasn't convinced that this helped, but he was impressed nonetheless with the man's folk knowledge. It was hardly the most well-known corner of Ukrainian history.

'There were never any czars or princes or princesses in Ukraine's past,' Ilko said. 'Those are Russian titles. In Ukraine we had the Hetman. It was a high military rank, second in nobility only to the monarch. This woman's father, Pavlo Skoropadsky, was the last of his kind. The last Hetman.'

'So what's she doin' 'ere?' said Kelly.

'For her sins,' said Ilko, 'she married a Yorkshireman.'

'An' what are we doin' 'ere?'

'Ssh,' said Cheslav

The three of them froze with their ears pricked up as footsteps approached along the path.

The man who hove into view, as large and lumbering as the prow of a ship, wore a long black overcoat unbuttoned and appeared out of the night conspicuously alone. His outline was big and blocky, like a giant robot. As he got closer, they saw his face. It looked jaundiced in the street light dappling through bare trees, enhancing the impression, created by the extensive scar, of something artificial and crudely patched together.

It was Kelly's first sight of Plotnik, and to him, the man looked like nothing less than a monument to over-eating topped by a face that resembled a vandalised concrete mask.

Ilko's thoughts, meanwhile, flashed back to the room of that mud house in Afghanistan, the brutish bulk pinning down the innocent child, welcoming her to a world of horror in which she had no rightful place at all.

To Ilko, Plotnik was the golem.

Cheslav had a different measure of the man again. To him, Plotnik was someone he knew not well but professionally, one for whom he'd always borne a grudging respect. The memory-whiff of that respect now served to engender caution, distrust – and a not inconsiderable helping of fear.

Cheslav was aware of Ilko's military training and experience, and Kelly didn't look like any kind of pushover either, but it was impossible for him to really tell how much their physical courage and fighting ability could be relied upon when it truly came down to the wire. If he had to go *mano à mano* alone with Plotnik, he honestly wasn't sure how much he fancied his chances against the lethal giant.

The four men stood facing each other across the final resting place of the Hetman's daughter. Or rather three men stood on one side facing one man on the other – though he was almost big enough to be three rolled into one.

Plotnik looked at Cheslav and Cheslav thought he noticed a slight nod from him, though he could be kidding himself. Plotnik was not renowned for his extroversion and sociability.

Then he moved his gaze onto Ilko.

'I know you,' he said.

'We met once,' said Ilko, 'a long time ago. Not long enough.'

'I remember you,' said Plotnik, nodding to himself now.

He cut the words off there but his expression declared that they had unfinished business.

Then he looked at Kelly.

'Who's he?'

'Does it matter?' said Cheslav.

'You've got my kid,' said Kelly.

It felt weird saying '*my* kid'. Disingenuous – but defiant, nonetheless. Besides, what else was he going to call him in front of this huge fucking gorilla?

'So where is 'e?'

'The pills first,' said Plotnik.

'Where are the two boys?' said Ilko. 'Let's stop fooling around.'

Plotnik pulled a mobile phone from his coat pocket and waved it in front of them.

'You give me the pills, I make a call and the boys will be released.'

'How do we know that?' said Kelly.

Plotnik looked at Cheslav. *Tell them*, his eyes were saying.

'This is how it's done,' said Cheslav. 'It'll be OK.'

'Good boy,' said Plotnik to Cheslav.

Cheslav kept calm. If he let Plotnik intimidate him, it would definitely give him the edge.

Ilko squatted down in front of the tomb and reached his hand through the gap in the broken lattice work.

Plotnik's gaze was drawn down to the inscription on the tomb and he noticed the details of the woman's Ukrainian birthright.

'Cute,' he said.

Ilko pulled out the Tupperware box that Kelly and Bea had packed the drugs in the day before, then stood up. He clutched the box to his chest, signalling his reluctance to hand them over until some guarantees were given.

Plotnik pushed a button on the phone and held it to his ear.

After a moment, he said, 'Release them.'

188

Then he hung up.

'What, that's it?' said Kelly. '"Release them"? How do we know 'e wan't talkin' to the speakin' clock?'

'Phone your boy,' said Plotnik.

'What?'

'Phone him. The boy, Damien.'

Damien's name on Plotnik's lips served to break Kelly out of a kind of spell.

He took out his mobile, feeling himself flush as he realised he still hadn't switched the damn thing on. The phone chimed its little signature tune as it came to life, and he called up the number.

Damien answered after just two rings.

'Hello?'

'Damien. Are you all right?'

'Kelly . . .'

Damien was at a loss for words. He sounded breathless, excited and a little emotional. Wherever he was, Kelly could hear music in the background.

'Where are yer? Is Stephen with you?'

'We're OK. They just let us go. We're outside the LGI.'

The LGI was Leeds General Infirmary. That music, Kelly guessed, must be the outdoor ice rink over the road that operated throughout the winter.

'Are you 'urt?'

'Not badly. 'Ang on.'

The sound went muffled while Damien presumably spoke to Stephen at the other end.

'Stevo says tell his mam 'e's down here at the hospital but he's OK. Listen, Kel, we're goin' inside. Can you send me mam down?'

'I'll get onto it. You sure you're OK?'

'Yeah, really.'

Kelly nodded at Ilko as he finished the call and Ilko passed the box of pills across to Plotnik.

'Tell Dmitri that concludes our business,' said Cheslav.

The three men turned around and began to walk away, leaving the big man with his prize, standing next to the illustrious tomb.

'Not quite,' they heard him say behind their backs.

As the three of them spun to face him again, Plotnik was spoilt for choice. He knew the boss wanted Cheslav dead but there was an old score to settle with the other Ukrainian. Plotnik couldn't work out how he had become involved in this business, nor how he had come back into his life after all these years and so far away from their last encounter, but the opportunity was too good to ignore.

He held out the Baikal at arm's length and pointed it first at one then the other.

Fuck it, he thought. He would have them both.

He let his aim settle on Cheslav – he would get him, as the bigger threat, out of the way first.

Without further warning, he squeezed the trigger.

There was a ragged explosion and the three of them ducked and flung up their arms in front of their faces.

When they looked a second later as the smoke was clearing, Plotnik was lying on his back on the ground at the foot of the tomb.

'Jesus fuck!' said Kelly.

'What—?' said Ilko.

They watched in disbelief for several seconds as the big man's arms and legs twitched.

Then, as all movement ceased, they crept towards the prostrate bulk.

Plotnik lay completely still now, and they looked down at him. Most of his right hand had gone, detonated to a bloody stump, and the old scar across his face was augmented with a cat's cradle of lacerating wounds where the faulty pistol had blown shot and shrapnel back into his face. His chest between the open flaps of the black coat was a wet mat of rusty redness.

The box of pills lay intact at a short distance from him in the grass, where it had flown from his grasp. Its lid was still clipped firmly in place, the contents unharmed.

'Did you get that?' said Ilko, raising his voice.

Denny stepped out of the cover of the foliage a few yards away from where the exchange had taken place. The Sony Handycam was still rolling in his hand as a look of amazement spread across his gaping face.

'That was fuckin' unbelievable.'

'Please tell me you had Night Shot switched on,' said Ilko as he went over and picked up the pills.

'Yeah,' said Denny glancing at the camera in his hand as if noticing it there for the first time. He switched it off and returned his stare to the body on the ground.

'Unfuckinbelievable.'

Cheslav went up and toed the body then bent down and scrutinised it for a moment without touching it. He smelt the odour of evacuated bowels coming off it and backed away.

'He's dead,' he pronounced at last.

'You don't say,' said Kelly.

'Unfuckinbelievable,' Denny said again, in case no one had heard him the first time.

42. Playback

IT WASN'T OVER and Cheslav knew it.

For a start, they still had the pills. This in itself was not an insurmountable problem – they could easily set up a way to surrender them to Dmitri or one of Dmitri's respresentatives, and that, in theory, should be that. End of story.

Of course, now that they were back in their possession, Cheslav was sceptical about how much Ilko was willing to hand them over anymore, and he was beginning to have the same doubts about Kelly. Neither of them seemed happy with the idea of this new drug hitting the streets, and despite his own personal disinterest, he was able to imagine without too much difficulty why not.

But it wasn't just that. It wasn't even mainly that.

Before Plotnik died, he had tried to shoot him. When Cheslav had said that the exchange concluded their business with Dmitri, he distinctly heard Plotnik say 'Not quite'. Then Plotnik had tried to kill him. Not for himself, not for any agenda of his own, but because Dmitri wanted it.

Whatever the outcome had been, and whatever it could ever be, Dmitri still wanted Cheslav dead. Hell, if Cheslav had been in Dmitri's place, *he* would want him dead.

He explained this to the others as they drove back to Kelly's house from the cemetery in Ilko's car.

When they got back, the women were gone, headed into town to join their sons who needed them at the hospital. They'd taken Casey and Chloe with them, both of the girls too concerned about Damien to be left at home.

But as Cheslav voiced his conclusion to the three other men, he knew that if Tracy had been there, she for one would have seconded his decision.

'We have to kill Dmitri.'

Kelly, Denny and Ilko had listened to his reasoning; now they stayed silent, knowing that every moral fibre should be crying out against this, yet unable to muster any genuine objection.

At heart, they knew that it wasn't just Cheslav's life at stake. Until Dmitri was stopped, and stopped for good, not one of them could rest easy. Further down the line, they would always be looking over their shoulders, fearing the threat to their loved ones and the unannounced bullet in the back of the head.

'What do you propose?' said Ilko.

'Let me see that camera.'

Ilko handed over the Sony that he'd given to Denny to secretly film their meeting with Plotnik. Together, they watched the playback, crowded around its small screen. Helped by the street lighting entering the graveyard, the Night mode had worked well enough to capture sufficiently clear images of what had taken place. Looking at it now, it became evident that Plotnik had pointed the gun not just at Cheslav but at Ilko too.

'We were old enemies from long time back,' said Ilko when they asked him if he knew why. 'It's a long story.'

'We can use this,' said Cheslav, indicating the film.

'How?' said Kelly. 'Surely, all this is gonna do is piss 'im off even more.'

'We don't send it to Dmitri,' said Cheslav. 'We send it to the Wainwright twins.'

'Who the fuck are the Wainwright twins?' said Denny.

'Look at the gun Plotnik used. It's a Baikal.'

'A what?'

'One of a consignment from Eastern Europe that Dmitri is about to sell to gangs in Manchester.'

'So?' said Denny.

But the others were starting to see his point.

'The Wainwright twins are Dmitri's most likely potential buyers. Now, would you want to buy a gun that did that?'

'How do we contact these Wainwright twins?' said Kelly.

'I have their number right here in my phone,' said Cheslav, 'along with all the other contacts Dmitri trusted me with.'

'I can see why he wants you dead then,' said Kelly.

Ilko said, 'Show me your phone,' and Cheslav handed it over.

'If we edit it down to when the gun explodes, we can upload the clip to your phone and you can send it directly to theirs. That's assuming they've got the new camera phones, of course.'

'They're supposed to be Manc gangsters, aren't they?' said Denny with perhaps just a touch of derision. 'Course they'll 'ave the new fuckin' phones.'

None of them for a second doubted that he was right.

43. Proof of Death

AFTER THE APPOINTED time for the exchange had come and gone, Dmitri waited.

Thirty minutes passed with no word from Plotnik. Still Dmitri waited. These things could take time: there was the exchange of goods, the arrangement for the release of the captives, the verification of their release that the other side would no doubt demand – the so-called proof of life. Dmitri had seen the movie, and Meg Ryan was beautiful in it.

Then, after all that, there was the business of eliminating Cheslav. His former righthand man had already proven too much of a liability to remain alive. His whisperings to Donna and to Dmitri's father were despicable – telling tales out of school – and put the ex-wrestler lower than a snake's belly in Dmitri's opinion. He had broken every point of honour in the code book as far as Dmitri was concerned, and already deserved everything that was coming to him.

The fact that Cheslav was privy to a great deal more of Dmitri's business made him not just a liability but a deadly threat. Getting rid of him by any means possible was not just desirable, it was essential. Dmitri had left the logistics of it up to Plotnik though, and so that was one more factor to account for the time it was taking him.

But after sixty minutes and still no word, Dmitri figured it was time to find out what was going on straight from the horse's mouth. He dialled Plotnik's number and let it ring.

After a dozen rings with no answer, he gave up, issuing one his customary curses and resisting the impulse to throw his beloved BlackBerry against the fucking wall. All his contact numbers were in it, and the only person who had a back-up was fucking Cheslav.

Instead of dashing it against the wall, he used it to call up the duty roster, saw that Gordy was on, got him on the phone straight away.

'All right, boss,' Gordy answered.

'Get over to Harehills. I've got Plotnik out on a job. See what's taking him so long.'

He gave Gordy the location of the cemetery and as much

knowledge as he needed to know. Then he brooded in his study for half an hour, listening to Donna potter around the house giving instructions to the au pair and putting the kids to bed.

'Are you going to say good night to them or not?' she asked him shirtily, sticking her head round the door. She was still in a mood with him from earlier, but he couldn't deal with that now.

'Donna, I'm busy,' he snapped back, making a point of looking occupied when in fact he was simply waiting and fretting.

'You're always fucking busy,' she said, and slammed the door on him.

Dmitri was still sulking over his concession to the tyranny of Friday nights and the unfairness of Donna's accusation when Gordy phoned back.

'It's a mess, boss.'

Not the words Dmitri wanted to hear.

'Go on.'

'Cops are all over t'place. Some'dy's dead by t'looks of it, but I think it's Plotnik.'

Dmitri closed his eyes and felt his heart rate go up several notches. He had to strain to hear Gordy's report through the blood pounding in his ears.

'You think? What d'you mean, you think? Just tell me what's fucking happening there, Gordy, or so help me God, I'll fucking—'

'They've got some bloke who found a body out walkin' his dog. I know, you cun't make it up, it's allus some'dy walkin' a—'

'Never mind the fucking dog. What's he saying?'

'It's just rumours, boss. There's a right crowd turned up but yer can't get near to see owt. They're sayin' it's a big fella, though.'

Dmitri's heart stirred afresh, this time with hope.

'Listen carefully, Gordy. Could it be Cheslav?'

'Not sure. They reckon the bloke who found him though tipped onto it when he heard a mobile phone ringing in t'dead bloke's pocket.'

'What time?'

'Eh?'

Gordy didn't seem to understand the question.

'When did he find the body? When did he hear the phone ringing?'

''Bout an hour ago, I think.'

Dmitri's hand fell to his side while Gordy's tiny voice continued squeaking a long way off.

An hour ago.

The same time he tried to ring Plotnik.

He lifted the phone back up to his ear. Gordy was still on the line.

'Get round to the safe house,' Dmitri told him. 'Take a team if necessary. I want it cleaned out thoroughly. If Plotnik isn't there, then I don't want any sign that he or anyone else ever was. You understand?'

'Got it, boss.'

After Gordy had hung up Dmitri dialled Cheslav's number. While the tone trilled at the other end, his mind continued to dwell in some remote measure of hope.

It was short-lived, less than a couple of seconds. Cheslav must have been waiting phone in hand for his call, he answered so fast, but Dmitri made sure he got in first.

'What the fuck happened?'

'You know what the fuck happened,' said Cheslav, 'or else we wouldn't be having this conversation.'

'I mean what the fuck happened to Plotnik? You were there, I take it. You saw him?'

'I saw him,' Cheslav said, and cryptically left it at that.

'So what the fuck did you do to him?'

'Nothing.'

'Don't play fucking games with me, Cheslav. Plotnik is fucking dead, and I'm fucking sure he didn't kill himself.'

'Well I'm glad one of is sure of that.'

'What's that supposed to mean?'

'Wait and see. I'm sure the coroner's verdict will be interesting.'

'All right.' Dmitri was at the end of his tether with this cat and mouse shit. 'Enough of this. Just tell me what happened to the fucking pills.'

'Your boy fucked up,' said Cheslav. 'We still have them.'

'What do you want?' said Dmitri. 'I gave you back the boys. What the fuck more do you want?'

'I want to live.'

Dmitri stayed silent for a beat, absorbing the implication of what Cheslav was saying. The bastard must know Plotnik's orders were to kill him. Other than that, Dmitri was still in the dark about what had happened in that cemetery, and how Cheslav had managed to get the better of the Carpenter.

'I need certain – assurances,' said Dmitri.

He made himself sound almost pathetic, playing a part for now. It was something he could make good later, when he had the pills back.

'So do I.'

'Can we make a deal? The pills, and your silence, and I'll forget about the whole thing. We'll call it quits.'

'I'll be in touch,' said Cheslav.

Then the line went dead.

'*MOTHERFUCKER!*'

Dmitri could palpably hear the rest of the household beyond his study door paying no attention to his outburst.

The kill was confirmed two hours later. Dmitri got a call from a friend of his, a high-ranking policeman in the West Yorkshire constabulary, wanting to know how the Ukrainian citizen that he'd helped secure a multiple-entry visa for as a favour to Dmitri Maximov was now dead on a slab in the police morgue, having been discovered in possession of a mangled gun smuggled in illegally from Russia.

It's not from Russia, you fucking moron, Dmitri was thinking as he listened to the terminal old bore witter on about it. But he didn't say that. Instead, he smiled and smiled while his brain and his tongue tried to wriggle out of the shit towards a credible solution.

44. Red Arrows

AFTER A RESTLESS night staring towards the back of Donna's head in the dark while she avoided brushing up against him, Dmitri rose before daylight, thinking about the calls he needed to make, the wheels he needed to set in motion.

Lillian cooked him some breakfast while she was feeding the kids before they went to school and he ate an egg and bacon sandwich standing up in the kitchen while Donna was taking a shower upstairs.

He didn't know whether it was him avoiding her or her avoiding him but he felt like getting out of the house and out of her way before she showed her face downstairs. He'd make it all up to her later: right now, he didn't have time for that shit.

'You be good at school today,' he said to Joshua and Carla while they were still making a mess at the breakfast table.

Then he heard Donna coming downstairs, and Lillian made them both kiss him goodbye before he swept out of the house.

It was a shit day, one of those days that made you ask what the fuck had happened to the blue skies and sunshine of the day before. He swung himself into the driving seat of the Merc, pulling the door mercifully shut against the freezing rain and setting the windscreen wipers going before edging the car down the drive with one hand while speed-dialling with the other.

'Gordy.'

'Here, boss,' a sleepy voice answered.

'You get it done?'

'Yeah. All sorted.'

'You clean everything good? I mean, no traces.'

'Had a team there till two. It's spick 'n' span.'

Dmitri hung up satisfied. As unlikely to occur as it was, the last thing he needed was some eager and clean young copper tracking Plotnik's movements to the address of the safe house and finding Dmitri's prints or DNA there and connecting him to the whale beached up in the morgue. In theory, there was nothing connecting Plotnik to the house anyway, no deeds, no papers, nothing. Dmitri wanted to keep it that way.

Next he phoned Madeleine, dialling the landline number of her apartment.

'Who is it?' she answered with her customary imperiousness.

One of the things he loved about her was her unwillingness to take any shit; ironically, it could be a total thorn in his side too.

'So where the hell were you?' she demanded when she knew who it was.

'Madeleine, I'm sorry. I'm floating up to my back teeth in shit right now. I just couldn't get away.'

'And I should care because . . . ?'

'Er, because I pay your rent?'

'Wrong answer, you fack!'

'OK, OK, baby, because I love you. OK? I love you. Is that better?'

'A little. Christ, Dmitri, it's so facking early.'

'Can I come over?'

'What? Now?'

'Is there any reason I shouldn't be able to come over now?'

'Like what?'

'You're on your own, aren't you?'

'No, Dmitri, I'm still in bed with the flight team of the facking Red Arrows. They're performing formation cunnilingus on my pussy right as we speak.'

Dmitri pretended to laugh while the blood jackhammered at his temples and he nearly ran the Merc into a lamppost.

'Ha ha. Really. I'm coming over.'

'If you know you're coming over, why ask permission?'

'In case you were about to go to work.'

'I've got a shoot on Wednesday. Till then, I'm a lady of leisure.'

'Then do me a favour. Stay in bed till I get there.'

He meant it to be business but the sight of her standing in the hall in her baby-doll nightie after he let himself in created a lengthy distraction.

She made love with him passively, almost disinterestedly, but he liked it like that. He could fuck her hard, taking out his frustrations on the world, and still she never complained. It was how she expected men to be, and he didn't disappoint. For her own part, she took it as though she were reading the paper over his shoulder but still had the good grace to give his balls an appreciative squeeze and stroke his hair like he was a little boy at the end of it all.

Afterwards, lying next to her in the bed, he got to the real point.

'Madeleine, I know you weren't happy with the apartment being used while you were away.'

'Mmm,' she murmured sleepily. 'Don't remind me.'

'The thing is, it's difficult sometimes, you know?'

'What's difficult?' she said, opening her eyes and raising herself up on an elbow to be able to glare at him properly. 'What's so difficult about not giving your facking key to someone else?'

'The place is – useful. What can I say?'

'Useful? It's my home, not a facking tool shed.'

'I know, I know, but – Listen, how do you feel about a new place? Somewhere better than this?'

Madeleine sat up, clutching the sheet to her breasts, and gestured at the opulence around them.

'Better how? What new place?'

'A house,' said Dmitri encouragingly, seeing now that he'd at least got her attention. 'Somewhere bigger than this. A proper house, in a nice part of town. And somewhere you won't be disturbed.'

'So what, you mean somewhere you can keep me even more hidden away?'

'No, no. It wouldn't be like that. I'm talking about a well-to-do area in a lively neighbourhood. Not this poky loft over the river.'

Dmitri pointed at the rain slamming against the windows, thinking the weather would help him prosecute his argument.

'This poky loft over the river is about as top end as you can get right now.'

'Exactly. And look at it. I'm not saying it's the money. It's not, that's of no importance, you know that. But don't you want more space? Somewhere with an upstairs and more light? Somewhere with a garden, a big garden, and a great view?'

She was quiet for a beat, so that he knew he was getting through her defences.

'Go on.'

'You can entertain your friends there. And I guarantee the

only other person who will ever have a key to it will be me.'

'Will you show me it first.'

'Whenever you like.'

'How soon? Today?'

Her interest was getting perkier by the second now.

Dmitri smiled.

'Maybe tomorrow? I've got a real busy day today.'

'Yeah, right,' she said. 'Looks like it.'

He laughed as he let her kick his arse out of bed.

'Tomorrow then?'

'Promise,' he said. 'And if you like it, it'll be like this place. I'll take care of everything. It'll be our little secret and you won't have to worry about a thing.'

'It better be good,' she said.

It's good, Dmitri was thinking.

One very careful previous owner. Who won't be coming back.

45. Meet the Wainwrights

It was well past eleven when Dmitri pulled up beneath a severely grey sky outside the York Road lock-up. Gordy was supposed to meet him there to do the donkey work, but was nowhere in sight yet.

'Where the fuck are you?' he said when he got him on the phone.

'Sorry, boss, I'm runnin' a bit late. Problems wi—'

'I don't want to know about your fucking problems.'

He paused and counted to ten. It was OK. He was nearly there. All he needed to do was get the guns off his hands then he could relax. The ball might be in Cheslav's court, but there would be no basket left to throw it in. Once the guns were out of the way, he just had to wait for Cheslav to surrender the pills. And if he never gave them up, then fuck it. Even that would not be the end of the world anymore.

'Listen,' he said to Gordy, 'I've got a key, I can let myself in. Just get here when you can, OK?'

'Yeah, sure,' said Gordy. He'd never heard the boss being so nice before. 'Anything you say.'

Inside the warehouse, Dmitri made himself a cup of tea from the boiler in the little scullery, listening to the amplified noise of the rain spattering the corrugated iron of the roof high above. The milk was powdered and the Styrofoam cup could hardly be said to enhance the flavour of the brew. In fact, he wondered how anyone could drink this piss. But having checked that the crate was all ship-shape and ready to be collected, and being there ahead of time, alone, for half an hour with just himself and the sound of the rain, he felt curiously satisfied, more so than he had in a long time. Like a soldier who knows that a ceasefire is only hours away, he felt heady with the prospect of a lasting peace.

He rummaged in the breast pocket of his suit and found a cigar that had been waiting there for a long time. Donna hated him smoking them in the house, ditto Madeleine in the apartment. Well neither of them was here now.

His spat with Donna would blow over before the day was out, he was sure of it, and installing Madeleine in the safe house would help to dissociate it from any investigation into Plotnik's demise and ensure that Cheslav, who knew nothing of its location or existence, would never be able to orchestrate that threatened meeting between his wife and his mistress.

He fossicked in another pocket for a lighter and applied the flame to the tip of the panatella. A minute later, he was leaning back on a rickety wooden chair with a cup of plastic-tasting tea in one hand and a lungful of satisfying smoke, wondering what life would be like twenty years from now when he was three hundred million pounds richer.

'Ey, Di-meetri, ma main man!'

The door banged open and two identical figures in hoodies waltzed in without bothering to knock. They were as skinny and floppy-fringed and acne-scarred as the first time he'd met them, and they crossed the floor of the warehouse with a tight-hipped swagger that made them look like they were taking the mickey out of paraplegics, but was probably caused by the unfeasibly low altitude at which they wore their jeans.

''Ow yer doin', man?' said the other one, whichever one he was.

'Davy,' said Dmitri, casting a noncommittal eye through his cigar smoke at the section of air floating midway between them. 'Dwayne.'

At least he knew he'd got the names right. He'd leave it to them to decide who was who.

'Weather's fuckin' well mardy out there,' said the one he suspected might be Davy, lowering the hood of his top and shaking off the raindrops it had collected between the car and inside. 'M62 were fuckin' lousy drivin', werenit, Ar Kid?'

'Too fuckin' right,' said the one he thought was Dwayne.

By all accounts, Davy was the elder of the brothers by twenty minutes – a sufficient hiatus for him to have claimed superiority in their subsequent business partnership and life dealings together.

'Well,' said Dmitri, feeling unusually magnanimous today for all the reasons he had previously inventoried to himself, 'can I offer you boys a cup of tea?'

Dwayne – the one he thought was Dwayne – laughed the kind of laugh that risked sending a blunderbuss-like discharge of snot shooting out of the nose, while Davy grinned and held his arms out in a gesture that under certain circumstances would signify 'Can I get a hug?' and under other others, 'Do you want some an' all?'

'Tea?' said Davy. 'Is that fuckin' Yorkshire tea by any chance?'

For some reason, this remark cracked his brother up. And one brother cracking up seemed to crack up the other one.

For some other reason, Dmitri failed to see the joke.

'Celebratin' already then?' said Davy, pointing to Dmitri's cigar.

'What?'

He looked at the cigar in his hand as though noticing it for the first time.

'No, not celebrating. Just – everyday smoking.'

He grinned, but he was getting tired of this. Tired of these fucking yokels from rainland. Was it these clowns who'd dragged this rotten weather over the Pennines with their sorry arses? Well, the sooner he off-loaded the guns and sent them back, the better for everyone then.

'So what's the story?' said Davy.

'Mornin' glory,' said Dwayne, and burst out laughing again – a hiccupping sound that put Dmitri in mind of either an exotic bird in a jungle or a mule labouring on a mountain pass in the hot sun.

'The story,' said Dmitri, ignoring whatever 'morning glory' might signify, 'is as we agreed over the phone.'

'Is that right?' said Davy. He wasn't really addressing this question to Dmitri; he was grinning over at his brother, who grinned back at him with a matching degree of inanity.

Whatever was going on between them was slowly beginning to piss Dmitri off now and sour the good mood he'd been in. He suspected the two of them were on some kind of drug – Davy kept sniffing and Dwayne seemed to be chewing on a mouth full of nothing. Which was fine, that was their business. But it wasn't really mixing well with his business.

'Look,' he said at last, 'why don't I just show you the merchandise and then we can pack it up for you?'

Surely, he was thinking, he couldn't be more reasonable than that.

'Oh yeah, the merchandise, man,' said Davy, 'the fuckin' merchandise.'

He had his hands clasped together over his balls and was weaving his head and shoulders from one side to the other like a stalking heron, or Ray Charles grooving at the piano to 'Unchain My Heart'.

'We've got a little query about the merchandise, 'an't we, Ar Kid?'

'Yeah, we 'ave, 'an't we, Ar Kid?'

'Yeah, we 'ave.'

Davy lifted one of his hands from his balls and pushed the screen of a camera phone towards Dmitri's face.

'What the fuck is this?'

He clicked a button and a video clip started to roll.

Dmitri smiled, thinking it was some joke – maybe some footage the two of them had made of some prank they thought he would find comical.

It took him a moment or two to realise that what he was looking at was a moving image of Plotnik.

His head actually moved back and a frown pounced onto his face.

Jesus, what the fuck was this?

He almost let the stub of the cigar burn his fingers as he watched Plotnik point a gun at somebody off camera, then evidently pull the trigger. There was a flash of brightness and a bang and Plotnik disappeared from view. After a couple of seconds, the picture shakily lowered to his massive body shivering on the ground without anything that one could clearly call a face.

'Yer know what?' said Davy. 'I've shit better guns than that.'

It was Dwayne who shot him while he was still looking at the camera in Davy's fist.

Pulled a pistol out of the pocket of his hoodie and put two bullets into him from six feet away, one in the chest, another one in the head.

To give the lad his fair dues, it was a skilful piece of work. Dmitri was already on his way to the ground when he made the head shot, so at that point he was technically dealing with a moving target.

Davy, hands clasped now behind his back, leaned over Dmitri and said, 'You an' yer mates, stay outta fuckin'

Manchester. We've got it covered, all right?'

Dwayne, tucking the gun away, looked at his twin brother like he was daft and said, 'I don't think he can 'ear you, Ar Kid.'

No, Dmitri could no longer hear anything. But he was certainly going to stay out of Manchester.

Permanently.

46. Telling

'OK, THANKS, OLEK.'

Cheslav pocketed the phone and returned his attention to the positioning of his napkin for dinner. Or tea, as they called it in Yorkshire. He knew that. It was like he'd always known that. After all, he'd been here long enough. Long enough to be considered an honorary Yorkshireman, at least?

'Dmitri's dead,' he said, keeping his voice down, not wanting to upset the nice people and families filling the tables in this nice conservatory at this nice hotel in the nice surroundings of 'God's own country'. As if God would have had anything to do with this business.

'Good,' said Tracy. 'I wish I'd fuckin' been there.'

Cheslav kept his head still, didn't look round, but he felt acutely aware of everyone around them. He imagined a dozen looks switching in their direction – a dozen looks that in reality were focused on nothing other than the soup on the table in front of them.

'Good,' she said again a minute later with acceptance and finality, and Cheslav could see the tears standing out in the corners of her eyes, quivering, but refusing to fall.

The eyes were bright. The bruising around them was beginning to fade at last. It looked less livid, less painful. Her wounds, the details of the world around them, were slipping back into soft focus. The luxuries and comforts of this country hotel were sliding into focus. He'd got them here at last.

'D'yer think we can go back home then?' Tracy asked, toying with her appetiser.

'What? You mean right this minute?'

Cheslav was thinking about the room upstairs that they had booked, the sweet thought of a night where it was just the two of them together, come what may.

'No,' she said.

She stretched out a hand to his forearm, placed it on top, let it linger there.

'Not this minute.'

He smiled.

And when he looked away from her, Sanjeev was sitting in a

chair opposite, making up the threesome at their table.

'Tell her,' said the ghost.

Cheslav kept looking at the Sri Lankan for a long time, but that was all he said.

Tell her.

He smiled at Tracy, and when he looked back across the table it was just the two of them once more.

'What is it?' she said.

His heart was thumping. For a moment, he wished he was facing some big ugly guy with a gun.

'Tracy,' he said at last. 'There's something I have to tell you.'

47. We'll Meet Again

'SO THAT'S IT,' said Denny. 'She knows anyway.'

Kelly had already been wondering what he was doing back in the Royal Park again. This time there was no Ilko, no excuse, just him and Denny, like the old times he'd promised himself he was never going to slip back into.

Fuck.

'She knows?' he said.

'Yeah.'

'Well 'ow the fuck does she know? Did you tell 'er?'

Denny lifted his fresh pint of Löwenbräu to his lips and looked around the big, still relatively emptyish room of the pub that was slowly filling up with early evening boozers.

'Does it matter?' he said. 'Personally, I think what really matters is that we should sink these an' then get the fuck out of 'ere before it fills up wi' students. Preferably to a curry somewhere, then a fuckin big fat hottie round at my place, or at the very least a fuckin' fat fuckin' spliff.'

'Denny. Can yer focus yer fuckin' thoughts on summat other than your appetites for one minute? What d'yer mean, she knows already?'

'I mean she fuckin' knows, Kel. 'Ow much more d'yer want me to spell it out? Tracy fuckin' Croft knows that it were us behind that petrol-station robbery. She knows that it were us who fuckin' kicked 'er kid's 'ead in. She knows that it were us that Baz were after when 'e copped a bullet.'

Kelly sat there for a minute gob-smacked. Like, a full minute.

''Ow long 'as she known?'

'Fuckin' ages, man. Since long before you came back on t'scene.'

'But – but – '

'Kelly, man. Don't fuckin' sweat it. It's cool. All right? She knows what kind a cunt Baz wa'. An' all right, her kid, what's 'e called – ?'

'Stuart,' said Kelly, a name that had been seared into his brain for three fucking years.

'That's the one, Stuart. I mean, it weren't like 'e were

permanently fuckin' brain-damaged or owt, is it? By all accounts, 'e's top dog at uni an' that.'

Kelly sat there silently for a moment, remembering the scenes between himself and Tracy during that fucking Ukrainian business – with her knowing, and him gormlessly fucking ignorant, as per usual, because Denny hadn't thought to open his fucking mouth and let him know what had been going on all along.

'Dun't fuckin' matter now, does it? DMT Dmitri's pushin' up daisies an' me an' you are sittin' in the Royally 'avin' a pint together an' it's all like nowt ever fuckin' 'appened.'

Great, thought Kelly. *Just what I always fucking wanted.*

'So what did Ilko do wi' all them pills?'

'Aw Jesus, Kel, I wish you 'an't fuckin' asked me that.'

'Why, what's up?'

''E only fuckin' went an' flushed the lot, din't 'e?'

'Fuckin' good,' said Kelly, and meant it.

'If that were the prototype batch an' Sanjeev were already dead, what d'yer reckon Dmitri were gonna do with 'em?'

'Fuck knoz,' said Kelly. 'Reverse engineer 'em, I suppose.'

'Reverse what?'

'If 'e'd found the right chemist, some'dy coulda taken them and worked out 'ow Sanjeev made 'em so they could reproduce the formula. Guess it's all a bit academic now though, innit?'

''Ave you been to fuckin' uni or summat in t' last three years? Academic?'

'What I mean is,' said Kelly, 'they're all gone. It dun't fuckin' matter, does it?'

'Right,' said Denny.

Something about the way he said it made Kelly look at him sideways.

'Aw, fuckinell, Denny, you 'an't.'

''An't what?'

'You 'an't still got any of 'em left?'

'Fuckin' chill out, man.'

Kelly kept looking at him.

'Just fuckin' chill, all right?'

Kelly fretted about it for a minute in his head, then thought about the firmness of Denny's grasp on the concept of reverse engineering, and the idea that if Denny still had even one of those pills left in his possession he wasn't going to take it before anyone would get the chance to do anything about the fact that it was the last one on earth.

'So,' said Denny, swigging the bottom half of his lager down in one go, 'are we off for that fuckin' hot knife or what?'

As the two of them started to stand up from the table, they became aware of an enormous figure looming over them.

They both looked up.

The figure looking down at them was like a ghost from the past.

Better, in fact, if it had been a ghost.

'Hello, boys, I'm back,' said Hamed, pounding down two meaty fists, one on Denny's shoulder, the other on Kelly's. 'Did you miss me?'

The End

Lightning Source UK Ltd.
Milton Keynes UK
UKOW050334161011

180359UK00001B/10/P